torn

Cat Clarke was born in Zambia and brought up in Scotland and Yorkshire, which has given her an accent that tends to confuse people. Cat has written non-fiction books about exciting things like cowboys, sharks and pirates, and now writes YA novels, usually about teenagers being mean to each other. Her first novel, *Entangled*, was published by Quercus in 2011.

Praise for *Entangled*

'Moving, thought-provoking, and truly gripping from start to finish' *Mizz*

'It isn't often you race through a book because you are desperate for the denouement, the truth . . . incredibly poignant and thought-provoking' *Birmingham Post*

'A fascinating and exciting read' *Belfast Newsletter*

'Grace's story is told with warmth, sensitivity and humour' *School Librarian*

'A most accomplished and daring debut' *Books for Keeps*

Also by Cat Clarke

ENTANGLED

UNDONE

A KISS IN THE DARK

torn

CAT CLARKE

Quercus

First published in Great Britain in 2011 by Quercus

21 Bloomsbury Square
London
WC1A 2NS

A CIP catalogue reference for this book is available
from the British Library

ISBN 978 0 85738 205 4

5 7 9 10 8 6 4

Typeset by Nigel Hazle
Printed and bound in Great Britain by Clays Ltd, St Ives plc.

For Dad, with heaps of love and a great deal of respect.
You really are quite marvellous, you know.

1

A funeral without a body is like a wedding without a bride. Or a groom.

Except this isn't officially a funeral – it's a *memorial service*. Instead of a coffin, there's an easel with a huge photo. She looks pretty. Hopeful, even.

The church is jam-packed. People standing at the back, craning their necks to get a good look at the family. There were even photographers outside when we arrived. It's a zoo. A snivelling, wailing zoo. Not that I can talk – I've been snivelling too. Dad pressed a hanky into my hand as soon as we got here. Now it's sodden and snotty, so I'm guessing he won't want it back.

No one's wearing black. Black is officially banned. Apparently she used to joke about her funeral, saying she hoped everyone would wear crazy neons and wave glow-sticks around. Well, no neons as such, but

1

I did manage to pour myself into my purple skinny jeans (*what* was I thinking?).

Sometimes I used to imagine my own funeral. It was nothing like this. And it certainly didn't involve the school choir singing 'Keep Holding On' by Avril bloody Lavigne. Polly Sutcliffe is centre stage. New haircut. Highlights too. She manages to get through most of the first verse before dissolving into tears. Real, actual tears, just like the ones I've been crying for days and days.

Tears of shock.

Tears of sadness.

Tears of guilt.

School has been weird since it happened. It's all anyone can talk about. The first day back, every teacher said a few words about her at the start of each lesson. Some were more convincing than others. Miss Daley hadn't even known her – not really – but you could tell she was genuinely upset.

Daley arrived at the start of the school year, fresh and new and vulnerable, a tiny bird-lady with *I'm a newly qualified teacher, please take advantage of me* tattooed on her forehead. So we did what we always do – try to find a weakness, see how far we can push her, wondering if she'll cry if we take things a little too far. But she held up pretty well. She took everything we could throw at her — even Tara's major attitude.

I keep looking over at Cass; I can't help it. She's picking cat hairs off her skirt, like she always does when she's bored. Except Cass hardly ever wears skirts. Her mum must have talked her into it. Looks like she's had a haircut too. It seems like everyone's got spruced up for the occasion. I catch Cass's eye and she half waves in my direction. I shake my head, just a tiny bit so no one else will notice. She shrugs and goes back to grooming her clothes. Jesus.

I shouldn't be surprised that she's not crying. I don't think I've ever seen her cry. Not even when Boots Mark 3 got run over last summer. And Boots Mark 3 was her favourite of all the Bootses. Boots Mark 4 isn't quite matching up, apparently. He's certainly hairier than the last one. I try to steer clear, since I'm sort of allergic to cats. Not properly — just enough to make my face itch when I'm around them.

Cass prides herself on being strong. She thinks girls who cry all the time are *pathetic*. Crying at the end of a Disney film? Pathetic. Crying because the boy you fancy doesn't even know you exist? Pathetic. The entire school crying on and off for the past couple of weeks? Pathetic pathetic pathetic.

Luckily she makes an exception for me. I'm allowed to cry whenever I want, and she'll do anything she can to cheer me up. Which usually involves making me laugh. She can *always* make me laugh. It's one of my favourite things about her. Although I hate it when she does it on purpose when I've got a mouthful of orange juice or something. That's just cruel.

The singing is over, thank God. I check the order of service: a reading by the three witches. Of course it doesn't actually *say* 'witches', but that's what Cass calls them. They're not *that* bad – individually, at least. Just normal girls: Gemma, Danni and Sam. But put them together and they transform into something bigger, something badder. And if you add their fearless leader into the mix, they mutate into a multi-headed monster of popularity. A monster that teachers *love*, for some inexplicable reason. A monster that boys love even more, for very obvious reasons. A monster that the rest of us bow down to – out of fear mostly, but also a kind of grudging respect. And jealousy.

But their fearless leader is no more.

4

The reading is surprising – a passage from one of her favourite books, apparently. A book I bought for her, a long time ago.

Dad whispers in my ear, 'Remember when I used to read this to you?'

I nod. Something tightens in my throat.

The witches get through it without the usual hair-flicking and pouting. Waterproof mascara was invented for days like this. I want to look over at Cass, but I don't. She'll probably be smirking and I couldn't bear that.

A boy stands up from the front row. Messy brown hair and sloping shoulders. He slowly makes his way to the lectern and takes a rumpled piece of paper from the back pocket of his jeans. He clears his throat and looks at us. His gaze roams the pews, not even pausing when it meets mine. It's five years since I last saw him. He's not a skinny little boy in too-big clothes any more. He's an almost-man. Jack.

'I'd like to thank you all for coming today. It means a lot to me and my family. I wish Tara could be here to see how much everyone loved her.' He smiles a tiny smile at the thought, and I do too. He looks down at the paper in his hands and everyone can see that he's shaking, trying to hold it together. He scrunches the paper into a ball and continues, 'Tara was the most annoying sister in the world.' Some people are shocked and frowning a bit; Cass looks interested. I'm definitely interested.

'I mean it. She drove me mental. She *never* let me have the remote control. She used to borrow my iPod without asking – and then I'd find it lying around with the battery run down. She listened in on my phone conversations and read my text messages. And she took the piss out of me *all* the time. She could rip me to shreds in any argument . . . and then she'd go running to Mum about it, saying that I was being mean and picking on her. She could wrap people around her little finger just like that.' He snaps his fingers. People don't know how to take this. It's brilliant.

'Tara was the best sister in the world. She used to bring me tomato soup and toast when I wasn't feeling well. And she'd make sure the butter went right to the edges too. She taught me to always say "no" when a girl asks if her bum looks big. She covered for me when I got wasted and was sick on the hall carpet – blamed the dog. Sorry, Mum. And sorry, Rufus.' Most people laugh – a muted, funereal sort of laugh.

'Tara was there for me whenever I needed someone to talk to. She didn't always say what I wanted to hear, but she was always honest. Totally, absolutely, brutally honest. The last thing she said to me was, "Get a haircut – you look ridiculous."' Jack laughs and runs his hand through his hair. I don't think he looks ridiculous.

'My sister was my very favourite person and I will miss her every day for the rest of my life. Now I've got the remote control whenever I want it and my iPod's always fully charged. But I just want my sister back. And that's not going to happen.' His voice cracks at the end, and he rushes back to his seat.

I'm finding it hard to breathe. I close my eyes and try to think of something else – anything else. It's useless. All I can think about is a brother grieving for his sister. And never knowing the truth.

Please, God, let this be over soon. I shouldn't be here. None of us should be here. Rae had the right idea. But then it's easy for her. She can get away with not turning up. She just has to play the depressed emo-girl card. The rest of us aren't so lucky.

Mrs Flanagan makes a speech. She talks about a Tara I don't recognize. *A shining star . . . always ready with a smile . . . helping others . . . a tribute to her school and her family . . . we're lucky to have known her . . . she'll be missed by each and every one of us.*

Why does being dead automatically make you a good person? Can't anyone see the truth? Tara clearly had Mrs Flanagan fooled. But then, she always did know how to handle teachers. They thought she was *wonderful*. The only one who ever seemed to have the measure of her was Daley. She wouldn't let Tara have her way just because she was Tara. It was like she arrived at Bransford Academy and no one had bothered to tell her the golden rule: Tara Chambers is God.

Daley stood up to her that first day of the trip. She didn't let Tara have her own way. Any other teacher would have backed down – Tara could be very persuasive. But Daley stood firm.

If only she'd let Tara have her way.

A couple more songs, a few words from the vicar, then it's over. We shuffle out of the church to the sounds of a piano playing a song that sounds familiar. It takes me a moment or two to place it: 'Don't Stop Me Now' by Queen. Except this version is orchestral and really slow. What a weird choice. Probably something else Tara joked about when she assumed that her funeral was a long way in the future.

It's good to get outside, to breathe again. Dad's arm hangs loosely across my shoulders.

'How you doing, kiddo? I know that must have been hard for you.'

He's been asking me this a lot since I got back. I think he's worried it's making me think about Mum. And it is. But Mum's death was very, very different.

I smile weakly at him. 'Yeah, I'm OK, I think. Thanks.'

He gathers me in a massive bear hug – his speciality. 'I think you're being really brave. I'm so proud of you.'

I feel sick but somehow manage to reply, 'Thanks, Dad. Listen, I'm going to find Cass. See you at the car in a few minutes?'

He nods and wanders off.

I scan the crowd looking for Cass. Stephanie de Luca is blowing her nose in a rather unattractive fashion. Her dad's suit is so shiny it almost blinds me, and her mum's hair is a black that's far from natural. A couple of photographers are milling around looking shifty. I keep well clear. I veer past Polly, who's huddled with a woman scribbling in a tiny notepad. Can't help but overhear a few words. 'Of course, we're all devastated. It's been such a shock.'

'And were you particularly close to Tara?'

'Well . . . yes. We *all* were, really. Tara was incredibly popular.'

Good grief.

A voice from behind hisses in my ear. 'Can you *believe* her? What the hell is she playing at?'

I turn around. 'I have no earthly idea. She must have lost her mind.'

Cass and I head towards a couple of tumbledown gravestones, away from the crowd.

'So . . . what did you think?'

'Of what?'

'Er . . . the saintification of Miss Chambers? Interesting, no?'

'Cass! The girl is *dead*. It's not funny.'

'I know. Sorry. It's just weird, that's all.'

Part of me agrees with her, but anger flares inside me all the same. 'There's nothing weird about it. Jesus, Cass! Don't you feel *sad*? Don't you feel *anything*?!'

I can tell I've gone too far, because she looks angry. And Cass never gets angry with me.

'Of course I feel sad! But there's nothing I can do about it. Just cos I choose not to wallow in it, doesn't mean I'm not upset! Stop telling me how I should be feeling, OK?'

For a second there I thought she was going to cry. But of course she doesn't. I still feel bad though. 'I'm sorry. I just . . . don't think you should joke about this.'

She shrugs and the anger is gone. 'You're right.

Listen, I have to go. Somehow I've been roped into helping at Jeremy's party. Twenty hyperactive six-year-olds running riot in Pizza Express — nightmare or what?'

I hug her goodbye, and I bet we look the same as any of the other multicoloured mourners. Clinging to each other for comfort. Wondering how such a terrible thing could have happened to someone so young. But we know.

We *know*.

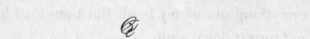

On my way to the car I see Tara's brother. He's sitting on the wall of the churchyard all by himself. He looks up just as I'm passing, and I'm sure that he's going to say something and I don't want him to. I really don't want him to. What am I supposed to say? *It sucks about your sister being dead*. He probably doesn't even remember me anyway.

An enormous woman swoops on Jack at that very moment. No — she doesn't swoop, she *envelops* him. She's wearing what appears to be a psychedelic tent. Jack disappears entirely in her embrace. Lucky escape for me.

Dad's having a sneaky fag, leaning on the bonnet of the car. As soon as he scopes me he drops the butt, grinds it underfoot and pops a mint into his mouth. We've come to an uneasy understanding about the smoking. He's allowed to do it as long as I'm not around. I don't want to see it, I don't want to smell it, I don't want to think about the state of his tar-stained lungs. If what happened to Mum didn't make him stop, nothing will. I'll let him off this time; I suppose the funeral *was* pretty stressful.

I crank up the volume on the stereo as soon as we're out of the car park. The music helps to clear everything out of my head. But then Dad has to go and turn it down again.

'So . . . how are you feeling?'

Not again. Please, not again. 'Fine, thanks.' I reach for the volume button, but I'm not fast enough.

'Her poor parents. They must be going through hell. I managed to have a quick word with Bob. Gave him our condolences. He looks . . . lost.'

Stop it stop it stop it. Please. 'I thought Jack did so well, keeping it together like that. I can't believe how much he's grown up! Last time I saw him he was a right scrawny little bugger.' He trails off into silence.

I have nothing to say, but I know he's waiting. Just try. Say something – anything will do. Here goes . . .

'Yeah.' Perfect. Non-committal. You can't read anything into a *yeah*, can you?

It seems to do the job. Dad carries on talking, and I carry on staring out of the window. From time to time I nod or say *yes* or *no* or whatever single word is required of me. Dad doesn't seem to notice that he's essentially talking to himself. Or maybe he notices but lets me get away with it because of the circumstances. I *am* supposed to be traumatized, after all.

There was a special session after school last week for the parents of the girls who were on the trip. Dad told me all about it afterwards. There was a psychologist who specializes in post-traumatic stress, talking about all the different ways this stress could manifest itself. Apparently 'there's no right or wrong way to grieve'. I'd have to disagree with that. Writing 'I misssss u so much. Ur in a betta place now. xoxo' on Tara's Facebook page pretty much sums up the wrong way to grieve as far as I'm concerned. There are also two 'R.I.P. Tara Chambers' pages on Facebook. One of them only has nine 'likes', but the other has 452 and counting. I'm ashamed to admit that I'll probably become number 453. I wouldn't want anyone to notice my absence.

I couldn't believe my ears when Dad came home spouting all that psychobabble bullshit. He's always going on about psychologists/counsellors/therapists being a waste of space. But for some reason this situation has changed his mind. Maybe he's wondering just how much death his little girl is going to have to deal with before her eighteenth birthday.

Bruno's waiting for us at the front door and I grab him and bury my face in his fur. I breathe deeply, pathetically grateful for his warm, comforting dogginess. It's over. The worst is over now. I got through it.

I take the stairs two at a time, desperate to take off these ridiculous jeans, which are (let's face it) too small for me. Bruno overtakes me and I know I'll find him on the bed, begging to have his belly rubbed.

But when I get to my bedroom Bruno's nowhere to be seen, which means he must be under the bed — his second favourite hiding place in the house.

And there's Tara, perched on the end of my bed.

2

Her hands are filthy and her fingernails are muddy
and bloody and ragged. She's picking at them, trying
to use a thumbnail to scour out the dirt from the
fingernails on her other hand. It doesn't seem to be
making any difference.

She glances up as I shut the door behind me. 'So
how was it?' Her voice has a croaky, hoarse quality
that it never had in life. I keep expecting her to clear
her throat, but she doesn't.

I ignore her. It's easier now.

I was terrified the first time she appeared – in
the middle of the night last Tuesday. For the first time
in days I hadn't woken up sweating or panicking or
crying. For the first time in days I'd dreamed about
something else. I stretched out under the covers and
breathed a deep sigh of relief. Maybe everything was
going to be OK. Maybe I wasn't going to be haunted

by this for the rest of my life. I tried to remember my dream, but it was already starting to slip away. I concentrated as hard as I could, but it was no good. Then a voice in the dark scared the life out of me.

'Er . . . you'd better not be over it already.' A voice I thought I recognized, even though there was something horribly different about it.

I scrambled to turn on the bedside light, wincing as light flooded the room. There she was. Perched on the end of my bed, right next to Bruno. I tried to scream but the only sound that came out was a tiny whimper. Bruno flicked his tail in his sleep, oblivious to my terror.

This is a dream. A new kind of dream. Focus really hard on it being a dream and you will wake up. I scrunched up my eyes really tight and pressed my fists into the sockets. *Just focus on breathing – in and out, in and out. That's it.* I felt calmer and better and . . .

'You know, it's not very polite to ignore people.'

Crap. Why can't you just wake up? You always wake up before the really bad things happen, don't you?

'Alice, for Christ's sake, you're boring me now. Don't be so pathetic.'

She didn't *sound* like a soul-eating monster from beyond the grave. She sounded exactly like Tara. If Tara had been gargling with gravel.

I opened my eyes and stared at her. Her hair was glossy as ever, highlights glinting in the light. Her face looked normal, if a little pale. Her vest and tiny shorts were pristine clean, unlike her hands. I tried my best not to look at the hands.

'That's better. God, anyone would think you'd seen a ghost!' She smiled at her own wit. 'So, as I was saying, you'd better not be over it already.'

'Wha . . . what?' I said, or rather croaked. Just like her.

'You were dreaming about something else. *Someone else.* Why weren't you dreaming about me?' She pouted.

I muttered to myself, 'You're not real, you're not real. I'm going to wake up now.' I closed my eyes and started humming a lullaby that Mum used to sing to me whenever I had a nightmare.

'You sound like a crazy person. Look at me, Alice, just look at me.'

I didn't want to but I couldn't help myself.

'There, that wasn't so hard, was it?' Now she was sitting cross-legged. Her toenails were painted candy pink. *But her hands . . . her poor hands. It almost looks like she's tried to claw her way out . . .*

I cleared my throat. 'What do you want from me?' *She's not real. Why are you even engaging with her? This is a dream, remember.*

Tara smirked. It was a smirk I'd seen countless times before. 'What do I *want* from you? Hmm. Interesting question. Let's see . . . someone to talk to, perhaps? Someone to share all my secrets with? A shoulder to cry on? Maybe just someone to sympathize with the fact that I'm *fucking dead!*' Anger flashed across her features so fast that I wasn't even sure I'd seen it. And then the smirk was back in place.

'You're not real.' The shakiness in my voice betrayed me.

'Sure about that, are you?'

'You can't be real. You're . . .'

'Dead? Tell me something I don't know.'

'Leave me alone. Please?'

'*Leave me alone. Please?*' She mimicked me perfectly. 'Now where would be the fun in that?'

'I'm closing my eyes now, and when I open them you're going to be gone. This is a dream or a hallucination or something, I know it is. When I open my eyes you're going to be gone.' *Deep breath. Close your eyes. Five more deep breaths. Now. Open your eyes now . . .*

'Boo!' Tara cackled, laughing so hard I thought she was going to choke. 'You always were an odd one, weren't you?'

'I'm going back to sleep now, or waking up, or whatever the hell it is that'll make you go away.' I sounded a lot more confident than I felt. I pulled the duvet over my head and snuggled down. My heart was drumming a wild beat inside my chest.

'Fine. Be like that. But I'll be back. You're going to have to talk to me eventually.' Then there was silence. All I could hear was the snuffly noises Bruno sometimes makes when he's having a particularly good dream.

I waited maybe five or ten minutes, almost sure she'd still be there when I peeled back the duvet. But she wasn't. The space next to Bruno was vacant. No ghost girls to be seen.

It had seemed so real. SO real. I replayed the conversation in my mind. Everything she'd said had been Tara through and through. But Tara was dead. *I am either a) losing my mind, or b) still dreaming.* I slapped myself across the face, hard. It hurt. A lot. *OK, so probably not still dreaming.*

I lay awake for hours, it seemed. *Her hands . . . how did her hands get like that?* Too scared to stay awake, too scared to go to sleep. But eventually I must have drifted off.

I woke up the next morning feeling completely exhausted. Bruno was licking my face. I shoved him off me and he retreated to the bottom of the bed. And then I remembered.

It was dream. It had to have been a dream. God, your brain must be seriously messed up.

But I was kidding myself. Even then I knew that it wasn't a dream. Not exactly.

So that was the first time, and she's been back twice more before today.

Thursday night was the same deal. I woke up from a rare non-nightmare to find her sitting at my desk on top of yesterday's clothes. I pulled a pillow over my head and pressed it against my ears, but I could still hear her. She wouldn't shut up. All she talked about was my bedroom and the fact that the décor hadn't changed since the last time she'd been here as a non-dead person. She couldn't believe I'd kept it pink, and kept asking when I was going to grow up. I wanted to scream at her. But there's no point screaming at someone who's not really there.

The pink bedroom was a surprise that Mum had organized when I was staying at Uncle Joe's one weekend. I came back and my room had been transformed into a riot of pink. A twirly curly dressing table fit for a princess. A bright pink fluffy rug. Pink bedding. And the odd bit of zebra print thrown in for good measure. I was ten years old and had been over the whole pink and girly thing for a good year or so. But Mum wasn't to know that. She'd been kind of busy with the whole 'trying not to die' thing. Her hair was just starting to grow back in little babyish tufts. She wore a pink headscarf the day of the Grand Bedroom Unveiling. We thought the cancer was gone for good – that she'd beaten it, just like she'd promised she would. She looked happy for the first time in months. I could learn to love my new bedroom because it had made her smile. And I *do* love it. I won't ever change it.

Tara went on and on about the room and the fact that the rug was a bit threadbare and weren't the curtains looking faded? I wasn't scared any more – just annoyed. I tried to focus on what I knew for sure: she was a figment of my imagination, conjured up by grief and guilt and lack of sleep. The human brain has some pretty impressive tricks up its non-existent sleeve. I've always suffered from an overactive imagination, and this was the result. I told myself this over and over again. I wasn't scared. I wasn't scared. I wasn't. OK, I was. Just a little. Especially when I thought about her hands.

Last night was different. I woke up in a panicky sweat, my vest top clinging to my skin. Another nightmare about that night. I turned the pillow over to get the cool side. For a moment it was bliss.

'Now that's more like it.'

Shit. Not again. Not tonight. It was hard enough getting to sleep knowing how horrific tomorrow's going to be. Keep your eyes closed. Don't look at her — it's better that way.

'I prefer it when you have nightmares. You *should* have nightmares. It's the least you deserve.' Her cheerful voice was at odds with her words.

I nearly spoke to her then, but what was the point? It was crazy. Whereas conjuring up a ghost girl in my mind meant I was only about seventy per cent of the way to crazy town. But my unspoken words were loud inside my head: *You're right*.

'So, tomorrow's my big day! Shame I'm not alive to see it really. They'd better do it right. Bet you're looking forward to sharing your grief with the entire school. You know you're going to have to rustle up some tears from somewhere. Maybe you should take a raw onion to help you out.'

Shut up.

Eventually she disappeared, but not before telling me to wear the skinny purple jeans to the memorial service.

How the hell did she know about the jeans? I've always been too embarrassed to wear them outside of the house. When I was rifling through my wardrobe this morning I was determined to ignore Tara's instructions.

22

But a little voice inside my head said *You might as well. What harm can it do? Maybe it'll make her go away.*

But now she's back and asking me about her own funeral. Changing into my trackie bottoms will have to wait. I ignore her, sit down at my desk and start making some notes for an English essay I should have done ages ago. You'd think Daley might have let us off, what with all that's happened. At least the essay is about a book I actually *like* for once – that makes it less of a chore. But it's impossible to concentrate with Tara chelping on. I can't make sense of the words on the page, but I stare and stare at them, desperately trying to block out her voice. I manage to ignore her for a grand total of twenty-three minutes.

I turn to face her. 'Please leave me alone. I just want to get on with my homework and forget all about today.' I have no idea why I'm trying to reason with a dead person.

She looks up, a triumphant grin on her face. '*Finally!* Watching someone do homework is even more boring than doing it yourself. So, what did you think of the turnout? Tell me *everything*.'

I sigh. If this is what it's going to take . . .

So I tell her all about it. I have a feeling she already knows. Who was there, who wasn't there. (She raises her perfect eyebrows when I mentioned

Rae's absence.) Who cried, who didn't. The music, the speeches, all of it. She asks a lot of questions, and I do my best to answer them. The only time her gleeful smile falters is when I mention Jack. But it returns when I recount Mrs Flanagan's speech pretty much word for word.

'God, that silly old bitch LOVES me. I mean, *loved* me.'

'Yeah, don't know why,' I mutter.

'You *do* know why. I played the game — it's as simple as that. It's all about telling people what they want to hear and being the person they want you to be — or at least making them *think* you're who they want you to be.' She's looking awfully smug. What does a dead person have to be smug about?

'Why can't you just be yourself?'

Tara shakes her head. 'Oh, Alice. How could you have forgotten? Being yourself gets you precisely nowhere. You are a nobody. You might as well not exist.'

'That's not true!'

'It is, and you know it. What do you reckon people would say at *your* funeral? "Oh, yeah, Alice. I think she sat behind me in history . . ."'

I've had enough. I head towards the door, pretty sure she (it) won't follow me downstairs.

'Where do you think you're going? I haven't finished with you yet.'

'Look, Tara, I'm really sorry you're dead.' Feels like something I should have said sooner. I slump back into the chair.

'Are you?' Her eyes lock onto mine.

'Of course I am! But I need to get on with my life. I can't have you popping up all the time, reminding me about it – making me feel worse than I already do. I'M SORRY! It was an accident!'

She says nothing.

I've never been good with awkward silences. 'An accident,' I say again. It sounds pathetically inadequate.

Tara fixes me with a withering look. 'Are you sure about that?'

'Of course I'm sure!' Yes. I am sure. Absolutely sure.

'Liar!'

My tears spring from nowhere. 'Shut up! Leave me alone leave me alone leave me alone!' Sobbing now, and trying to ignore the voice inside my head.

'You have to find out what happened,' she says.

'I know what happened!'

'Do you?' Her tone is reasonable.

'Yes! No . . . I don't know.' My thoughts are tumbling and stumbling and scaring me.

'You *have* to find out. You owe me that at least.'

She's right. I don't want her to be right.

'Tell me what to do.' Resigned now.

'Why don't you start by talking to that dykey best friend of yours?'

'She's not a . . . don't say that!' I hate that word.

'Yeah, whatever you say. Just talk to her.'

A shout from downstairs makes me jump. It's Dad, bellowing that dinner's ready. I'm suddenly aware of the garlicky oniony aroma wafting into the room. It usually makes my saliva glands go into overdrive, but today it turns my stomach. I wonder if I can get away with skipping dinner. Doubtful. Dad's been watching carefully, making sure I eat. Cooking all my favourite meals. He says I've lost weight; he can be so clueless sometimes. How can he not notice the flesh spilling over the top of these bloody jeans?

Tara's gone. Of course she's gone. I can't pinpoint the exact moment it happened. She didn't disappear in a puff of smoke, or dissolve into nothingness or walk through a wall. She was there and then not there, but I don't know what happened in between. I must pay attention next time. But maybe there won't be a next time. Maybe my madness is over. Please let it be over.

3

I'm meant to be hanging out with Cass on Sunday. We usually watch a DVD in her room or something. That is what my life is supposed to be like: spending time with my best mate, going shopping in town and maybe going to the cinema with a boy. Not going to funerals (or memorial services or whatever). Not talking to dead girls. Not thinking the unthinkable.

I told Cass I might go round later. But it doesn't seem right somehow, us getting back to our old routine. How can it be the same as before? Are we supposed to just pretend that nothing's changed?

Dad made me eat an extra helping of roasties at lunch. My stomach feels stretched tight like a drum.

I'm lying on my bed, trying – and failing – not to think about Tara. Why does she want me to speak to Cass? What could she possibly tell me that I don't already know?

I was there. I know exactly what happened.

Except I wasn't there when it *actually* happened, was I? When Tara Chambers breathed her last breath.

My phone rings and rescues me from my thoughts. I don't recognize the number.

'Hello?'

'Er . . . hello. Is that Alice?' It's a boy. A boy is calling me. Boys don't call me.

'Yeah, it is.'

'Hi. It's Jack — Tara's brother.'

I stop breathing for a second. 'Hi.' My voice sounds impossibly vacant.

'I hope you don't mind me calling. I saw you yesterday after . . .'

'I'm so sorry about your sister. I don't really know what to say.'

He laughs, but not like he finds it funny. 'No one does.'

'Sorry. I . . .'

'You don't need to apologize. I've had enough of people apologizing. I think it's starting to drive me a bit mental.'

'Sorry.' Now he laughs for real and I like the way it sounds — rich and warm, like the very best hot chocolate, the posh stuff Mum used to buy.

'Listen, Alice, I hope you don't mind me calling like this. It's just, I'd really like to talk to you.'

'No, of course I don't mind, but . . . um . . . what do you want to talk about?' The answer is obvious, but I cling to the hope that it might be something else. Anything else.

'You were in Tara's cabin on the trip, weren't you?'

'Yes. Not just me though.' Maybe he doesn't notice how defensive I sound.

'I know, but I need to know what happened. I mean, I know what the police say. It's just . . . I'd like to hear it from someone who was there. And you used to be such good friends with her . . . Sorry, this must be hard for you too. But maybe it would help for you to talk it through as well.'

No. Say no. You're too upset to talk about it. 'OK.' *What?* No!

'Thanks, Alice. I really appreciate this.' He pauses for a second. 'You know, I sort of missed you when you stopped coming round to our house. You were the only one of her friends who didn't ignore me.'

'I . . . thanks.' He's talking nonsense though; I *did* ignore him.

We arrange to meet up after school on Tuesday, and then say our goodbyes.

Shit. What am I going to do? I can't face him. I *can't*. It's one thing pretending in front of Dad and everyone at school. But he's her *brother*. I can't just lie to his face. He'll know something's up. And it's not right. He deserves to know the truth. But he never will. We promised. We ALL promised.

There's no way I can go through with it. I was just too taken aback and cowardly to tell him. I'll call him on Tuesday and say I'm ill or something. Yes. That's what I'll do. It'll be fine.

Cass texts me later: *Soooooo bored! When u coming over?*

It's easier for me to go rather than have to explain why I don't want to. Not sure that my reasons would go down too well . . . *I'm kind of knackered cos a dead girl keeps hounding me. You see, she wants to find out exactly why she died and for some reason she wants me to talk to you about it and I really REALLY don't want to.*

So I hop on the tube and arrive at Cass's just as they're clearing away dinner. Her brother is home from uni for the weekend. I used to have the biggest crush on Matt, but I never told Cass. She'd have taken the piss something chronic. Anyway, the crush has faded now. He smells funny, and I don't like the way he looks at me. He *leers*. I'm pretty sure he never used to leer.

Cass drags me up to her room and launches into a full-on tirade about how annoying her brothers are and how she can't wait to leave home and how she can't wait for Matt to go back to uni tomorrow and why does he have to come home so often anyway. I'm semi-sympathetic. Three brothers is really more than anyone should have to cope with. Tom's OK though – as far as I can tell he hardly ever leaves his room. And Jeremy is cute as anything. But he won't be six years old forever. It's only a matter of time before he grows into a big stinking leering oaf like Matt. Still, I wouldn't mind having at least one annoying sibling to keep me company sometimes. There will be no one to make a speech like Jack's at my funeral. Jack. I wonder if I should tell Cass about Jack.

I tune back in and Cass is moaning about dirty pants on the bathroom floor and burping at the dinner table.

'Ha! You can talk . . . you're hardly the Queen of Hygiene yourself.'

She throws a pillow at my head. 'Shut it, you. You don't know what it's like. I could *kill* them sometimes.'

We're both silent for a second.

'So . . . anyway, what have you been up to since yesterday?'

31

'Nothing much. Dad keeps watching me. I think he's waiting for me to have some kind of breakdown. And he made me eat a fried breakfast AND roast chicken for lunch.' *And by the way, Dead Tara told me to ask you about the night she died.*

'God, your dad's such a feeder. Still, I reckon you could do with some more meat on your bones.'

I throw the pillow back at Cass, but it misses and knocks a picture frame off her bedside table. Cass picks up the frame and sets in back in place. It's a photo of me and her taken a couple of years ago on a school trip to France. We're eating gigantic ice creams and we're both sticking our tongues out. You can see other people in the background. Tara's there, her perfect profile visible over my shoulder.

I have to tell Cass, even though I know exactly what she'll say. 'Jack called. He wants to talk to me about it.'

'Jack? Who's . . . what? Her *brother*?' I've noticed that Cass doesn't like using Tara's name these days. As if it makes a difference. I'm tempted to remind Cass that Tara is/was not Lord Voldemort. But maybe she doesn't even realize she's doing it, and maybe it doesn't matter if it makes her feel better.

'Yeah. He called me earlier. He wants to meet up on Tuesday.'

'You're not going to? *Are* you?' Cass is horrified.

'I . . . I don't know. I said yes, but . . .'

'You can't! Have you lost your fucking mind?'

'No, but . . . I couldn't say no to him.'

'Why not?! It's not hard. Tell him you don't think you can talk about it. You're *traumatized*. Yeah, no one can argue with that.'

'Don't you think he deserves . . . ?'

'Deserves what? To know the truth? You *have* lost your mind, haven't you? How many times am I going to have to say this to you: no one can find out what happened. No one. You KNOW that, don't you? If anyone finds out, we'll be in deep, deep shit. They're not going to say, "Oh, it's OK. We understand it was an accident and you were scared and panicked and did the wrong thing." We'll go to prison. All of us. For God's sake, Alice. I can't believe you're even considering this.'

I'm stunned by her viciousness. I know it's driven by fear, but it's still horrible to see her face all twisted up. I can feel the tears start to well up. I can't help it. 'I . . . wasn't going to tell him anything. I would never do that.'

Her face softens. 'Alice, we have to be careful. If you talk to Jack, you might let something slip by mistake. We have to be on our guard all the time, at least until all the fuss dies down. I really, really don't think you should do this.'

'I don't think he's going to interrogate me or anything. Maybe he's got no one else to talk to.'

'But why does it have to be *you*? Of all people?'

'Because he knows I was in Tara's cabin? Because I used to be friends with her, I don't know. I think I owe it to him to at least talk to him. It seems like the least I can do, after—'

'It was an *accident*, remember?' I swear, if I hear Cass say the word *accident* one more time . . . It's been her mantra since it happened. She holds onto it like a life raft in a storm.

'It was still our fault. And we could have told the truth about what happened. We should have told the truth.' She knows how I feel, and I know how she feels, and we're so utterly opposed that I wonder how things can ever be the same between us. How can we possibly get back to normal after something like this? We don't deserve normal.

Cass sighs and flops back on the bed. 'Let's not talk about it any more. I can't have this conversation again. You do what you want. Talk to Jack, whatever. Just be careful, OK?'

We sit in silence for a while. I shouldn't have said anything. I was going to bail on Jack anyway. But now I'm not. Telling Cass has made me absolutely certain that talking to him is the right thing to do. I'm not stupid enough to think it'll make up for what happened, not even a little bit. But somehow I've got to get back on track. Back to who I am. I've always thought of myself as someone who does the right thing – or at least tries to.

I really hope I can be that person again one day.

4

Jack's due any minute. I'm early, of course. I'm sitting in some little coffee shop that I've never noticed before even though I must have walked past it a thousand times.

I order a hot chocolate with extra marshmallows; it's sweet and creamy. The door chimes every time someone leaves or enters, and I look up every time. Half expecting Cass to storm in and drag me out by my hair. But I managed to successfully evade her in the chaos at the end of the school day. And I didn't tell her where I was meeting Jack, thank God.

I check my watch; he's late. I gulp down my hot chocolate before it turns into cold chocolate. I wipe my mouth extra-carefully, and resist (with difficulty) the temptation to nip to the loos to check myself out in the mirror. *This isn't a date, remember? In fact, it's the exact opposite of a date, if that's even possible.*

I study the menu, even though I've already done that for a good five minutes or so. Then the door chimes again and there he is. He's wearing his school uniform, but he wears it well. The top button of his shirt is undone and his tie is loose. A messenger bag slung over his shoulders and black Converse on his feet. He scans the room and smiles when he spots me.

'Alice, hi. Thanks for coming.' Instead of sitting opposite, Jack sits next to me. The waitress appears from nowhere and he orders a black coffee, and another hot chocolate for me before I can protest. My stomach hurts.

'So . . . how are you doing?' For a second I think he's going to touch my arm, but he doesn't. Instead, he rests his hand near my elbow on the table.

'I . . . How are *you* doing?'

'OK, I suppose.' He rubs his face. 'I'm glad the funeral's over with. I was dreading it.'

'Your speech was lovely.'

He grins. 'Really? Thanks. Dad didn't think so. He was all "Why did you say those things about Tara? You shouldn't speak ill of the dead." He thought it was completely inappropriate.' The grin dials down to nothing. 'I suppose I can hardly blame him though. It's not the way he wants Tara to be remembered.'

'Things must be difficult at home right now . . .'

Jack shrugs. 'Mum spends most of her time in Tara's room, staring into space. Tara had this hoodie that she wore round the house all the time, and Mum sits with it on her lap.' I haven't seen Tara in a hoodie for years. The image of Tara's mum fills me up with a sadness that seeps into every corner of me. I fill in the extra details myself: raindrops drizzling down the window, tears drizzling down her face, Jack watching from the doorway.

'And Dad's not much better — just different. I can't seem to do anything right at the moment as far as he's concerned. I try to stay out of his way as much as I can.'

'I can't even imagine what it must be like.'

'Your mum . . . she died, didn't she?'

'Yes.' What else is there to say?

'So you kind of know what it's like, don't you?' NO! I want to scream. That was different.

I say it gently. 'That was different. She was ill for a long time. In the end it was almost a relief.' This is a lie. Even though I knew how much pain she was in, I still begged her not to leave me. It haunts me nearly every day.

This time Jack reaches out for my hand, and we sit in silence for a little while. I like the way it feels: my hand feels warm and safe, and the rest of me would like to feel that way too. It doesn't feel weird or strange or embarrassing like I would have imagined (if I could ever have imagined such a thing happening to me).

Jack's phone rings and he lets go of my hand to retrieve it from his pocket. I wonder how long we would have sat like that if we hadn't been interrupted.

Jack looks hard at the display on his phone, before sighing. 'Sorry, Alice. I've got to take this.' He half turns away from me, pointlessly trying to shield me from the call. 'Hello? Yes, I'll be home for dinner . . . I'm at Freddie's. Yes . . . OK . . . Right. Look, Dad, I've got to go . . . Yes. Before seven, I promise.' He disconnects the call with another sigh, deeper and longer than the first. He looks exhausted – weighed down with it all.

'Sorry about that. He wants to know where I am twenty-four hours a day. It's starting to drive me up the wall. He never used to bother where I was from one day to the next, not like with Tara. She always had to tell him where she was going and who with and when she'd be back.' I find this hard to believe; Tara always gave the impression she could pretty much do whatever she wanted. 'I was allowed to just get on with things. Dad always said it was different for boys. Tara hated it. But it's different now. I'm gonna have to say something if he doesn't stop it soon. It's not as if I'm going to go and drown in some loch, is it?'

He registers the shock on my face and winces. 'Sorry. I shouldn't have said that. Got to stop feeling sorry for myself.' He tries to smile, but it doesn't quite work out for him. More than anything I want to reach out for his hand, but I would never do something like that.

'So . . . do you think you could tell me about the trip?' I knew this was coming, but it still feels like all the air has been sucked out from my lungs with a turbo-boosted vacuum cleaner. I want to run away and hide and never come back. But I nod.

'I know it must be hard for you, but I just want to know about . . . her last few days, you know? I *need* to know.'

One last try to get out of this: 'Have you tried talking to Danni or Sam or Gemma?'

'I learned not to waste time talking to those bitches a *long* time ago. No. You're the one, Alice.' My heart thuddunks inside my chest, even though I know he doesn't mean *I'm the one*. Because that would be ridiculous: we hardly know each other, and even if we did, there is precisely no chance that *I* would be the one.

Jack's eyes are intense. I can't look away; I don't

want to look away. 'You're the only one I trust to tell me the truth.'

I can barely speak or think or do anything, but somehow I manage to choke out a few words. 'Where do you want me start?'

'How about at the beginning?' His smile is encouraging.

So I think back to that first day, setting off in the darkness. None of us had any idea that we were heading into a nightmare.

I start to talk and talk and talk – editing myself as I go.

Here's what actually happened.

This is not what I tell Jack.

5

None of us was looking forward to the trip. It wasn't skiing in Austria, or checking out the sights in Brittany. It was Scotland. Doing outdoors stuff in Scotland. An adventure holiday, for Christ's sake.

Abseiling and caving and orienteering in the rain. I was not a happy bunny. I tried to wheedle my way out of it, but Dad wouldn't listen. He thought it would be *good* for me. 'Life is all about new experiences.' Thanks, Dad. I got a new experience all right.

Seems like most of the other parents thought the same thing: it would be good for their little darlings to get out of the big bad city and explore the great outdoors. Still, I was surprised that Tara and her sidekicks had signed up. These were not the kind of girls who did things they didn't want to do. But it was an opportunity to get away from the parentals for a week, and who'd turn that down? (Apart from me, that is. I actually quite like spending time with Dad. When he's not watching me, hawk-style.)

The coach set off before dawn. A nine-hour journey. I don't like long journeys – never have. I used to get sick just going along the motorway to see Uncle Joe. In our family, no journey was undertaken without several plastic bags in Mum's handbag, just in case. Weirdly, I stopped getting carsick after she died. But I still have to be careful on long journeys and sit in the front seat, sipping water all the way, no reading.

I felt sorry for Cass having to sit next to me. I wasn't exactly chatty. Just wanted to close my eyes and go to sleep until it was over. Except I can't sleep on any journey; I can't really sleep anywhere but my own bed. And now I can't even sleep there.

Cass was the one person who wasn't completely hating the idea of what was to come. All that *being active* sort of stuff comes naturally to her. Cass is mega-sporty. She's on the hockey team, she does athletics AND she's in the swimming club. God knows where she finds the energy. Organized sport is just so . . . blah. If I'm going to exercise, I prefer to do it alone so that other people are spared the gasping and general ineptitude. But not Cass – she's up for any sport (except for netball, which is another thing she thinks is beyond pathetic). Plus she was glad to get away from her brothers for a while.

The journey seemed never-ending. I was glad we were sitting near the front. Near the teachers. The back of the bus was Tara territory. I knew what it'd be like: Gemma, Sam and Danni hanging on her every word, laughing at things that weren't funny. Well, that's not exactly fair – Tara *was* funny. Mean, but funny. Unless her humour was at your expense, in which case it was just . . . horrible.

It was Miss Daley's first school trip. She'd bought a new Berghaus fleece just for the occasion. Shame she'd forgotten to take the price tag off. I was worried that Tara (+3) would eat her for breakfast, so I leaned over and told her. She blushed something fierce and thanked me. Cass didn't look impressed. Being nice to teachers is not a quality Cass appreciates in a best friend.

I wondered how old Daley was, and if she'd always wanted to be a teacher. When she was our age did she dream of supervising a bunch of over-educated, over-privileged teenage girls on a trip to deepest, darkest Scotland? Or maybe she wanted to be a doctor, or a rock star or a housewife? I finally settled on the idea that she'd wanted to be a writer, but being an English teacher was the next best thing. Maybe she taps away at her laptop late into the night, long after she's finished marking our essays. Maybe she sips a glass of Pinot Grigio and dreams of the day she can give it all up and write full-time. Or maybe my imagination just runs away from me sometimes.

About three hours into the journey, Polly Sutcliffe came and asked Daley when we'd be stopping at a service station. Daley told her we'd be stopping in an hour or so, and asked if she'd forgotten to bring any food.

Polly shook her head, embarrassed. 'No, I've got food. Um . . . Tara just wanted to know.'

'Well, if Tara wanted to know, then Tara could have got up off her backside and come to ask me herself, couldn't she?'

Cass and I smirked at each other.

Polly blushed. 'Oh I don't mind. I fancied stretching my legs anyway.' *Yeah, right.* She scurried back up the aisle.

It was hard not to feel sorry for Polly. But it was just as hard to be entirely sympathetic. Polly had never been popular. She wasn't one of the pretty girls or one of the sporty girls or even one of the super-brainy girls. Not that I was, either. But Polly was just *there*. On the edge of things, without any real friends. She got nasty bouts of eczema from time to time, which made her even more awkward and self-conscious.

Whenever Polly was around, I felt bad. Like I should try and be her friend because no one else would. But I just couldn't bring myself to do it. We probably didn't have anything in common anyway. I was a coward. Everyone knows that your friends reflect on you, and I was worried about people lumping me in with Polly — one of the Untouchables. I'd been there before.

At least I tried to be nice to her. I smiled and said hello in the corridors, which is more than most of the others did. I let her borrow my notes when she was off sick that time last year. But that was as far as I was willing to go. And if I'm honest, Polly made me feel slightly uncomfortable. She was always *watching*. You'd be chatting and having a laugh in the canteen or the common room or the courtyard, and then you'd look round and there she'd be, sitting in a corner — watching . . . listening. It was as if she could blend in with her surroundings somehow and I was the only one who noticed. Sometimes I wondered if she was studying for some kind of How-To-Be-A-Normal-Teenage-Girl test. And then I'd feel mean and think that she was only watching because that was all that they (we) *allowed* her to do. She was not allowed in.

The only thing that Polly had going for her (in our eyes at least) was the fact that she could sing. Like, really well. And she wasn't shy about doing it either. She would perform at the end-of-term concert and everyone would be amazed. It was almost like we forgot, year to year, that she had this incredible talent that made us all jealous. When Polly sang, she looked sort of beautiful.

As far as I was aware, Polly didn't even cross Tara's radar until about a year ago. Cass was the first one to notice that Polly had started following Tara around, acting like a little lapdog. Tara seemed to tolerate her, but that was all. She'd let Polly sit at her table at lunch. Polly would sit at the end of the table, reading (or pretending to read) a book, while Tara and Gemma and Sam and Danni chatted and laughed and ignored her. Everyone thought it was weird. No one else had sat at that table for at least two years. Cass's theory was that Tara saw Polly as a pet. I wasn't so sure.

I craned my neck to watch Polly head back to her seat. She stopped and said something to Tara, who was presiding over the coach from the middle seat right at the back. Then she sat down in the empty row just in front of Tara's crew. Just before I turned away, Tara caught my eye. We looked at each other for a second or two before Cass thumped me on the shoulder, wanting to show me a video on her phone.

That happened sometimes. I'd notice Tara looking at me or she'd notice me looking at her, and whenever it happened I thought, *I can't believe we used to be friends*.

The rest of the journey was uneventful. Cass let me sit next to the window as soon as we got to the Scottish border and I gazed out at the passing scenery. It was like England, only wetter. There was crap music blaring out from the back of the bus. I *hate* being forced to listen to other people's music, so I plugged myself into my iPod and turned it up loud. The rest of the world disappeared for a while.

6

I opened my eyes when the coach stopped. Cass
laughed at me and said I'd been snoring. Which was
a load of crap – I hadn't even been asleep. A quick
glance out the window confirmed it was still raining.
We milled around getting soaked while the driver and
Mr Miles pulled out our rucksacks and Daley went
looking for the person in charge of the place. It wasn't
much to look at; a few cabins in the soggy woods. I'd
checked it out on Google before we left. The middle
of nowhere – lots of mountains, a creepy forest and
a loch. I looked at my phone and sure enough, there
was no reception. Not that it mattered, as Mr Miles
had already made it very clear that this was to be a no-
tech holiday. We'd be handing in our phones, iPods,
BlackBerrys and anything else that would make the
week even slightly bearable.

We eventually got out of the rain and into the

biggest of the buildings, which turned out to be a pine-panelled hall where we'd be having our meals. Rows of chairs were laid out facing a stage, and Daley told us to sit down. Cass and I sat in the back row. Three people were up on the stage, all looking super-outdoorsy in their primary-coloured fleeces. Daley had clearly made the right style choice.

A woman stepped forward and introduced herself. Her name was Jess and she had greying dreadlocks and a friendly face. She welcomed us to Loch Dunochar and told us what the next week had in store for us. Basically a lot of being outside in the pissing rain, running around in the woods and embarrassing ourselves in front of our peers. Well, that's not exactly what she said, but that was pretty much the gist of it. *Getting back to nature* – that's what she said. 'How are we supposed to get *back* to nature when the closest we've ever been is London bloody Zoo or Camden on a Saturday night?' I whispered to Cass. She rolled her eyes.

The guy standing next to Jess was clearly bored – he must have heard this spiel a hundred times before. He looked way too cool to be there: shaved head, eyebrow piercing and a tattoo peeking out from the sleeve of his fleece. He was wearing baggy shorts and flip-flops and his legs were tanned. *God knows how he got a tan like that around here*. I couldn't help staring at his calf muscles.

His name was Duncan and he had the nicest accent I'd ever heard. Turned out he was going to be in charge of most of the activities we'd be doing. I looked around and pretty much all of us were hanging on his every word. Tara was eyeing him up like a tasty snack. Clearly we were all thinking the same: *Maybe this week isn't going to be so bad after all.* As soon as I thought that, a new worry came crashing down on me: *You are going to embarrass yourself in front of the hottest man you've ever seen in your life.*

The only ones who seemed immune to Duncan's charms were Cass, who was staring out of the window, and Rae who was (as usual) surreptitiously plugged into her headphones and nibbling at her fingernails. A week without music was going to be a total nightmare for her. *She might actually have to talk to real people.*

The other guy introduced himself as Paul, but we were so not interested. He was older and beardy and not Duncan. He went on about safety and making sure we listened carefully to our instructors and he told us not to go wandering off into the woods on our own.

Cass put her hand up to ask a question. 'Why

shouldn't we go into the woods on our own? Is there some mad axe-man out there or something?'

Paul and Jess exchanged looks which obviously meant *This one's trouble*.

Danni nudged Tara and then mouthed the word *pathetic* in Cass's direction. Cass none-too-subtly stuck up her middle finger at Danni.

'No, there's no mad axe-man . . . that we know of anyway.' And he laughed a stupid horror-movie laugh. We stared at him until he stopped. 'No, but seriously, it can be dangerous out here. This area is riddled with caves and potholes, as you'll be finding out for yourselves tomorrow, courtesy of Mr Fletcher here.' He gestured towards Duncan before carrying on. 'If you don't know where you're going, you could easily find yourself falling down a hole and breaking a leg. Or a neck. And with all this lovely weather we've been having, the rivers are in full flow, so no late-night fishing trips for you ladies, OK?' *This guy is a weirdo*. 'And I won't even mention the lions and tigers and bears.' *Yep, a proper weirdo.*

Polly's hand went up. 'Are there really bears around here?' she asked hesitantly. Everyone laughed and I felt bad for her. When would she learn that it's *always* best to keep your mouth shut?

Paul tried his best not to smile. 'No, there are no

bears. And no lions or tigers for that matter. There *are* supposed to be wildcats in this area, but I've never seen one. The most fearsome creatures round here are the midges, which will eat you alive if they get half a chance. Lucky for you lot, they're only a problem in summer.'

'Yeah, like Scotland even *has* a summer,' I muttered to no one in particular.

And then the introductions were over and we lined up to hand in our phones and stuff to Daley. Tara tried to pretend she hadn't brought her phone with her, but Daley just stood there waiting until Tara gave up and handed it over. She flounced away, going on about it being an infringement of her civil rights and what if there was some kind of emergency? She had a point. I felt kind of anxious that I wouldn't be able to speak to Dad for six days. I'd always been able to ring him before, just to check things were OK.

Then came the part I'd been dreading: sorting out the sleeping arrangements. There were six cabins, each sleeping five girls. Everyone looked around, sizing each other up, ready for a free-for-all. I edged closer to Cass. Tara and Danni and Gemma and Sam looked ready to audition girls for the coveted (or not) fifth spot in what would no doubt be the cushiest cabin of the lot.

But Daley surprised us by taking a piece of paper from her pocket. 'I've already allocated each of you to a cabin, so if you could go and stand with your cabin-mates when I read out your name.'

'AW, MISS?!' The chorus included pretty much everyone. I was too horrified to speak. Tara was giving Daley *major* evils.

I felt nauseous as the names were read out. One by one, everyone went and stood together in their little groups, some looking happier than others. The witches had managed to wangle a cabin together, but their fearless leader was left out in the cold. And then there were five:

Tara. Polly. Rae. Cass. And me.

Hardly what you'd call a dream team, but I was relieved that Cass and I would be together. And although Tara was the last person I wanted to share a room with, I *did* find it funny that she'd been separated from her loyal followers.

Tara was NOT happy. She stormed right up to Daley and gave her some spiel about this being completely ridiculous. We'd always been able to choose our own rooms before, and she wasn't with any of her friends. She gestured towards us and didn't even bother to disguise her disdain. 'But I barely know these people!' Not strictly true. She was on the swimming team with Cass, Polly was her new puppet, and I was . . . I don't know . . . a little piece of history? The only one she genuinely didn't know was Rae, but then no one really knew Rae.

Tara tried her best to convince Daley to let her swap cabins. She used some of her classic tricks: charm, logic, and a weird semi-flirtatious thing that works on all the teachers. When it was clear that Daley was having none of it, Tara tried for extreme petulance.

Daley cut her off. 'Tara, is this really such a big deal? Can't you bear to be separated from your entourage for a few nights? It might do you good to spend time with some different people for a change.'

I thought Tara was going to deck her. No one ever talked to her like that. Daley was fast becoming one of my very favourite people.

Tara looked around, well aware that she was looking like an idiot, and that if she carried on, Daley might humiliate her further. She shrugged. 'Whatever. Who cares, anyway? This whole trip is a joke.' She flicked her salon-perfect hair as she meandered over to stand next to me.

Daley smiled at us. 'Right, so everyone's happy then? Marvellous! Off you go to your cabins. I think you'll find your names already on the doors.'

Tara shook her head, hardly able to believe what had just happened.

I smiled at her in what I thought was a sympathetic way. She didn't smile back. *Bitch.*

7

Our cabin was . . . cabin-y. More pine. Five uncomfortable-looking beds with matching tartan blankets which looked mega-scratchy. At least there was a bathroom. That was another thing I'd been dreading: some kind of outdoor shower/toilet-block situation. So the bathroom was a big relief, and it was actually pretty nice too.

Of course Tara was the first to bagsy a bed. She went for the one nearest the door, all the better to make her escape. She dumped her rucksack on the bed and did just that – escaped. No prizes for guessing where she was going – the witches were in the cabin next to ours.

I took the bed furthest away from Tara's. Not on purpose, it just worked out like that. Cass had the bed next to mine. Polly started unpacking her stuff straightaway, laying out clothes on her bed and

57

carefully refolding them before putting them away in the drawers underneath. If you listened carefully, you could hear her singing under her breath.

I started to unpack, just dumping the stuff from my rucksack straight into the drawers. Nothing was ironed anyway. I always ironed Dad's clothes because he needed to look semi-presentable for work. But by the time I'd finished with all his trousers and shirts (shirts were the worst), I could never be bothered to do mine.

Cass lay on her bed, alternating between muttering about having to share a cabin with *that bitch* and getting excited about the potholing tomorrow. She'd done it a few times before. Cass and her family never go on normal holidays like normal people. They always have to *do* stuff, like horse-riding or climbing or sailing. Weird.

Potholing was probably near the bottom of my list of things I ever wanted to try in my life. I get claustrophobic in lifts, so underground caves and tunnels and tiny crevasses are hardly my idea of a fun time. Cass tried her best to convince me that it was 'a total rush', but I wasn't buying it.

Cass stopped mid-babble and shouted, 'Oi! Rae!' across the room. I had no idea why she was shouting until I saw that Rae was plugged into her iPod.

Huh? She was lying on her bed and staring at the ceiling.

Rae turned to Cass and pulled off her headphones. 'What?'

'How did you manage to get that past Daley?'

Rae smiled. I don't think I'd ever seen her smile before. 'Brought a spare. Nicked it off my sister last night. She's gonna kill me for wiping her music, even if it was just a lot of electro-crap.'

'Nice one,' said Cass, as Rae plugged herself back in. I was annoyed I hadn't thought of smuggling in a spare phone. I could have brought Mum's. I keep it in my desk drawer – not sure why.

I noticed that Polly had stopped unpacking and was watching us. As soon as she realized that I'd noticed her, she looked away. She arranged an alarm clock, some moisturizer and a book on her bedside table, then went into the bathroom, probably to arrange some stuff in there.

We didn't see Tara again till dinnertime. As I was tucking into my not-too-bad tuna bake I saw her making a beeline over to a table in the corner. A table where Duncan was sitting, alone, with a book propped up behind his plate. He didn't seem bothered at the interruption. Why would he? What hot-blooded male could resist the charms of Tara Chambers? None that

I'd ever met, that was for sure. Tara's posse wasn't far behind, and he didn't seem to mind that either. I couldn't stop watching them: the way Tara touched Duncan's shoulder on more than one occasion; the way her hair fell in front of her face before she oh-so-coyly tucked it behind an ear; the way she took dainty bites of her salad and dabbed at her mouth with a napkin.

I was so intent on watching Tara's table that a great big dollop of cheesy tomatoey tuna escaped from my fork and landed on my lap. Cass laughed so hard she choked on her water. I watched as she coughed and spluttered.

'Serves you right for laughing at me. And don't think I'm going to Heimlich you. If you die, it's your own fault . . . I might come to your funeral though – if I've got nothing better to do.' This made her laugh and choke even more, so I gave her a couple of half-hearted pats on the back, which did precisely nothing. Eventually Cass was able to breathe again. She punched me on the arm. It hurt.

'*Thanks!* Some friend you are. Next time you're dying, I'll be right there . . . not caring.'

'Whatever. I've got a serious tuna-crotch situation going on here.'

Cass wrinkled her nose. 'Gross. You'd better go

and change before Tara notices and gives you a new nickname.'

I stood to leave. 'A *new* nickname? What's the old one?'

But Cass wouldn't tell, and I didn't push her. Sometimes ignorance is bliss, I guess.

They put on a film for us later that night – not my cup of tea at all. Tara and her posse sat directly behind me and I had to listen to them whispering all the way through. I tried to ignore it and concentrate on the painfully predictable events unfolding on-screen, but it was impossible. Duncan seemed to be the main subject of the conversation, which started like this:

Danni: *He totally fancies you.*

Tara: *Do you reckon?* (Could no one else hear how disingenuous that sounded?)

Danni and Sam and Gemma: *Totally!* (Did they practise speaking in chorus?)

Tara: *He is pretty hot, I suppose.*

Danni: *You should totally go for it. You know, his cabin is the one just behind yours . . .*

Tara: *How do you know that?*

Danni: *I make it my business to know the exact location of all hot men within a one-hundred-metre radius.* (This

was perhaps the funniest thing I'd ever heard Danni
say. Except she wasn't joking.)

Sam: *I reckon you should pay him a visit one night . . .
say, if you had an insect bite that needed some lotion rubbing
on it . . . ?*

Gemma: *Yeah! You SO should!*

Tara (sounding thoughtful): *We'll see.*

The thought of Tara creeping into Duncan's cabin
made me feel sort of sick. *He wouldn't actually do
anything with her . . . would he? He'd lose his job for sure.
And probably get arrested or something. Maybe I should
warn him? Don't be so ridiculous. What would you say? 'The
hottest girl in our school wants to get in your pants. And I
don't think you should let her.' Yeah, that'd work.*

I looked to see if Cass was listening too, but she
was engrossed in the film. She has a bit of a penchant
for lame rom-coms, a fact that never fails to surprise
me. I can't stand them – there are only so many
ridiculous coincidences a girl can take.

I was the first one back to the cabin after the
film. At least I *thought* I was – but Polly was there,
scrabbling around on the floor near Tara's bed.

'Lost something?'

'What? Oh, yes.' She stood up and went over to
her bed and started fluffing up the pillows. 'It doesn't
matter though. It was just a hair grip – I've got lots.'

She was wearing a long nightgown, the sort my nan wears. I felt bad for her; Tara would have a field day.

The rest of us were all in bed by the time Tara swanned in. No doubt she'd been busy planning her assault on Duncan. Without a word, she started stripping off her clothes. Not an ounce of self-consciousness. I was kind of jealous of that. She seemed to take ages getting changed, like she was enjoying showing off her body.

'You can stop staring at me now, Cass,' she said as she pulled a teeny-tiny vest over her head. 'I'm decent.'

'Fuck you, Tara.' Cass looked over the top of the map she was studying.

'You'd like that, wouldn't you?' She laughed and blew a kiss in Cass's direction before flouncing into the bathroom.

'Bitch,' Cass muttered.

'Just ignore her,' I said.

'Easier said than done. You know, one of these days she'll get what she deserves.' Cass was always saying things like this. I never thought anything of it.

8

Cass was in the foulest of foul moods the next morning. At breakfast she munched her cornflakes in such an aggressive way that I thought she might break a tooth. She hadn't bothered to wash her hair and it was all over the place. I'd shampooed my hair twice, conditioned it, straightened it . . . and then tied it back in a boring old ponytail.

The more I thought about it, the more freaked out I became. *What if I get separated from the group somehow? What if they leave me down there? What if I can't find my way out and I starve to death after days and days lost in the darkness?*

I tried to talk to Rae, who was scrawling something in her notebook in between bites of toast.

'God, I'm not looking forward to today. Have you done potholing before?'

It took her a moment or two to realize I was

talking to her. She shut her notebook and put it on her lap. 'Nope.'

'I don't know why anyone in their right mind would want to do it. Anything could happen down there. But I suppose they wouldn't let us do it if it wasn't one hundred per cent safe, would they?'

Rae shrugged. 'You'd be surprised. Accidents are always happening on trips like this. You hear about it all the time.'

'What? Seriously?' It was hard to tell from her expression whether she was joking.

'Yup.' She wasn't joking.

'Great. Thanks. I feel so much better now.'

'You're welcome.' And with that, she got up and left. *That's what you get for making an effort with people.*

'I . . . I'm nervous about it too.' Polly. I'd forgotten she was there. Easy to do.

'Well, we can be nervous together.' I smiled at her and she smiled back shyly.

Neither of us had any idea just how bad it was going to be.

It started off OK. The caves were a couple of miles away from the camp, so we had to trek through the woods. The rain had yet to put in an appearance, and the sun was at least making an effort to shine through the grey. The forest floor was covered in a thick bed of pine needles; I liked the way it felt springy under my feet. I almost managed to forget that we were headed into the bowels of hell. Almost.

Tara was up ahead with Duncan, who was carrying a massive rucksack. Miss Daley walked a few steps behind, dwarfed by her own rucksack. If she fell over she'd never be able to get up again. We'd leave her there, flailing and floundering like a distressed tortoise.

Everyone was wearing waterproofs and helmets with lights on – like miners' hats. Some people managed to carry off the look better than others. Cass was practically born to wear this stuff. Her mood had improved and she was prattling on about the last time she'd been potholing and how deep she'd gone and stalactites and stalagmites and other subterranean things I had no interest in. I just wanted to get the morning over and done with as quickly as possible.

Duncan ran through his safety spiel again and Paul checked the lights on our helmets, but my mind was elsewhere. I was weighing up my options:

a) *Tell Daley you can't do it. You're claustrophobic. This is your worst nightmare. You should go back to camp and help make lunch or something.*

b) *Just get on with it and stop being so pathetic.*

No matter how tempting option a) was, I couldn't bring myself to do it.

I refused to look that weak in front of the others, no matter how scared I was. *It'll be fine it'll be fine it'll be fine. Nothing bad is going to happen. You are NOT going to die.*

Tara asked Duncan to double-check the chinstrap on her helmet. He had to stand really close to do it and she was loving every second. Daley was watching though, so that was good. Maybe she knew what Tara was up to – or at least suspected it. Or maybe she was jealous. Daley and Duncan had to be about the same age. *Now there's a thought: Daley bagging the hot guy before Tara can get her hands on him. That would be very cool indeed.*

The thought of doing a little matchmaking for Daley was enough to distract me for a couple of minutes. Until we actually entered the cave. Then the panic set in, as I'd known it would.

It was dark and damp and dripping. Awful. I stayed as close as I could to Cass. Kept bumping into her every time she stopped. She was surprisingly patient with me; she knew how scared I was. Every step I took was one step further away from light and fresh air and normality.

Paul was right behind us and kept on pointing out

different rock formations and interesting (his word) algae. I concentrated hard on what he was saying, trying to ignore the panic crawling up my throat. On either side of us the walls of the cave seemed to be creeping closer together, preparing to crush us to a mushy pulp.

I could hear Tara up ahead, laughing crazily so that her voice echoed all around us. *Trust her to be enjoying this. Maybe she's just pretending, to impress Duncan. Or maybe she's just fearless these days.* It seemed like I was the only one who was terrified at being down there. Everyone else was completely at ease, as if they spent every day in a confined space hundreds of metres below the ground. (The Tube doesn't exactly count.)

We stopped in a massive cavern and gathered round so Duncan could tell us about how it was formed. *WHO CARES? JUST GET ME OUT OF HERE!* I couldn't even ogle his calf muscles to distract me – he wasn't wearing shorts. Tara & Co. were right at the front, trying their best to look hot in their caving gear. Tara was the only one to manage it. She looked like an advert for Caves R Us or something.

I turned round and saw that Polly was standing apart from everyone else, staring into space.

'Hey Polly, how are you doing?'

'Fine. I'm fine.' She looked anything but fine.

Hard to tell in that light, but I thought I could detect a greenish tinge to her face.

'It's just you look a bit . . .'

'I said I'm fine.'

'OK, as long as you're sure.'

'I said so, didn't I?' *Ouch. Being nice really isn't working out for me today.*

I meandered back to Cass just in time to hear Duncan describe the next stage of our wondrous adventure. He expected us to crawl through a TINY little tunnel. When he stepped aside to show us the entrance, I actually laughed. I was so sure he was joking. It was a mouse hole. Or maybe a badger hole. But in no way whatsoever was it a person-sized hole.

Duncan explained how we should use our elbows to propel ourselves through the tunnel. It was only about fifteen metres long. *Only* fifteen metres. *I am going to die.*

Paul went first. Even though he was a proper medium-to-large-sized man, I wasn't reassured. There was no way I would fit in that tunnel. I'd get stuck like a cork in a wine bottle, no question. One by one the girls disappeared down the hole of horror. There were just a few of us left: Tara, Danni, Rae, Polly, me and Cass. And Duncan and Miss Daley.

Daley suggested Polly go next, and Polly looked questioningly at Tara, as if asking permission. Tara ignored her.

I whispered to Polly. 'You don't have to do it if you don't want to, you know. Tell Daley you're not feeling well.' I refrained from telling her I was thinking of doing exactly that.

'No. I'm doing this.' Her voice was shaky, but she looked determined. *So I'm the only pathetic coward here? Wonderful.*

Polly paused for a few seconds in front of the tunnel.

'Get a move on, Sutcliffe. We haven't got all day. I want to make sure I get through before the tunnel collapses,' Tara piped up in an overly cheerful voice.

Daley scowled at her before going to Polly's side. 'Don't listen to her, Polly. You take your time.'

Duncan joined in. 'It's perfectly safe. There's nothing to worry about. I've been through this tunnel like a hundred times, and I'm still here, aren't I?'

In she went. *If Polly can do it, so can I. There's no way in hell I'm going to be the only one to chicken out. I have to do this.*

And then she got stuck.

9

'Help!'

We all gathered round the tunnel's entrance.

'I can't move. I can't move. Oh God, I can't move.'

Duncan stuck his head into the tunnel. 'Polly, calm down! You need to calm down. You're not stuck.'

'I am! I can't move!' Polly screamed. Danni and Tara exchanged a bored look.

'OK, I'm coming in. Just breathe, OK, Polly? Breathe. Everything's going to be fine.' He disappeared into the tunnel, and we could hear him trying to calm her down, encouraging her to move down the tunnel. It was no good. She was crying now, whimpering and sobbing.

'I want to go back. Let me go back.'

'Polly, it's much easier if you go forward. I promise you.'

'No! I need to get out NOW!' Her voice was completely panicked.

Daley looked helpless, wringing her hands together and hopping from one foot to the other. Even Cass looked a bit freaked out.

'OK, OK. See if you can shuffle backwards a bit – just a little. That's my hand you can feel on your ankle. I'm here. Nothing's going to happen to you.' Duncan sounded super-calm. Not fazed at all.

It took maybe ten minutes, but Duncan managed to coax her back out of the tunnel. Polly emerged feet first, gasping and crying. She collapsed on the ground and Daley rushed over. The rest of us crowded round, but Duncan told us to give her some space.

Polly looked terrible. Her hair was all sweaty and stuck to her blotchy red face. She whispered something to Daley, and Daley grimaced. It was only then I noticed the smell. Polly had wet herself.

Danni whispered in Tara's ear. Tara's eyes lit up with glee.

Daley and Duncan decided it'd be best for us all to head back the way we came. Tara and Danni made a big fuss of being disappointed while I managed not to faint with relief. Duncan scooted down the tunnel to tell Paul to carry on with the others, then we headed off. Daley had her arm around Polly, who clung to her, shuffling like a little old lady.

Duncan tried to keep things light-hearted on the way back, chatting with Tara. Cass and I hung back behind the others.

'Well that was fun, wasn't it?' said Cass.

'Poor Polly. It must have been awful for her.'

'She shouldn't have panicked. That's the last thing you should do down here.'

'She hardly did it on purpose.'

Cass shrugged and then lowered her voice. 'Still, I can't believe she wet herself! Embarrassing or what?! She'll never live it down.'

'No one else has to find out.'

'Alice, you can be so dense sometimes. Hmm . . . now how could people *possibly* find out? It's not as if Motormouth Danni and Bitchface Tara were down there with us. Oh wait, they *were*. Everyone will know before the end of the day, I can promise you that.'

I caught up with Tara and Danni on the walk back to camp. 'Hey, Tara. Wait up a second.'

Tara and Danni both treated me to their finest *You are a nobody, how dare you interrupt our conversation?* look.

'Um . . . I just wanted to say . . . I think it would be good if no one said anything, about what happened.'

'You mean about Polly pissing her pants?' Danni laughed hysterically before looking at Tara to check that was the right thing to do.

'I don't think anyone else needs to know. It's not fair.'

'What's not fair is us missing out on potholing and hanging out with Duncan in the dark, all because Polly was too pathetic to crawl through a poxy tunnel. Now, if you don't mind, Danni and I were in the middle of a *private* conversation.' She made a gesture to shoo me away. I swear I hated her right then. Completely hated her. I trudged back to Cass.

'Looked like that went well,' said Cass.

'Oh, fuck off,' I said wearily.

Polly ran into the bathroom as soon as we got back. She emerged a few minutes later in her dressing gown, oozing shame from every pore. Daley took her clothes away to wash, but not before pulling me aside and asking me to keep an eye on Polly.

'I've already had a word with Danni and Tara. We don't need to tell anyone else what happened. It's no one's business.'

I nodded, but there was no question in my mind — Cass had got it right. *They WILL know. One way or another, they will know. A secret like this doesn't get kept.*

We heard everyone else get back to camp a couple of hours later. They sounded excited and loud and full of life. The contrast with us lot couldn't have been greater. Cass was snoozing with a pillow on top of her head. Rae was listening to music and reading a book. Polly was under the covers with her back to the rest of us. I'd tried talking to her, but she insisted she was fine.

It was only a matter of time. I knew it. Cass knew it. Polly knew it.

10

We were the last ones to arrive at dinner. Daley and Mr Miles were in the kitchen serving us, since the catering staff had Sundays off. Jess, Paul and Duncan were nowhere to be seen. Maybe they were having a debrief about the day's events. So there was no one to supervise the dining hall. Otherwise it wouldn't have happened.

I was behind Polly in the queue and noticed that Daley gave her an extra portion of mash. When it was my turn, Daley asked me how Polly was doing. I shrugged. That's when I heard the crash.

I left my tray in front of Daley and rushed round the corner into the dining hall. Polly was standing there, her hands balled into fists at her sides. Her dinner (complete with extra mash) was sloppily sliding down the wall to her right. The upturned tray was on the floor. EVERYONE was staring at Polly.

And Polly was staring at the piles and piles of toilet roll that were on the table in the corner. The table she'd sat at last night. There was a teetering pyramid on her chair too. Someone had even gone to the trouble of spelling out Polly's name in toilet paper, just in case we didn't quite get the message. There must have been a hundred rolls or more. It looked like the whole camp had been raided for bog roll.

Polly barged past me. Daley came out to see what the commotion was just as the whole room erupted into laughter. She took one look and then hurried out after Polly. Mr Miles came out and stomped straight over to the table. He flicked a hand at the pile on the table and toilet rolls tumbled to the floor, revealing Tara and the others looking the very picture of innocence.

'Who did this? Tara? Danni? Tell me who did this!' The room fell silent.

Tara spoke up. 'I don't know, sir. It was like this when we got here.'

'And you didn't think there was anything strange about that? Didn't think it was maybe worth mentioning to me or Miss Daley?'

Tara shrugged. 'Not really. I thought maybe someone was doing some kind of inventory.' Anyone else would have burst out laughing. But Tara was cool as ice – staring him down, daring him not to believe her. I wanted to shout: YOU KNOW IT WAS HER! OF COURSE IT WAS HER! But I didn't.

Mr Miles told everyone to get on with their dinner, and Tara offered to clear things up afterwards. That was the masterstroke that convinced him she had nothing to do with it. Tara Chambers was some kind of evil genius.

The only topic of conversation at dinner was Polly. Somehow *everyone* knew what had happened at the caves. Well, they knew the basics. Some people had added their own little details to the story. My particular favourite: Duncan had given Polly mouth-to-mouth resuscitation and she'd thrown up in his mouth.

It was awful. Rae and Cass and I sat in the middle of the gossiping maelstrom, trying not to say anything that would add fuel to the fire. Polly would never live this down. Not ever.

Daley came back after dinner and gave us a lecture: 'I will not tolerate bullying blah blah blah. If anyone knows who did this blah blah blah.' We'd heard (and ignored) it all before. There was nothing she could do. Polly had been chosen for this years ago. She was the sacrificial lamb. We ALL let it happen – every single one of us. We were just relieved it was someone else. *Anyone* else, as long as it wasn't us. Nothing Polly could do would ever be good enough for us to accept her.

By some sort of unspoken agreement, Rae, Cass and I headed straight back to the cabin after dinner. I passed Tara on the way out. She was armed with black bin bags to gather up the bog roll. I glared at her. It was the best I could do. She smiled back. I didn't punch her in the face.

I'd expected to find Polly a sobbing, broken heap on the bed, but she was sitting cross-legged on the bed looking perfectly perky. She was putting moisturizer on her hands. Something about the care she was taking made me think of surgeons scrubbing up on those medical dramas on TV.

'Polly, hi. How are you doing?' I sat down on the bed next to her.

'I'm fine.' Before I could express my scepticism, she continued, 'Really. I'm not going to let it bother me any more. They're the pathetic ones, not me.'

'Then why did you decorate the wall with your dinner?' asked Cass, her usual diplomatic self.

Polly shrugged. 'For dramatic effect?'

We laughed. *Wow. She's handling this way better than I would. I'd never want to show my face in front of that lot again.*

'You know who it was, right? That fucking bitch. Someone really needs to teach her a lesson sometime.' Cass was properly indignant.

Polly shrugged again. 'Maybe they will. One day.'

'It'd be nice to wipe the smirk off her stupid, perfect face.' Cass had her 'thinking' look on. It was so obvious when she was plotting something; she was like a bad cartoon sometimes.

'Cass, just leave it. Polly's OK, and that's all that matters.'

'I *won't* leave it. Tara can't keep treating people like this and getting away with it.'

'She's been doing it for years and no one's ever bothered about it before.' I wanted this conversation to stop.

'Well, it's about time someone did,' said Cass.

'And I suppose you're that *someone*, are you?'

'Maybe I am.' Cass grinned at Polly and Polly smiled back.

'Whatever. I'm going to take a shower.'

I gathered my stuff and headed for the bathroom, glad to escape for a while. Why couldn't they just accept that Tara was Queen Bee and that was just the way things were. Nothing was going to change – not now. No one was going to be able to embarrass her the way she'd embarrassed Polly. *I doubt Tara's felt*

embarrassed for years. Except for that time she called a
teacher 'Grandma' by mistake. But even then she managed to
laugh it off in a way I never could have.

I took the longest shower I could get away with,
relishing the peace. When I eventually came out of
the bathroom, Rae was listening to her iPod and Cass
and Polly were sitting on Polly's bed, whispering. It
was good to see Cass being nice to Polly, especially
since she'd never been particularly nice *about* her. But
Cass had a natural sense of what was right and what
was not. And the way Polly had been treated most
definitely fell into the 'not' category.

Cass scooted back over to her own bed. She was
looking very pleased with herself, which made me
suspicious. Before I could ask what she was up to, Tara
came sweeping in.

'What's up, ladies?' I could hardly believe her
nerve.

Cass's face transformed from smug to scared
quicker than you could blink. 'Tara! Did you see him?'
Eh? What is she on about?

Tara was as confused as me. 'What? Who?'

'The man . . . there was a man. Outside. Looking
in the window.'

'Bullshit!' Tara laughed. 'You probably just saw
your own reflection, loser.'

'No. It was a man. I SAW him, I swear it.'

Tara stood with her hands on her hips. 'Oooh! A man! That must have been particularly terrifying for you . . . given your *preferences*.'

A timid voice piped up from the corner. 'I saw him too.' So Polly was in on it. Whatever *it* was.

Tara rolled her eyes. 'It was probably Mr Miles, or Duncan or Paul.'

Cass shook her head, all solemn. 'I don't think so. Unless one of them would have a good reason to be wearing a balaclava and creeping round our cabin.'

Tara looked from Cass to Polly and then back again. Then she looked at me for verification. 'Did you see this mystery man then, Alice?'

'I . . . just got out of the shower.'

Tara glanced over at Rae, but she was oblivious to everything. For just a second, I thought Tara looked unsure. But only for a second. 'Well, if some perv wants to check us out, then let's give him a proper show.' She whipped off her T-shirt and jiggled in front of the window.

'Tara! Don't!' Cass jumped up and pulled the curtains together violently.

'*Tara! Don't!* Don't be so pathetic, Cass. It was probably just some local yokel getting his jollies. I mean, who can blame him.' She gestured at herself and laughed.

'I think we should tell someone,' said Polly.

'I'll tell Daley in the morning, but I don't think we should tell any of the others. No point scaring everyone.' Cass looked serious. Her face didn't particularly suit serious.

Tara snorted. 'No one would believe you anyway. Right . . . if you lot have quite finished wetting your pants over nothing . . . Oops, sorry, Sutcliffe – bad choice of words. Anyway, I'm going to bed.' Polly's face was expressionless. The words just bounced off her; she had a force field now. And an ally.

We all got ready for bed. I was trying to work out what the hell was going on. Obviously Cass and Polly were lying about the man at the window. But why? It'd take more than the idea of some peeping Tom to spook Tara.

When I was sure the others were asleep I crept over to Cass's bed and shook her.

'Wha . . . ?'

'What was all that about? That "man at the window" crap?' I whispered.

Her grin shone bright white in the darkness. 'Oh, that. Just something me and Polly came up with.'

'Since when have you and Polly been partners-in-crime?'

'Since she decided to fight back against Tara the super-bitch.'

'Making up some story isn't exactly what I'd call fighting back.'

'Don't you worry – that was just Stage One.' She was completely awake now and the glee was bursting out of her voice. 'Wait till you see what we've got in store for her. It'll be epic.'

'What are you going to do?' I tried my best to sound bored, but I was desperate to know what she was up to.

Cass tapped her nose. 'I'm afraid that's classified information.'

'*Classified!* You're so ridiculous. Look, Cass, just tell me.'

'Nope, sorry. No can do. You'd only try and talk us out of it. I *know* you.'

'Fine. Be like that. See if I care.' I scampered back to my own bed and flung the covers over my head. I was fuming; I hated being out of the loop. Cass usually told me everything. Which meant this plan of hers had to be A Bad Idea.

11

I couldn't sleep that night and woke up feeling mega-cranky. Tara was the only other one awake. She was looking out of the window at the misty morning. She looked like a normal human being, a *nice* normal human being. She heard me emerging from my cocoon of tartan.

'Morning, Alice.' This was maybe the nicest thing she'd said to me for four years or more, but I tried not to read too much into it.

'Morning.'

'Wow. You look like shit.' *Ah, that's more like it.*

'Thanks.'

'Do you believe that bollocks Cass was on about last night? Some crazy psycho stalking us?'

The way I saw it, I had a choice: a) tell her that of course I didn't believe it. Cass was just trying to wind her up, or b) lie. It was not a difficult decision to make.

'Well, Cass seemed pretty freaked out about it. And it takes a lot to freak her out.'

'I wouldn't worry about it,' she said.

'I'm not.'

'Oh.'

I felt like I'd scored a point. The score currently stood at: Tara — 13,472 points (give or take a few), Alice — 1.

Tara meandered over to my bed and lowered her voice. 'You know, just for the record, it wasn't me who told everyone about Polly.'

'I don't believe you.' I felt terribly brave, saying those words out loud.

'You can believe what you want. I couldn't care less.'

'And I suppose you had nothing to do with the toilet roll in the dining room either?' *Shut up, Alice. This cannot end well for you.*

Tara looked me in the eye, and I felt like she was seeing the inside of me. *All that is Alice.* I was sure she was going to say something that would cut me to the core, leaving me feeling hollow and worthless. But she just smiled at me. Not a smirk this time, a smile. But it was a sad sort of smile. A smile that hinted at what used to be. What might have been.

I had no idea what to make of it, and was relieved

when she released me from her gaze and headed into the bathroom. I didn't believe her. It *had* to have been her who told everyone about Polly.

Monday was mercifully less eventful than the day before. We went kayaking on the loch, which turned out to be almost fun. I shared a kayak with Rae. Cass was with Polly, which made me uneasy.

Tara had managed to wangle her way into Duncan's kayak. She kept on asking him questions, and you could just tell he was loving the attention. He was careful not to act too keen when Daley was around, but that wasn't too much of a problem – Daley and Mr Miles were woefully inadequate at manoeuvring their kayak. They couldn't paddle in time to save their lives; whenever she wanted to go left, he wanted to go right. It was a total shambles.

The afternoon brought orienteering in the rain. The rain was different from London rain: icy needles flying horizontally at your face. Once again I found myself paired with Rae, who could at least read a compass. I let her lead the way, making sure she knew I wanted to get back to camp and get dry as soon as was humanly possible. We even talked a bit. I asked her what kind of music she was into, and she went off on one – talking a million miles a minute. It was as if the words had been all bottled up and she'd just been waiting for someone to actually ask before popping the cork. I'd never heard of half the bands she mentioned, but I nodded in all the right places.

We managed to finish the course before I got hypothermia, which was a relief. Tara and Danni had somehow managed to get back first. They were looking mighty pleased with themselves, huddled over their mugs of hot chocolate. They must have cheated. Tara looked up when I came squelching in. She gave me a little wave, and I waved back, not wanting to look rude. *Idiot.*

The other girls came in two by two, laughing and bitching and moaning. Daley checked them all off on her list. Until there were only two missing: Cass and Polly. We waited. Everyone had an extra hot chocolate. We waited some more. Miss Daley started to look restless. Jess told her to give them another ten minutes or so, but it was obvious she was worried too – she kept on fiddling with her dreadlocks. Still, we waited. Just as Daley was about to burst a blood vessel from stress, in they strolled. Soaked to the skin and looking sheepish.

'Where on earth have you two been? We were worried about you!'

'Sorry, miss. But map-reading is haaaaaard. We ended up going in completely the wrong direction. It was totally my fault,' said Cass. Polly nodded fervently.

I wondered why Cass was lying. She knew how to read maps the way I knew how to read the back of cereal boxes.

They came over and sat with me and Rae in the corner.

'So you got lost, did you?' I didn't try to mask the scepticism in my voice.

'Of course not! We were exploring.' Cass looked at Polly and they both laughed. I think I preferred the old Polly.

'In this weather? Cass, you're crazy.'

'It's only a bit of rain! Besides, it'll be worth it.' More secret looks between Cass and Polly.

OK, I'll admit it: I was feeling kind of left out. I didn't like this new alliance one little bit. Yes, it was cool that Cass was being nice to Polly. But she didn't have to be her NBF, did she? *What about me? OLD Best Friend.* I knew I was being stupid. There was no way Polly was going to replace me. Their blossoming friendship was temporary, borne out of mutual Tara-loathing. It would be over soon, I was sure of it.

Rae and I found ourselves alone in the cabin. It seemed like we were doomed to spend the rest of the trip in each other's company. We played cards in silence, sitting cross-legged on my bed.

'They're up to something, aren't they?' She swiped at her fringe, which was always falling in front of her eyes. It promptly fell right back again.

I picked up an ace from the deck. 'Yeah, I think so.'

'I overheard them talking about balaclavas or something this morning.'

I filled Rae in on what she'd missed last night.

She nodded thoughtfully. 'And Cass won't tell you what's going on? I thought you two were supposed to be best friends or something.'

'We *are* supposed to be best friends or something. I mean, we *are* best friends.' I sighed. 'She thinks I won't approve, which is stupid.'

'Sounds like she's got something pretty major planned . . .'

'I hope not. It's a waste of time trying to get one over on Tara.'

'Why? Don't you think she deserves it? The way she swans around, acting like she's Queen of the fucking Universe.' Rae sounded bitter. 'You used to be friends with her, didn't you?'

I was surprised – I thought this little nugget had been erased from the consciousness of the entire school. 'Yeah. She was . . . different back then.'

'I'd bloody hope so. Otherwise I'd be seriously questioning your taste.'

'God, I want to go home.' *Where did that come from?*

'But why? Aren't you having, like, a super-fantastic time?' Her voice was a perfect imitation of Gemma (or Sam – they were kind of interchangeable). 'You know what they say: "Your school years are the best years of your life." To which I say, "If that's true, I might as well kill myself now."' I laughed, and Rae looked sort of pleased.

Cass and Polly came crashing into the cabin, slamming the door behind them. Cass was hiding something behind her back in a none-too-subtle fashion. I didn't even bother to ask. It was too tiresome for words.

But that didn't stop Rae. 'What's that behind your back?'

'Nothing!' Guilty as anything.

'If you didn't want us to ask then you would have hidden it a bit better, wouldn't you?' *Nice one, Rae.*

Cass shrugged. 'It's just a couple of props, that's all.'

'For what?' asked Rae.

Cass looked over her shoulder, as if worried she might be overheard. 'For getting Tara back. Didn't Alice tell you about the man who's been watching us?'

'The fake man you made up to try and scare Tara? Yeah – pretty lame, if you ask me.'

'Ah, but you don't know the half of it. That was just laying the groundwork. Wait till you hear the rest!'

'Oh great, so you'll tell Rae, but not me. That's charming.' I sounded like a five-year-old.

'Aw, don't be like that, Alice. I was always gonna tell you! And besides, we're going to need your help. Both of you.'

Rae and I looked at each other. I don't know what was going through her mind, but I was thinking *Uh-oh*.

Rae retreated to her bed and picked up her iPod. 'I can't be arsed. Sounds like more trouble than it's worth.'

'But don't you want to teach her a lesson? Show her she's not as great as she thinks she is? Get her back for everything?' Cass's voice was fierce and her eyes were shining with excitement.

'Get her back for what? She's never done anything to me,' said Rae.

'But she's *ignored* you, hasn't she? She's ignored all of us. And look at what she did to Polly!' Polly nodded along with Cass's words, looking more like a lapdog than ever.

I had to say it: 'Actually, Tara told me it wasn't her.'

Cass's laugh was an ugly bark. 'Since when do you and Bitchface share heart-to-hearts? Oh wait, I forgot you two used to be like *that*.' She crossed her fingers together to show just how close Tara and I supposedly were. I had no idea why Cass was suddenly throwing this back in my face.

Polly spoke up. 'It was her. I know it was her.'

We all fell silent. She was probably right. And if it wasn't her, she could have stopped it. Any decent person would have stopped it.

'So what do you say, Alice? Are you in or out?'

A lot rested on my answer. If I said no, Cass would take that as a sign of some kind of loyalty to Tara, which wouldn't be true at all. It would just mean that I didn't want to get involved in some stupid schoolgirl prank – one that would only end badly, for us. Even if we managed to 'get' Tara, she'd only end up getting us back. She'd go bigger and better and make us all social outcasts forever. But Cass would never forgive me for chickening out, and she'd go ahead with the plan anyway.

And if I said yes, well, who knew what was going to happen? And that was the problem: I *like* knowing what's going to happen. I like planning and organizing and all those things that just aren't very cool. Cass is all spontaneous and reckless. She lives in the moment, and I live next Wednesday at precisely 2.30 p.m.

I needed to loosen up – live a little.

'I'm in.'

12

I regretted the words as soon as they were out of my mouth. I wanted to stuff them back in and swallow them, but I didn't get the chance because Tara, Danni, Sam and Gemma chose that exact moment to invade our cabin.

Our reactions were very different: Rae immediately plugged herself into her iPod. Polly picked up a book and you could tell she was trying really hard to concentrate on it and not look at the witches. Cass did her best to stand her ground and treat them all to her special evil glare, but it just bounced off them and smacked her in the forehead. And I . . . did nothing. Sat there on my bed, wishing I was invisible.

'So, welcome to my humble abode. Not up to much, is it?' Tara looked round at each one of us, just in case it wasn't painfully clear that she included *us* in that assessment.

'Nah, ours is way nicer. And I don't think much of the locals – they're not very friendly,' said Danni. The others laughed. Gemma laughed a little bit too much, as usual. She sounded like a hyena with learning difficulties.

Cass stepped forward. 'Oh, I'm sorry, Danni. Please accept my apologies for not meeting your high standards.'

'There's no need to apologize, Cassandra. You can't help it.' Danni smiled brightly.

'Fuck off!'

'Now there's no need for language like that. Danni was only joking.' Tara stepped in and patted Cass on the cheek. Cass flushed fierce red with anger. 'There's no reason we can't all get along, is there? Polly, I'm *so* sorry for what happened to you the other night. If I find out who did it, I'll sort them out. I promise you.'

Polly looked up from her book with a gormless expression on her face. She didn't quite know what to make of this. None of us did. 'I . . . thanks.'

The four of them crowded onto Tara's bed and proceeded to talk about Duncan. The rest of us did our best to studiously ignore them, but it wasn't easy. They dissected him from head to toe, detailing every inch of his hotness (but neglecting to mention his calves – I guess that was just *my* thing). Tara stayed

strangely quiet at first, letting the others build him up
to full-on Adonis status. And then . . .

'He kissed me.'

'*What?*' 'When?' 'No way!' That was the three of
them. I'm not sure who said what, because my mind
was too busy shouting *LIAR!* to listen properly.

She was lying. She had to be. There was no way
that could have happened. Why was she saying it in
front of us anyway? Why wasn't she just whispering
it to the others in the cabin next door? Wasn't she
worried that one of us might tell Daley or something?
*Of course not. As far as Tara's concerned, we'd never dare to
grass her up. She's probably right.*

Tara didn't even bother to lower her voice as
she gave them the gory details. She *wanted* us all to
hear. She wanted us to be jealous. And I was – until I
remembered that she had to be lying.

Here's what happened, according to Tara . . . She
volunteered to help him put the kayaks away that
morning. They talked about all sorts of things (they
had *loads* in common, apparently). He talked about
his ex-girlfriend and their messy break-up. He talked
about free climbing (whatever *that* is, but Tara seemed
to know). He asked her lots of questions, including
'Do you have a boyfriend?' She said no. Then, just as
they were about to head back up to camp, he came

up behind her and said, 'You seem a lot older than sixteen.' *Urgh!* And then she'd turned around and he was standing so close and he just kissed her. Just like that!

'Was he a good kisser?' 'Did anything else happen?' 'Ohmygod!' Reactions from Danni, Sam and Gemma respectively. Tara's responses were: 'He was amazing.' 'That would be telling.' And 'I *know*!'

She looked as smug as I've ever seen her, basking in the glow of their admiration. It was sickening. She whispered something in Danni's ear, and Danni hit her lightly on the shoulder. 'You filthy girl! You're so lucky!' Gemma and Sam clamoured to find out what had been whispered, so Danni whispered it to both of them. 'Tara! OMG!' They all fell about laughing. Once they'd recovered their composure, Danni caught me staring at them in disbelief.

'Can I help you?'

I blushed and said nothing.

'Awww, Tara! Look what you've done! You're embarrassing poor Alice here.'

Sam joined in. 'Yeah, Tara. Not in front of the children!'

Danni was gleeful. 'It's OK. I'll explain: When a mummy and a daddy — or a girl and a really hot Scottish guy — love each other very much, or just fancy the pants off each other, they have a special cuddle.' Now they were hysterical with laughter.

Bitches. Hideous bitches. Every single one of them. Why couldn't I stand up for myself? How did they manage to make me feel so small and pathetic? Why did I *let* them?

Cass spoke up. 'Shut up, Danni. You're so fucking boring.'

Tara stood up and stretched, revealing her perfectly toned stomach. 'C'mon, ladies. Let's go for a walk before dinner.' They all jumped up and trotted out of the room after her. They were very well trained.

Rae took out her headphones and we told her all about Tara and Duncan. She was sceptical, big time. After much discussion and analysis, we were divided. Cass and Polly thought Tara was telling the truth, and Rae and I were almost certain she was lying.

Tuesday was hiking and archery. Archery was OK, but I was crap at it. Cass was a natural – like Robin bloody Hood or something. When no one was looking, she pointed her bow at Tara and mimed shooting her. Tara was having trouble holding the bow properly, or at least she was pretending to. Duncan had to stand right behind her, practically enveloping her with his body. I watched them closely. *Maybe something* is *going on between them after all. Look at the way he's got his hands on her waist to steady her. Inappropriate?! I wonder what I'd do if he touched me like that* . . .

Danni, Gemma and Sam seemed to have bought into Tara's story all right. They were watching with barely disguised envy. Miss Daley didn't seem to have noticed anything was up though – she was laughing and joking with Mr Miles. *Maybe teachers have holiday romances too? Urgh. Miles is OLD. And he has a moustache, for crying out loud. Surely Daley wouldn't go there.* Suddenly I was obsessed: watching Tara and Duncan, Miles and Daley, even checking to see what Beardy Paul was up to (helping Polly, as it turned out). I was reading too much into everything and it was all making me feel strange and lonely somehow.

I sat at a different table at dinner. Not quite sure why. Cass raised her eyebrows at me inquisitively as I walked right past my usual spot. I shrugged. I went and sat next to Saira, who was sort of the new girl. I say 'sort of' – she'd been at Bransford Academy for over a year. And that meant she was still a bit of an outsider. It took a *long* time to be accepted at Bransford. And some of us never would be – not really.

Chatting to Saira made me feel more like me again, after the afternoon's weirdness. I'd had enough of speculating about who was trying to get into whose pants. Or who had already *been* in whose pants. Saira and I talked about books we'd read, and which TV programmes we were missing – nice, normal things.

Dinner was also a blessed escape from The Pointless Plan to Get Back at Tara. It was all Cass wanted to talk about. She'd been on and on about it all day, filling me in on the details whenever we had a moment alone. And when she hadn't been pestering me about it, I'd seen her bugging Rae. Polly obviously already knew the ins and outs. We were going to do it tomorrow night – Wednesday. Anxiety bubbled up inside me every time I thought about it. So I tried really hard not to.

13

There was a film to watch after dinner — some crap horror movie where everyone ran around in the woods, screaming for no reason. Well, there was a mad psycho killer on the rampage, but the screaming wasn't doing anyone any good.

I had no idea why people would actively choose to watch something like that. Real life is scary enough, surely. Bad things happen all the time. Cass was loving it: she whooped like a crazy person every time another hapless girl got killed. Everyone else seemed to be enjoying it too, but I had a headache. I told Cass I was off to get some painkillers. She nodded distractedly, already salivating over the next gruesome murder that was about to happen on-screen. *How is it possible for one person to love cheesy old Hugh Grant films AND gorefests like this? Surely the two should be mutually exclusive?*

I ran to the cabin. The woods looked different,

threatening. Anyone could be out there watching you, and you'd never know. Not until it was too late. *See? Horror films mess with your head. Yesterday you'd have thought the woods were darkly romantic or something. But today . . .*

I slammed the door shut behind me and flicked on the light switch. *Made it, safe and sound.* I laughed at myself for being such a loser. And then a voice behind me scared me half to death.

'Leave me alone.' There was a person-shaped lump under the covers on Tara's bed.

'Tara? Is that you?'

'Who the fuck did you think it was, the Gruffalo?' Her voice was muffled by the blankets.

'I thought you were watching the film with the others.'

She said nothing, and I went over to my bed and started rummaging for ibuprofen. I swallowed the pills dry, wincing. I had my hand on the door handle, ready to head back to murder and mayhem, when I said, 'Tara . . . are you OK?' *Who cares?*

'I'm fine.' And then there was a too-long pause. 'Thanks.'

'Are you sure? Do you want me to get Danni or someone?'

'No. I just want to be left alone.'

'Is it something to do with Duncan?' I have no idea why I said that.

'Look, Alice, could you just piss off and leave me alone . . . please?'

She didn't emerge from under the covers. So I did as she asked. It was only later that it struck me that the person-shaped lump under the covers might have in fact been a two-person-shaped lump. But I couldn't be sure.

Another sleepless night. My head was full of Tara and Duncan and The Plan. I tried to think about mundane things like whether Dad's big presentation at work had gone OK, and if he'd take me to our favourite Indian restaurant when I got back, and was Bruno missing me as much as I was missing him?

I managed to trick my mind for approximately thirty seconds at a time before the worries came crashing back. I don't know why the idea of Tara and Duncan bothered me so much. It was really none of my business if they wanted to shag each other senseless. And they very probably *weren't*, anyway. Maybe I was just jealous.

The Plan was another matter. I didn't want to go

through with it, but I knew I would. I'm not going to pretend I had some kind of premonition or something, but I definitely had a bad feeling. In my mind it was a terrible idea, no matter how much Cass tried to convince me otherwise.

The next day arrived way too soon. Jess interrupted our breakfast to tell us that we were supposed to have been going on a gorge-walk (what even *is* that?), but because it had rained so much overnight it would be too dangerous. Paul had organized a nature trail for us instead. There were a few groans and mutters around the tables. Everyone thought a nature trail sounded really lame. I wasn't bothered. *Sounds a lot safer than gorge-walking, that's for sure.*

We were divided into groups of six, roughly along the lines of our cabin groups. Unfortunately for us, we got the addition of Danni the Delightful. Miss Daley would be leading our group, which wasn't so bad. At least it wasn't Duncan. I wouldn't have to worry about him and Tara ripping each other's clothes off in the middle of some sunshine-dappled glade.

The sun *was* shining for once, so the walk was actually kind of nice. I stayed at the front with Daley. She was surprisingly knowledgeable, but I guess she'd been swotting up for the occasion. It was more interesting than I'd expected – I even managed to forget about what we'd got in store for Tara that night. For a little while, at least.

Tara and Danni hung back, not the slightest bit interested in anything Daley had to say. We had to keep stopping so they could catch up. It was annoying, but Daley let them get away with it. Maybe she was starting to realize that you really didn't want to make an enemy out of someone like Tara.

Towards the end of the trail we came across an old tumbledown cottage in the darkest part of the woods. The sunshine barely managed to make it through the treetops. It was properly creepy, like something out of last night's film. The empty windows looked like the eye sockets of something long dead. No one else seemed to think it was creepy. They all set about exploring while Daley sat down on a tree stump and munched on an apple. I stood watching the cottage warily, half expecting to see a ghost appear in one of the windows.

'Alice! Get over here!' Cass shouted from the other side of the house. I sighed and headed in the direction of her voice. They were gathered round something, but I couldn't see what it was. It was strange seeing Tara and Danni there too. If you didn't know better, you might think all of them were friends.

It turned out to be a well. Nothing more than a low, moss-encrusted wall with a great big hole in the middle. Big deal. I leaned over and peered down into the black. I couldn't see the bottom and it smelled dank. Cass grabbed my shoulders as if to push me in. I yelped – I couldn't help it. Tara and Danni laughed, and Cass looked supremely smug. *Traitor.*

Meanwhile, Polly had found a grapefruit-sized rock and was holding it above the well. We all fell silent and watched as she dropped it. We didn't hear it hit the bottom for a good second or two. And when the sound came, it wasn't a splash like I'd expected. It just sounded like a rock hitting more rock. Cass reckoned that whoever had lived in the tumbledown house had left when the well dried up. Cass has a theory for almost everything. And she has a way of sounding ultra-convincing, even when she doesn't know what she's talking about.

It only took us about ten minutes to get back to camp from the Creepy House in the Woods. *Who in their right mind would choose to live all the way out here on their own?* I mean, I like my privacy, but that kind of isolation is just plain odd. Thinking about it made me feel cold and strange in a way I can't quite explain.

14

Midnight. A suitably sinister time to be putting The Plan into action. As discussed, we'd all come back to the cabin early and changed into plain black clothes. The black seemed a bit unnecessary to me, but Cass insisted. Rae had to lend me a pair of black jeans (I couldn't do up the top button). Cass had gone over everything again and again, making sure each of us knew what we had to do. Essentially, Rae and I were going to be there as an extra couple of pairs of hands. Our instructions were clear: we were to stay silent the whole time. I was fine with that.

We were all huddled up in our own beds by the time Tara came back. She switched on the overhead light so we all had to try extra-hard to look like we were asleep. Switching on the light was such a typically inconsiderate Tara thing to do. I was beginning to think this plan might not be such a bad idea after all. That didn't stop me feeling nervous as hell though.

I didn't think I'd be able to fall asleep, but I suppose I must have done. Next thing I knew, Cass was shaking me awake and handing me a balaclava (definitely overdramatic – Tara would know it was us for sure). Reluctantly I pulled it over my head. It smelled of stale smoke and made me gag a little. I grabbed the torch from my bedside drawer and crept over to the door where Rae was waiting with a rope Cass had stashed under her bed earlier. Cass had a rope too. She'd been raiding the storerooms over the past couple of days; God knows how she'd managed it without getting caught.

Rae and I headed out into the darkness while Cass and Polly stood over Tara's bed whispering. Sleeping, Tara looked impossibly beautiful. It was hard to believe she could ever be mean or spiteful.

The night was colder than I'd expected, and we weren't really dressed for it. Cass had said our jackets would be a dead giveaway if anyone spotted us. I cursed her for thinking of everything as my teeth started to chatter.

The stars were out in full force and the moon seemed to be making a concerted effort to illuminate us. Almost like it wanted the world to know we were up to no good. Rae led the way along the path away from camp and I hurried after her, tripping over the occasional tree root. She was the first to recognize the tree that Cass had pointed out on the way back from the nature trail. I didn't think it was particularly distinctive, but Rae seemed sure it was the right one. Cass had said we needed to be far enough away from camp that no one would hear Tara if she screamed, but not so far that we risked getting lost in the dark ourselves. I really hoped there wasn't going to be any screaming.

Rae leaned against the tree to wait. I jumped up and down on the spot, trying in vain to get some warmth back into my body.

'You look like some kind of insane ninja keep-fit guru.' Rae did a little kung-fu move to demonstrate. I laughed, which made me feel a bit more normal in the midst of the craziness.

A few minutes later I heard them coming along the trail. Polly and Cass were on either side of Tara, their hands gripping her arms. At least I *assumed* it was Tara — kind of hard to tell with a pillowcase over her head. Tara was barefoot and wearing the skimpiest vest and a tiny pair of shorts. *She must be freezing.* I hadn't really thought about the fact that she wouldn't be dressed. I wondered if it was something

Cass had overlooked or if she'd planned it this way. The latter option seemed most likely – she'd thought of everything else.

Tara's shoulders were hunched against the cold. Her hands were tied behind her back. Cass and Polly weren't exactly being gentle with her as she stumbled her way towards us. *I can't believe I agreed to this.* I wanted to turn and run back to camp.

They led Tara to the tree and forced her into a sitting position with her back to the trunk. Polly grabbed the rope from Rae and proceeded to wind the rope around the trunk and Tara. The rope made her vest ride up; Tara's belly was white and goose-bumpy.

I grabbed Cass by the arm and pulled her away from the others. I yanked off my balaclava. 'Right, I think that's enough. We should stop before she freezes to death. She must be scared out of her mind,' I hissed.

'I know! It's awesome.'

I couldn't see Cass's face. It felt like I was talking to a stranger. 'No, it's *not* awesome. We should stop now. Let her go.'

'What the fuck?! We're just getting started. Don't you go wimping out on me now, Alice. Don't you dare . . .'

I sighed. 'All right, five more minutes. But then I'm untying her, OK?'

Cass glared at me before holding up her hands in a gesture of surrender. 'OK, OK! Five more minutes, I promise.'

We turned back to the others. Rae was standing a little way away, her arms folded across her chest. Polly was crouched down in front of Tara. There was an awful muffled sound coming from beneath the pillowcase – halfway between a moan and a scream.

I grabbed Cass again. 'Did you *gag* her?'

'Of course we fucking gagged her! Otherwise she'd have screamed bloody murder and woken up the whole camp! What did you think we were going to do, Alice? Ask her nicely to be quiet?'

I was out of my depth. This wasn't at all what I'd expected. Either I just hadn't thought it through properly, or Cass and Polly had kept things from me on purpose, knowing that I'd never go through with it otherwise. I thought we were going to bring Tara out into the woods, give her a bit of a scare, have a laugh at her expense. I hadn't thought about gags and pillowcases and just how scared she would be. It was my own fault. I'd just gone along with it all, because it was easier that way. And because a part of me really did want to get Tara back. For everything.

Cass knelt down in front of Tara, and I moved a little closer so I could hear.

'We've been watching you.' Her voice was gruff. There's no way I would have recognized it as Cass's. She sounded mega-pervy. Cass ran her fingers up and down Tara's arm. Tara squirmed this way and that, trying to escape her touch. 'Aw, what's the matter? Don't you want to play? Hmm? You *look* like the kind of girl who likes to play. What do you say I untie you and you show us what you can do? My mate Baz here has been *aching* to get to know you a little better . . . and he hasn't had any in a long time, have you, Baz?' *Where is she getting this stuff from? She's depraved.*

Cass moved her hand to Tara's leg and traced her fingers up Tara's thigh. A thought popped into my head and I did my very best to squash it down, hard. But it bubbled up again, spilling over the sides of my brain. *Cass is enjoying this, isn't she?*

A louder, more desperate whimper from Tara as her heels scrabbled against the muddy forest floor. She tried to kick out at Cass, but Cass managed to dodge her. Although I couldn't see Cass's face under the balaclava, I knew she was grinning. Her eyes were glittering in the darkness. She high-fived Polly. Rae was standing a few metres away, her back to us. I could hardly blame her.

Tara's head thrashed from side to side. I was worried she'd knock herself out on the tree trunk. Her body was bucking and twisting against the ropes. There was a sound coming from her that I didn't like one little bit. A terrible wheezing gulping sort of sound. *Enough's enough.* I shoved Cass out the way and knelt down in front of Tara, wrenching the pillowcase off her head.

Tara's eyes were bulging out of their sockets and her nostrils were flaring madly. The ugly wheezing sound was getting worse. Somewhere in the back of my mind I recognized that this was really bad. The gag was on tight, Tara's mouth pulled into a grimace. I did my best not to dig my fingernails into her face as I tried to loosen the cloth. I vaguely heard Cass's voice — her normal, everyday voice. 'What the hell are you doing? Shit! She's seen you now! You've ruined everything.' I ignored her. Tara didn't look right. Something wasn't right.

I eventually pulled the gag away from Tara's face. The wheezing sound was different now. Rattling. Tara's eyes were glassy and unfocused. 'Tara! TARA! Look at me.' I grabbed her face and forced her to see me. There was a flicker of recognition. 'It's OK, Tara. It's only us. We were just messing around. Come on, just breathe now. It's OK, calm down.' She was shaking her head wildly, still panicking.

Rae was at my side now. I looked at her helplessly. 'What's the matter with her? What are we going to do?' My voice sounded jittery and unnaturally high.

'Tara? Try and breathe slowly. Through your nose. Just breathe.' Rae sounded calm and in control.

Tara was still shaking her head, gasping for air. Her chest was heaving. 'I . . . I . . . can't!' The words were barely audible.

'Tara? Have you got asthma?' asked Rae.

Tara nodded frantically.

'Have you got an inhaler?' Another nod.

'Where is it? Is it in your rucksack?' A shake of the head.

'Bedside table? No, no, wait, in your spongebag?' Tara nodded, and something approaching relief flitted across her features. But she still couldn't catch her breath. And even in the darkness I could see that her lips were turning blue.

I leaped to my feet. 'I'll get it – give me the torch. NOW!' Cass was standing a few paces away, looking gormless. She handed it over without a word. 'For Christ's sake, Cass, untie her!' She snapped out of it and started working on the rope.

Polly spoke up. I'd almost forgotten she was there. 'Rae, you go with her. Two of you will be able to find it quicker.'

Rae looked unsure. 'I think I should stay here with Tara.'

Polly was fiddling with something in the pocket of her cardigan and I had this bizarre thought that maybe she was about to pull out a magic wand and make everything all better. She didn't. 'No, go with Alice. I'll look after Tara. I've done first aid. She'll be all right.' That made up Rae's mind. She sprang to her feet and we sprinted off together, without a backwards glance.

15

The run back to camp lasted forever. I was ahead of Rae on the narrow path, the beam of my torch flailing wildly. My hands were shaking. *Oh fuck oh fuck oh fuck please let her be OK please God let her be OK I'll do anything if only she's OK.* I blinked away tears, not bothering to wipe them from my face.

Eventually we burst out into the clearing. The cabins were all dark. Everything was quiet and peaceful and everyone was asleep. When we reached our cabin I scrabbled for the light switch before realizing it was on the other side of the door. Another two seconds lost.

Rae took control. 'You check the bathroom, I'll check by her bed.'

'OK, OK, OK,' I said over and over as I sprinted into the bathroom. I slipped on a wet towel on the floor. *Fuck fuck fuck.* Four sponge bags on the cabinet.

Not hers though. Probably didn't want us rooting through it, checking out her expensive shampoo.

A triumphant shout from Rae. 'Got it! It was under the bed.'

'Thank God for that. Quick, let's get back.'

Rae paused, clutching the inhaler in her fist. 'Maybe one of us should get Daley or something? Call an ambulance?'

The next words out of my mouth were ones I will always regret. 'No, there's no time. Let's get the inhaler to Tara, then bring her back to camp. The four of us can carry her if we have to.'

Rae shook her head. 'I don't know. I think . . . Don't you think we should tell someone?'

'Rae, we haven't got time for this. We need to go!' I grabbed her arm and pulled her towards the door.

Her lips were fucking blue. Don't think about it. Run faster.

Rae shouted from behind me, 'Did you know? That's she's asthmatic?' I hoped I was imagining the hint of accusation in Rae's voice.

'No! Did *you*?' She didn't answer.

And then we were back at the tree, and Polly and Cass were crouched over Tara. These were the things

I noticed: the muddy, bloody soles of Tara's feet, the candy pink nail polish on her toenails, the birthmark on her thigh, her pink *Little Miss Naughty* vest. And her eyes, staring but not seeing. Dull and lifeless. Dead.

Tara was dead.

Rae fell to her knees at Tara's side and started doing CPR – pumping Tara's chest, then breathing into her mouth. I just stood there, looking at Tara's eyes. She was gone. Anyone could see she was gone. But Rae didn't give up until Polly grabbed her arms and pulled her away.

'Rae, stop it! It's no good. She's dead.' Rae crumpled to the ground, sobbing. Polly patted her back awkwardly. Cass was still as a statue. I was floating somewhere high above us. Maybe Tara was too.

Suddenly I came to my senses. 'I'm going to get Daley.' I backed away from the others, desperate to escape from this place.

Cass flinched as if she'd been slapped. 'No!' She came towards me. Slowly, slowly, as if I was a frightened animal that might bolt at any moment. 'Alice, stop. Come back. We need to talk about this.'

'No, I've got to get Daley.' I stumbled over a tree root and fell. Pain shot up my spine; I welcomed it.

Cass stood over me, her hand outstretched. 'C'mon, Alice. We don't want to do anything hasty now, do we?' She thought her voice was soothing, but it sounded like poison being poured into my ears. I wanted her to stop saying my name. She grabbed my elbow and hauled me to my feet. She steered me back towards the others. Towards Tara.

Rae looked up at me, eyes red. 'Go, get Daley. Get . . . someone.' She stood up unsteadily, as if she was drunk.

'No.' Polly's voice was firm and sure.

'Why not?' My voice was shaky and pathetic.

'Because if you do, we're going to get blamed for this.' Now Cass was the one looking like a frightened animal. A cornered animal that would do anything to protect itself. Somehow Cass and Polly were standing together, and I was next to Rae. A line had been drawn between us.

'It was an accident. We'll explain everything.'

Cass laughed mirthlessly. 'Yeah, like they're really going to believe us. She's fucking dead, in case you hadn't noticed. This is serious.'

'I *know* — that's why we have to get help!'

Cass was looking at me like I was insane.

'No one can help her now,' said Polly.

There was silence for a moment or two. Over Cass's shoulder I could see Tara's feet. Muddy and bloody and dead. A wave of nausea engulfed me and I stumbled away from the others and puked. I heaved over and over again until there was nothing left. A hand was rubbing my back and a voice was murmuring words of comfort. Rae.

I don't know how long the argument went on. Rae fought pretty hard, but the other two wouldn't budge. I said nothing. I think I knew I was already beaten. Maybe I could have got through to Cass if I'd persisted, but I guess I'll never know.

After a while I could tell Rae was beaten too. Beaten into submission by Cass's talk of trials and prison and murder. *Murder*. It seemed that Polly agreed with everything Cass said.

Eventually I spoke up. 'So what do you want us to do?' I swallowed down the sourness in my throat.

Cass started to pace back and forth, nervously rubbing her hands together. 'OK, OK, let me think . . . let me think. We have to get rid of . . . the body.' *The body*. Tara was no longer Tara, no longer a person.

This cannot be happening. This is a school trip, not some stupid horror movie. We cannot be talking about getting rid of bodies. This does not happen in real life.

'We could take it to the loch,' said Cass.

'Don't call her that. She's not an "it".'

'Alice, you'd better listen to me. It doesn't bloody matter what we call her. She's dead, and *we* might as well be, unless we figure out a way to make sure no one finds out what happened.'

'Can't we just . . . leave her here? Maybe they'd think she was sleepwalking or something?' I knew how lame that suggestion was before I'd even finished speaking.

'We can't! There's all sorts of evidence and stuff. Your pile of puke for a start! They'd work it out eventually. No, we have to make her disappear.'

'The loch won't work. They'll find the body,' said Polly.

'Right, yes, of course. We'll have to bury it.' Cass at least had the decency to look appalled at her own idea.

'Cass, listen to yourself! We can't do this! It's not right. Think about Tara's family . . . never knowing what happened,' said Rae.

'Rae's right,' I said.

'Think about *our* families! Alice, think about what this would do to your dad. It would kill him!' I hated her right then. Suddenly I knew that Cass would do or say *anything* to keep this quiet. And I realized that I would too, and I hated myself even more.

'What about the well?'

It was Polly's idea. The well wasn't far. Between the four of us we'd be able to carry Tara. The well was deep. No one would ever find her. Hopefully.

Before we knew it, Cass had a plan. We'd chuck the pillowcase and rope into the well – no one would notice they were missing. She'd put the balaclavas back where she'd found them. She would hide Tara's swimsuit and goggles somewhere, and take her flip-flops and towel down to the jetty by the loch. Everyone would think that Tara had gone for an early-morning swim and got into difficulty in the water. I wasn't sure people would believe that, since Tara was one of the strongest swimmers in school, but Polly said that maybe they'd think she'd had an asthma attack. *She did have a fucking asthma attack. Because we tortured her!* I wanted to scream. Cass would back up the story by telling everyone she'd seen Tara creeping out of the cabin at dawn. The loch was huge. They'd give up looking for the body eventually.

I felt like I'd disappeared completely and left some amoral Alice in my place. I was going along with this even though I knew it was wrong. Evil, even. But I was scared. So scared. I didn't want to go to prison. I didn't want to break Dad's heart. Cass had known full well the right buttons to push to make me do what she wanted.

Carrying Tara to the well was harder than you'd think. It was as if she was suddenly three times heavier than she would have been alive. I was stationed at her right arm. I kept on having to put my hand in her armpit to hoist her higher – to stop her from slipping from my grasp. Her skin felt wrong somehow, cold and clammy. Cass kept swearing under her breath. The other two were silent the whole way, like me.

Tara's eyes were still open. I wanted to do that thing I've seen on TV, where some kindly doctor just passes his hand over the eyes of a dead person and the eyelids close as if by magic. But I wasn't sure if it would work like that. And if it did, Tara would look like she was only sleeping. And I knew that wasn't right.

We reached the well just as I was convinced that my arms were about to be yanked out of their sockets. We laid Tara down on the grass, as carefully as possible.

'Right . . . OK, let's do this.' Cass's voice was shaky as she dropped the pillowcase and rope into the well.

'Are you sure? It's not too late to . . .' I didn't even try to finish the sentence.

Cass put her hand on my shoulder. 'It *is* too late. Alice, I'm so sorry. This should never have happened.' Her voice was wobbly, but she didn't cry.

We manoeuvred Tara over the wall and held her there for a few seconds before lowering her as far as we could. I didn't want to let go. As her hand slipped through mine, I felt a ring come loose and I grasped it tightly in my fingers. I don't know why.

There was a sickening sound when she landed at the bottom of the well. There was no going back now. We couldn't pretend it had been an accident. We were covering up a crime. I prayed that God would forgive us – and I haven't believed in God since Mum died.

Cass and Polly were peering over the side of the well so I took the opportunity to pocket the ring. Before I knew what was happening, Cass had picked up a huge rock and dropped it over the edge. Another sickening sound, even worse than the first.

'What are you doing?' I shouted.

Polly gestured at me frantically to be quiet, and Cass ignored me. She was scouting around for more rocks. I grabbed her arm. 'Stop that!'

There was a horrifying blankness in her eyes when she looked at me and explained that we had to cover up the body. Just in case. Another prayer to a God I didn't quite believe in.

We all helped to find rocks around the clearing. I couldn't bring myself to drop any into the well. The thought of the havoc they were wreaking on Tara was unbearable. I had an image in my head of her beautiful face all caved in. Pulpy and ruined.

Cass kept on working, throwing rock after rock into the well. Eventually Polly put a hand on her shoulder. 'That's enough. We should go now.' Cass didn't seem to hear; she carried on.

Polly, Rae and I stood a few feet away, waiting. Eventually Cass fell to her knees, her shoulders slumped. I crouched down beside her. 'Cass, we have to go.'

Cass looked at me, her eyes wide and terrified in the moonlight. 'What have we done?'

I had no words.

16

Cass was back in control by the time we got back to the cabin. Or at least doing a very good job of pretending she was. She set about grabbing Tara's swimming stuff while Polly and I watched. Rae had run to the bathroom as soon as we'd got back. A couple of minutes later I heard the shower running.

'Give me your balaclavas. I'll put them back on the way to the loch.'

I pulled mine from my pocket and handed it to her. 'I'll come with you.'

'No. You won't.' She wouldn't look me in the eye.

'I want to.'

'No. You don't.' She was right, of course.

Rae came out of the shower after Cass left. Her skin was ruddy from scrubbing. She got into bed and plugged in her headphones without even looking at me or Polly. I glanced over to check Polly's reaction, but she was staring at Tara's bed. The sponge bag and its spilled contents were on the bed where Rae and I had left them. *The inhaler. Shit.* Rae's jacket was slung over a chair by her bed. I rifled through the pockets and was practically dizzy with relief when I found it. I tossed it over to Polly, who'd put everything else back into the spongebag in the meantime. Then she zipped up the bag, put it back under the bed and smoothed down the rumpled blanket.

We got ready for bed in silence. I lay in the semi-darkness and let the tears try to drown me. They trickled down and settled in my ears. It tickled.

Cass crept in after about half an hour. I sat up and wiped away the tears. 'Cass,' I whispered.

She came over and sat on the edge of my bed.

'Are you OK?'

The corners of her mouth turned up, acknowledging the banality of my question. 'Been better.'

'Do you think . . . anyone will find out?'

'I have no idea. I'm not exactly an expert in this kind of thing. Alice, I'm so sorry.' She took my hand in hers – a completely un-Cass-like gesture. 'Do you think you can ever forgive me?' Her voice was small and weak.

'It wasn't your fault,' I whispered, but a voice

inside my head screamed *IT WAS YOUR FAULT. IT'S ALL YOUR FAULT!*

There's not much left to tell. At breakfast Cass asked Danni if she'd seen Tara. Danni went to Miss Daley. Miss Daley spoke to Jess and Paul. No one was worried – not really. Not until they found Tara's stuff on the jetty. Of course, they didn't tell us what was going on. They kept us all together in the hall. Everyone huddled in little groups, wondering what the hell was going on. Rae sat as far away from us as she could possibly get. Polly kept glancing over at Danni, Sam and Gemma, and I found myself doing the same. They probably thought Tara was up to something. That's what everyone else seemed to think – at least at first. Then Daley came in looking frantic. She took Cass away with her. I wasn't worried that Cass would give anything away. Cass has always been an excellent liar.

And then the police arrived in three huge 4x4s. That's when the mood changed. Some people started crying. I didn't. It seemed like hours before Daley came back to tell us what was going on. Cass didn't come back with her.

Daley told us that Tara was missing and we

needed to keep calm and not panic. We had to stay there and let the police do their job. Search parties were being assembled. 'I'm sure we'll find her . . . I'm sure . . .' Her voice trailed off and a tear trickled down her face. That nearly broke me. I wanted to tell her everything. *Surely she'd understand? Everyone would understand. No one would blame us.* But then a policeman in a Day-Glo jacket appeared in the doorway. His face was craggy and serious, and his laser eyes scanned the room. I could have sworn he looked at me for half a second longer than he looked at everyone else.

It was way too late to tell the truth.

Lunch came and went; no one ate very much.

They put on a DVD – a comedy; no one laughed very much.

Dinner came and went and it was just the same as lunch.

Then Daley told us. They were working on the theory that Tara had got into difficulty swimming in the loch. The search had been called off for the night. Our parents had been informed, and we'd be travelling back to London overnight.

I sat with Saira on the coach. She was upset, but in a strange, excited sort of way. The horror of it all was fascinating to her, and I was disgusted. Still, it was better than sitting next to Cass. She sat near the back with Polly. Rae sat by herself.

All the parents were in the school car park when we arrived at dawn. Dad gave me the kind of fierce hug he used to give me when Mum was dying. Those hugs always scared me a little.

I saw it on the news two days later. 'The search has been called off for missing London schoolgirl Tara Chambers. Police divers have been combing Loch Dunochar for the past three days, but this evening Detective Inspector Marshall, the officer in charge of the investigation, announced that the search would not continue. It's thought that Tara went for an early-morning swim in the loch and got into difficulty in the water. Although a strong swimmer, Tara suffered from asthma, and there's been speculation that her condition could have played a part in this tragedy.'

Then there was an outside broadcast with a correspondent standing on the shore of the loch. He was standing next to the craggy, laser-eyed police-man.

'Detective Inspector Marshall, are you saying that you believe Tara is dead?'

Ouch. That was blunt. Marshall gave the stupid reporter a hard look before answering.

'I'm saying that the search has been called off. Unfortunately we believe that the most likely scenario is that Miss Chambers drowned while swimming in the loch.' His voice was soft and his eyes were sad. 'This is not the first time a tragedy like this one has happened here. Fifteen years ago a man in his twenties was lost in Loch Dunochar. His body was never found.' Cass would be relieved — there was a precedent. I was not relieved. A part of me wanted them to keep looking and realize she wasn't there and . . . and what?

The reporter asked DI Marshall a few more questions before handing back over to the studio. They'd set up some kind of debate about safety on school trips. A woman with red poodle hair tried to blame Tara's death on the teachers. She kept saying the words *in loco parentis*, and you could tell it made her feel clever.

'Al, you shouldn't be watching this.' The screen faded to black and Dad slumped down next to me, remote control in hand.

'It's OK, Dad. I'm OK. Really.' I held his gaze and tried my best to transmit my okayness straight into his brain. It didn't work; it never worked.

'I just wish you didn't have to go through this. You've had so much to deal with already. It's not fair.'

Dad put his arm around me and I nestled into him. His sympathy was hard to bear, but the thought of him knowing the truth was much, much worse.

17

I finish talking and Jack says nothing. He's picking at his fingernails. The weight of everything I haven't told him is like a thousand tonnes on my shoulders. Except that's not where I feel it. It's there in the pit of my stomach, as if I've swallowed a boulder.

Jack will never know about Duncan, or about how hideous Tara was to Polly after she got stuck in the cave. And he'll never know how his sister died. Maybe it's better that way. A tragic swimming accident has got to be easier to deal with than the truth. *Yeah, nice try, Alice. You keep telling yourself that.* The voice in my head isn't mine. It's Tara's.

My hot chocolate has gone cold and gross, but I take a sip anyway just for something to do.

Jack looks up at me and his eyes are shiny. There are tears there, but he's not going to cry them. I don't know what I'll do if he cries them. 'Thank you. I really appreciate you talking to me. It . . . it helps.'

'How?'

'Well, I feel like I can picture her there now, doing all that mad outdoorsy stuff. I bet she hated it, didn't she?'

He smiles, and all I can do is shrug.

'Alice, it's OK. You don't have to pretend with me.'

'What . . . what do you mean?'

'I know you didn't exactly get on with Tara. Not many people did.'

'What are you talking about? She had loads of friends.'

'Not anyone close though. Not the way you two used to be.'

'But Danni and Sam and . . .'

'Dopey and Sneezy and Bitchy?' We laughed and it felt good. 'I'll let you in on a little secret. That's if you promise not to tell anyone . . .'

I nod, and he leans in close.

'Tara didn't even really like that lot. In fact, I'd even go so far as to say she kind of despised them.' He's understandably pleased with this little nugget of information.

'What? No way!'

'It's true, I swear!'

I take a moment to roll this idea around in my head. Half of my brain thinks this makes no sense whatsoever, and the other half is nodding along as if it's always suspected as much. 'Why does she . . . I mean, why did she hang out with them all the time then?' I wince at my mistake, and Jack waves it away like it doesn't even bother him. I suppose he's been making the same mistake a lot over the past couple of weeks. I know I did after Mum died.

'Maybe she didn't have any better options. Not since you two fell out anyway.'

'That's ridiculous. She was the most popular girl in the whole school. She could have been friends with anyone she wanted.'

'Even you?'

'What are you trying to say?' I don't like the way this conversation is heading, and considering where it's already been, that's saying something.

'She missed you. It really upset her when you two stopped being friends.' He sees me wince. 'Sorry, I know it was a long time ago and everything. I just thought you should know. The Tara that the rest of the world saw was different to the Tara I knew. God, I miss her so much.' He rubs his face with his hands. 'Does it get any easier? I can't imagine ever not missing her.'

'It will get easier, I promise. You'll always miss her, but there's nothing wrong with that.'

He reaches for my hand and squeezes it. 'Thanks for this. I owe you, big time.' I can't speak. His hand on mine has pushed all coherent thoughts out of my head.

He doesn't let go of my hand, and all of a sudden he looks shy as anything. 'Maybe, I dunno . . . maybe I could take you for a pizza or something sometime? I mean, it doesn't have to be pizza . . . Just to say thanks, y'know.'

Did he just ask me out? Not a chance. He just feels bad for grilling me about Tara. Of course he doesn't want to go out with me. His sister's just died, for Christ's sake. But all I can think about is holding his hand and what it would be like to kiss him. He'd never be interested in me. Not in a million years. Stop this train of thought right this second.

He's looking at me strangely and I realize I need to actually say something out loud. 'Pizza's good. I like pizza. As long as there's no anchovies.'

A perfect smile from Jack, followed by a perfect grimace. 'Urgh. Anchovies are the food of the devil. No worries there. We'll make an anti-anchovy pact. Let's shake on it.'

We both look down at our hands and they're still

entwined, so we kind of move them up and down in a lame handshaking action. We laugh, and all of a sudden it's not awkward at all. Just the opposite in fact: it feels like the most normal thing in the world.

She's there when I get home. Scaring the crap out of me when I open the wardrobe. She's tucked away in the corner next to some shoeboxes. I slam the door, and turn on the radio as loud as it'll go.

But I can still hear her. 'You fancy him, don't you?'

I sing along to the song that's playing, even though I don't know the words. It's some crappy ballad with a lot of warbling in it.

'I *said*, "You fancy him, don't you?"'

More singing from me. Louder and louder.

'You should audition for the school choir. Who knew that beneath that mousey, incredibly *average* exterior lurks the voice of an angel? Truly.'

This shouldn't hurt me. Insults from a figment of my imagination should bounce off me like bouncy things. But they don't.

Suddenly she's not in the wardrobe any more but sitting cross-legged on my bed. 'I can't believe I'm sitting here, all dead and gross, and you're creaming yourself over my little brother. It really doesn't bear thinking about.' A shudder runs through her – a big fake shudder. 'Haven't you got anything more important to think about than getting into Jack's pants?'

I know I'm blushing. I *must* be blushing. 'Shut up!'

'*Shut up?* Jesus, Alice, you are so pathetic it hurts. It actually physically HURTS. And it takes a lot to hurt me now, trust me on that one. All I'm saying is that I can't believe you're obsessing about Jack when you really should be spending at least one hundred per cent of your time feeling bad about me. And don't forget the whole working-out-exactly-how-I-came-to-be-quite-so-dead thing. It's important, Alice.' Her voice has changed. It's slower and lower somehow. Her eyes are steady on mine. They don't *look* dead. Not like they did that night. These eyes have a spark: a bright, fierce spark that won't let me go.

'I don't fancy him.'

'Liar, liar! Pants on fire!' She giggles like a small child and then launches into that god-awful Kings of Leon song. She always loved to sing. When we were nine years old we formed a girl band called 2 Awesum. Our singing voices weren't all that great, but that didn't stop us performing at Dad's fortieth birthday party. He danced and laughed and said it was surely only a matter of time before we signed a recording contract.

'Admit it! You like him, don't you? It's nothing to be ashamed of – it's perfectly natural. Although he IS younger than you, which is a bit ick. But it's about time you got some action. I was beginning to think you'd be a virgin forever.'

I can feel my cheeks burning burning burning. 'What makes you think I'm a virgin?'

She doesn't even dignify that with a response, unless you count a classic Tara eye roll. Which I don't.

'I've had . . . boyfriends.' I couldn't sound less convincing if I tried.

'Yeah, I hate to tell you this, but snogging Neil Bagshaw round the back of the bowling alley when you were twelve doesn't count as "having a boyfriend".'

I hate her. She's dead and I'm sorry about that, but I HATE her.

My phone rings and I pounce on it. A teeny-tiny part of me hopes that it's him. It's not. It's Cass – which is almost as surprising. Cass doesn't *do* phone calls. Texting and emailing and Facebooking and IMing, but not phone calls. I've stopped bothering to phone her – monosyllabic doesn't even begin to cover it.

'So, did you do it then?' Straight to the point. Typical Cass.

'Did I do what?' Let's see if I can make her say Tara's name.

'Talk to her brother.' Nope, guess not.

'Yeah, I saw him after school.'

She waits for me to continue, but I won't. I don't know why, but I've suddenly come over all stubborn. Maybe Ghost Tara is rubbing off on me. Speaking of Ghost Tara, she's gone of course.

'And?'

'And what?' I think I'm actually starting to enjoy myself – just a little.

Cass sighs a huge long staticky breath down the phone. 'What did you tell him?'

'I told him we killed his sister and chucked her down a well.' I don't mean to say this out loud – honestly I don't.

'You're fucking hilarious. I can't believe you're joking about this.'

'Oh, so it's OK for *you* to joke about it, but I'm not allowed. Yeah, fine, that makes total sense.'

She says, 'Alice, please . . .' with just enough imploringness to make me feel guilty.

'I told him about the trip. Nothing bad – *obviously*. It was fine. Sort of nice actually.'

'Oh God.'

'What? Everything's fine. He doesn't suspect a

thing.' Saying those five words brings it all crashing back down on me. I lied to him. I can never *not* lie to him. Even if we . . .

'You like him, don't you? He's her fucking brother, for Christ's sake! How can you like him? How can you even *think* about liking him? Nothing can ever happen with him – you do realize that?'

Of course I realize that. Mainly because he DOESN'T FANCY ME. He doesn't. He just wants to take me for pizza to thank me for talking to him about Tara. And he probably wants to talk about her some more. There's no one else to talk to. I am The Last Resort. Nothing more.

'Alice? Are you still there?'

'I'm here.'

'You have to stay away from him. It's way too risky. You'd have to lie ALL the time.'

'I lie every day – to everyone. We all do.'

'Yes, but this is different, and you know it. I'm warning you, Alice, you have to stay away from him. For all of us.'

18

All anyone can talk about at school is Tara. Still. By lunchtime on Friday I've gleaned the following information from various sources:

1. The swimming team wore black armbands at the weekend – in memory of Tara.
2. Two pages will be reserved in the yearbook for some kind of Tara-related memorial thing.
3. The school dance WILL go ahead after all, much to the relief of everyone. (Apart from me, of course.)
4. Polly Sutcliffe is forming something called the Tara Chambers Memorial Society.

This is the one that floors me. What is she playing at? Could she possibly draw any more attention to herself? On my way to lunch I see her putting up pastel-coloured flyers on the noticeboard outside the cafeteria. There are loads of people milling around, so I can't do what I want, which is to shake her – hard.

'What are you *doing*?'

She turns and I notice that her hair really does look a lot better than it used to. Her eczema seems to have cleared up as well. Either that or she's discovered some new miracle foundation. She looks like a different person almost.

'Putting up flyers. Why, do you want one?'

I lower my voice. 'No, I do not want one! What exactly is the Tara Chambers Memorial Society?!'

'It's a charitable foundation. Anyone can join. The plan is to raise money for Tara's favourite charities. It's going really well already – I've arranged with Daley for us to get the proceeds from the dance.' I do not recognize this person. It's not the hair or the skin . . . it's everything.

'Why are you doing this?' I don't even try to hide the fact that I'm looking at her like she's a crazy person.

'Don't you think it's a nice thing to do?' She looks all serene and weird. She staples a duck-egg-blue flyer right next to a baby-pink one. She's careful to make sure the edges match up exactly.

I'm finding it hard to find the words I want to say. 'I think it's a lovely thing to do.' This is sort of true, even though I find it hard to believe that Tara had *one* favourite charity, let alone charities *plural*. I lower my voice. 'I just . . . don't think *you* should be doing it. I thought we were all going to lay low for a while?'

Polly laughs. At me! 'Lay low?! You're being a tad over dramatic, don't you think? There's no harm in it at all, silly. In fact, do you want to join? So far I've got Sam and Gemma, and Danni'll definitely join, won't she?' She pauses and puts her hand on my arm. 'I'm just trying to do the right thing, you know?' Her eyes are glistening, like she's about to cry on me. I can't be doing with that.

'I've got to go.' I turn so abruptly I practically bump noses with Cass.

'What are you two whispering about?' I have no idea what possesses her to say something like this. There's only one thing I would be whispering about with Polly Sutcliffe.

'Nothing. Let's go.' I drag her away, leaving Polly and her perfectly symmetrical flyers.

The cafeteria is pretty much full, but I manage to find a free table for Cass and me. Rae is sitting a few tables away. She's spread her bag, coat and some books around her to make sure no one sits too close.

I bring Cass up to speed on the Polly situation. She's as surprised as I am. After a bit of speculation over what charities Tara could possibly have been involved in (during which Cass wonders if giving blowjobs to half the sixth-form at Knox Academy counts as charity), we fall into silence. I munch on some sad-looking iceberg lettuce. Cass eats her lasagne – with chips.

'You know, it may not be such a bad thing after all,' she whispers as she squirts yet more ketchup onto her plate.

'How can it be anything *but* a bad thing?' I try (and promptly fail) to resist nabbing a couple of her less ketchup-splattered chips.

'Well, I mean, it sort of puts them off the scent, doesn't it? Not that there IS a scent, but if there was . . . if someone thought there was something suss about what happened, they'd hardly suspect someone who was the president of the Chambers Appreciation Society or whatever it's called.' She looks almost impressed with the idea. 'Maybe we should join?'

I can't tell if she's joking. 'Don't be ridiculous. We're supposed to be staying away from each other, *remember*?'

'Then why are you having lunch with me, eh? Quick! Someone might see! Run away!' We've discussed this a hundred times already. It's OK for me and Cass to hang out, because we did *before*. It would be more suspicious if we didn't hang out (as she keeps reminding me whenever I show any sign of wanting to be alone for two minutes). But we should steer clear of Polly and Rae, just to be on the safe side.

'Cass, you drive me insane. You do realize that, don't you?'

'Ah, but you love me really.' She tries her best grin on for size. That grin used to make me laugh. It used to charm me. Things have changed.

I have English straight after lunch. It's a relief to escape from Cass. I used to hate the fact that we weren't in any of the same classes any more, but now I'm glad. It means I don't have to sit there looking at Cass and wondering *What kind of person are you, really?*

I think I'm doing a pretty good job of hiding my feelings. Cass has no idea how good I am at lying. Nobody knows but me.

We're studying *Much Ado About Nothing*, and it seems like the stupidest play in the world. I detest each and every one of Shakespeare's comedies. Random misunderstandings, mistaken identities and overheard conversations do not, in my opinion, equal hilarity.

Daley's got us reading out loud, which I've always

hated. I've never seen the point of it — everyone reads in a bored monotone and no one actually listens. It's impossible to concentrate on the words being spoken when you're checking a few pages ahead to see what *your* next line is. I usually try to volunteer to read a small part early on. Servant #3 or third-lady-on-the-left. Otherwise there's a real danger you'll end up being Juliet or Lady Macbeth or whoever.

Today I'm finding it especially hard to concentrate. My gaze is constantly drawn to Tara's desk. Danni has to sit by herself now. She's staring out of the window. To be honest, she's looking sort of rough. But rough for Danni is not the same as rough for normal people. She still looks ten times better than I ever could. It's not that her hair looks greasy or anything, but it's definitely on the turn. Nothing like her usual just-stepped-out-of-a-salon silky mane.

She's wearing a lot less make-up than usual, which would perhaps be a good thing if she was one of Those Girls — those orange idiots with fat spidery eyelashes (yes, I mean YOU, Sam Burgess and Gemma Jones). But Danni's make-up has always been perfect. I've lost count of the number of times I've wanted to ask her exactly how she manages to get her eyeliner to look like that. But that's not the kind of conversation you have with someone who can't stand you (and who you're a bit scared of, if you're being totally honest). I'm not even sure she's even wearing any eyeliner today, let alone her trademark emerald green (sounds wrong, looks right). Her face looks like all the colour has been drained out of it. She's in black and white and everyone else is in colour.

I've given up trying to follow the play. I can't stop staring at her. I'm sure she must be able to feel it; I'm sure any second she'll turn around and catch me watching. But she doesn't. She is elsewhere.

A thought smacks me round the head and makes me feel worse than ever. It's a strange, obvious thought: Danni is a real person, with real feelings.

I've felt guilty about the grief we've caused Tara's parents. I've felt guilty about the grief we've caused Jack. Christ, I've even felt guilty about the grief we've caused Tara's bloody dog. But it never even crossed my mind to feel bad for Danni or Gemma or Sam or anyone else Tara was friends with. Is it just because I know they wouldn't give me a second thought if something happened to Cass? Or is because I am fundamentally a bad person with all the empathy of a paper clip?

I'm sure Tara slagged off her friends to Jack all the time, but I don't buy what he said about her not actually liking them. Maybe she *said* that, but why would you spend all your time with people you despised? It makes no sense.

But it doesn't matter how Tara felt about Danni. What matters to me, suddenly more than almost anything else I can think of, is how Danni felt about Tara. How Danni is feeling right now.

I have to talk to her.

19

OK, so I didn't talk to Danni. She made a super-speedy exit and Daley caught me as I was heading out the door.

'Alice, I've been meaning to talk to you. How are you?' Her voice is soft and oozing with sympathy, and, sure enough, her head is tilted to one side. The head tilt: the international symbol for *I feel your pain*. As soon as this thought pops into my head, I feel bad. She's only being nice. EVERYONE is only being nice.

'Fine, thanks, miss.'

'Now that's not true, is it?' This is new. Most people are relieved to get a 'fine'. You can see it in their eyes. They don't want to talk about it – not really. Because they don't know what to say. I don't blame them, because I wouldn't know what to say either. Death is weird that way.

'Um . . .'

'It's OK, Alice. You can be honest with me. Do you think I didn't notice you staring out the window for the whole lesson?' Thank God she didn't realize it was Danni I was staring at. That would have led to a completely different conversation – perhaps even more awkward than this one.

I say, 'Sorry about that,' at the same moment she says, 'Don't worry, you're not in trouble or anything.' This makes her laugh a little. I wait for her to speak next. It's safer that way.

'This must be especially hard for you.' There's a definite emphasis on the 'you'. I'm sure I didn't imagine it. I can barely disguise my surprise when she says, 'I know you and Tara were close.'

How the hell could she possibly know that? She's been at Bransford all of five minutes, and Tara and I were most definitely NOT close in those five minutes.

I muster up superhuman levels of nonchalance. 'Not really. What makes you think that?' I try to sound light and airy and fine and dandy, but I'm sure I sound suspicious – with a dash of petulance thrown in for good measure.

'I thought I heard that somewhere.' Now she stares off into space, searching the murky corners of her Shakespeare-addled brain.

I say nothing.

'Maybe I was mistaken. But I thought . . .'

Still nothing from me. It's not easy to keep quiet in situations like this. You want to say something – anything – to fill the quiet. Normally I'd start babbling like crazy, but I have to be careful here. Very careful.

Daley shakes her head as if to clear it and starts to gather up her notes. 'Never mind. Anyway, if you need to talk to anyone – about anything at all – my door is always open.'

I thank her and head for the door as fast as my legs will propel me, but once again she foils my escape plan.

'I can't help thinking . . . I can't help thinking there must be something I could have done.' Her voice is shaky. She sighs deeply and her shoulders slump, like her body has decided to fold in on itself. She's been putting on an act for us, that's as clear as anything now. It must be exhausting for her. I try to look at it from her point of view. Her first trip away in her new job, and one of the kids goes and dies on her. Of course she'd blame herself. Even if a giant cartoon anvil had fallen from the heavens on top of Tara's head, she'd *still* feel responsible. Because that's the kind of person she is.

I want to reassure her that there was nothing she could have done. Whichever version of Tara's death you choose – swimming accident or practical joke gone wrong – there was nothing she could have done.

But I don't reassure her. I turn my back on her and leave.

By the time the bell rings at three thirty I am dog-tired. Every day is the same now, and I can't help wondering how long it's going to last. It takes all my energy – and then some – not to shout out, 'WE DID IT! IT WAS US! IT'S OUR FAULT!' I wonder what would happen. Would it be the second biggest mistake of my life? Or would there be an epic sense of relief? An unspeakable, unthinkable weight lifting off my shoulders.

I head to the local library. It's one of my very favourite places. Mum used to bring me here after school on Fridays. Then we'd pick up fish and chips on the way home and watch a film with Dad.

For ages after Mum died I couldn't bear the thought of coming here. Dad met me at school one Friday and tried to bring me. There was a scene – not quite a tantrum, but pretty close. He never mentioned it again. We still kept up the tradition of fish-and-chip Fridays, but the library was *our* place. Mine and Mum's. It didn't seem right going there without her.

This particular library is a beautiful old red-brick building, slightly worn around the edges. I used to think it looked like a magical castle or Hogwarts or something (I was sort of stupid that way). About a year ago I was wandering past, trying to ignore it as I always did. But my legs betrayed me and wandered me right up the steps and inside. My legs obviously knew it was time for me to get over it, even if my brain didn't. And it was OK; I didn't break down sobbing at the enquiry desk or anything. I stood just inside the entrance and breathed in that perfectly musty book smell. I felt like I was home.

I could picture Mum with her specs propped up on her head – making her hair go every which way. I called it her mad-professor look (and she called me a rude little oik). Mum would always head straight for the new releases and I'd head for the children's section, which was down some spooky stone stairs in the basement. I would spend half an hour (no more, no less) picking three books for the week, and we'd meet up on the front steps. It always made Mum happy that I was a reader, so it made me feel hideously bad that I read a grand total of nothing in the year after she died. Mum loved stories. She loved escaping from reality. It's only now that I wonder if she loved escaping so much because she wasn't exactly happy with her real life. Maybe she hated her job. Maybe one day she'd have got bored with Dad and run off with Mr Humphries from next door. Maybe I'd have been a huge disappointment to her. Except there's no 'maybe' about that last one.

Today the library is pretty much deserted – everyone else in the world is gearing up for the weekend. I am learning German vocab. Truly pathetic. But it's better than being stuck in my room with Ghost Tara. Or hanging out with Cass, trying to pretend that nothing's changed. Or sitting in front of the telly with Dad, dreading what he's going to ask me next.

My phone buzzes, scaring the crap out of me. It's a text from just about the only person in the world I want a text from. Jack: *How about tomorrow for that pizza? J.* My heart starts racing a billion beats a minute. My heart is clearly stupid. It has a tendency to get overexcited for no reason.

I wait a few minutes before texting back, so he doesn't think I'm a total desperado: *Can't do tomorrow – sorry. Next Sat?* Of course, I *am* free tomorrow. I have zero plans for the whole weekend. Unless you count surfing the Net, writing an essay and playing Scrabble with Dad. Which I don't. But I have to at least pretend not to be a complete loser.

Next Sat works for me. Want to meet at Nat. History Museum at 2? Pizza later?

The Natural History Museum? *WTF?*

OK! See you there! I debated about using two exclamation marks in one text. It seemed a bit overenthusiastic, but I didn't want him to think I *wasn't* enthusiastic either.

I'll be waiting by the dead diplodocus – you can't miss it. :)

There I was being all impressed that he didn't use text speak and he goes and ruins it with a smiley face. But the idea of Jack smiling at me, even in a text message, pleases me more than I'd like to admit.

I sit back in my chair, German vocab leaking out of my brain at an alarming rate. There's no room for it in my head now that Jack's taken over. So, we're going to a museum. That's . . . different. I've only been to the Natural History Museum once, on a school trip years ago. All I remember is that it was big and busy and we were supposed to go round filling in some sort of activity sheet. I think I got lost.

The Natural History Museum. Clearly Jack is not interested in me. At least not in that way. No one goes to a museum on a date. You go to museums with your mum or your gran or your school. Not with someone you fancy. He really *does* just want to take me out to say thanks. My overexcited heart shrinks back inside my chest, feeling sheepish.

I chuck down my phone and it slides right across the table and onto the floor. Stupid phone. Here I was, perfectly happy, doing my homework like a good little girl, minding my own business. And then my bloody phone has to go and ruin everything. *Jack* has to go and ruin everything. Why couldn't I have enjoyed that teeny kernel of hope for a few more days before it went POP?

The truth is, I hadn't even realized that I'd *had* any hope until it was gone. Now I can admit to myself that a part of me (and not even a small part) had thought that something could happen between us. And that part of me wanted it to happen so badly that it forces a couple of tears out of my eyes before I can do anything about it.

A museum. A stupid, dusty, boring museum full of hyperactive kids. Fantastic.

20

I'm going to have to spend Saturday with Jack,
knowing that a) I as good as murdered his sister, and
b) he does not want to kiss me. A normal person might
not be able to think these thoughts simultaneously.
A normal person might be more concerned about
a) than b). Clearly there is something very, very
wrong with me.

I *know* I should stay away from him. I should
make up some excuse and bail. He might text me
for a bit, eager to thank me for telling him about the
trip. But I could make up more excuses, and then
he'd surely stop bothering after a while. It would
be simple. I'd never have to worry about saying the
wrong thing or giving anything away or accidentally
confessing. This would be the right thing to do, no
question.

But I want to see him. Even if it has to be at some

stupid museum . . . as *friends*. I just want to be near him and I'm not entirely sure why.

Ghost Tara tries her best to annoy me about the whole thing, but I'm getting better and better at blocking her out. One of her barbed comments will occasionally hit the mark, making me feel ugly and worthless and guilty. Like when she points out that my new top looks fine . . . as long as I suck my stomach in and don't make the mistake of breathing. I scrunch the top into a ball and chuck it in the bin in the kitchen. Dad finds it (of course he finds it), but I think he buys my story about dripping olive oil all down it. And since the top is now spattered with leftover curry and soggy teabags, he can't really tell.

I tell Cass that Dad is taking me to visit Nan and Grumps. She smirks and says, 'Rather you than me.' Cass only has one grandparent left – her mum's mum, who lives in Sydney. Cass has seen her three times in her whole life. Old people freak Cass out, whereas I kind of like them. They always seem so . . . sedate. Well, maybe it's just the ones I know, but Nan's always all *What's the hurry? You've got time for another cuppa, haven't you?*

I wish I *was* going to see Nan and Grumps. They live near the beach in Sussex. It's a pretty chilled sort of place too – the kind of place I could really do with being right now. Nan's been phoning since I got back from Scotland, trying to get me to go and visit, 'to get away from it all'. If only it was that easy.

It takes me ages to decide what to wear on Saturday, particularly with Tara wittering in my ear the whole time. 'Hmm . . . I don't think Jack will like that colour,' and 'Well, if *you* think that top goes with those jeans then I'm sure it's fine. Really.' I went for the nicest clothes I could go for without tipping over into Date Territory. Not that I know all that much about what people actually *wear* on dates. So I'm wearing my favourite jeans and a red top. People always tell me I look good in red. I don't know why and I'm not sure I believe them.

I check myself out in the mirror (with Tara smirking over my shoulder, of course) and I think I look fine. Not crap, not amazing – just fine. I suppose the red does look sort of good against my super-pale vampire skin. Minimal make-up: a couple of swipes of mascara and a dab of lip gloss. I tie my hair back in a messy ponytail and I'm good to go. Nearly. I open up the top drawer of my dressing table and grab Mum's necklace. It's an emerald on a silver chain – very simple and completely beautiful. Mum said the emerald matched my eyes, and I always wished that was true. Whenever I admired it, she'd say, 'This will be yours one day.' We never thought *one day* would arrive quite so soon.

I fasten the necklace and it sits in that perfect spot on my collarbone. The one perfect place on my body. I shut the drawer, but not fast enough to ignore what's nestled there among the rest of my jewellery. The ring. Tara's ring.

It's beyond risky keeping it here, but I don't know what else to do with it. I can't just get rid of it. That wouldn't be right. And I don't want to hide it in my sock drawer or something. It's precious and it deserves to be looked after.

I check over my shoulder – Ghost Tara is gone. I open the drawer again and take out the ring. It's slender and pretty – three strands of silver plaited together. Tara wore it on the pinky finger of her right hand. She never took it off – not even when she was swimming. Back when she and I were friends, she wore the ring on her index finger. She used to twist it round and round when she was nervous about something. I don't think she does (I mean, *did*) that any more. Not so much to get nervous about when you're reigning supreme at the top of the social pyramid, I suppose.

Before I can think about what I'm doing, I slip the ring onto my pinky finger. It fits perfectly and looks just right. Strangely, the idea of wearing it doesn't creep me out in the slightest. Something about it makes me feel a little less wrong, a little less . . . Alice. I twist it round my finger, just like she used to do. It's comforting. But of course I can't ever wear it, and especially not today. So I put it back where I found it and shut the drawer more firmly than I need to.

On the way to meet Jack, the ring is all I can think about. Specifically, how it slid off Tara's finger into my hand as we let her go. What were the chances of that happening? It's almost like I was *meant* to have it. So I'd never be able to move on. Never be able to forget.

London's looking beautiful today – not grey and grimy like usual. The first bit of sunshine we've had in weeks, and I'm going to be stuck in a museum. Fabulous.

There are loads of people sitting on the steps outside, even though it's pretty cold. A boy and girl are snogging as if they're going for some kind of world record. It's hard not to stare. I think for a second that maybe museums *are* date-worthy after all, but then I notice their rucksacks and cameras. Tourists. They don't count.

I head for the door before the boy-tourist and

girl-tourist decide to get horizontal and make me puke. It takes a couple of seconds for my eyes to adjust after the brightness outside. The place is completely rammed. People *everywhere*. And it's loud. It makes me feel a bit panicky for a second, but then I see him. And the panic melts away.

He's sitting on the floor next to the massive dino skeleton. He's reading a battered old paperback and he's completely oblivious to everyone and everything around him. His hair keeps falling down over his eyes and he keeps pushing it back in a battle he's never going to win.

I know I should go over and say hi, but I don't want to – not yet. It feels like there's a *possibility* in this moment. Not a real possibility, but if I pretend hard enough I can imagine that I'm his girlfriend and he's waiting for me, trying to get lost in his book when really all he can think about is me. Or something.

He looks up and catches me staring. Embarrassing. He waves and clambers to his feet. I make my way towards him, nearly colliding with one of those scary off-roader-style pushchairs. Jack doesn't notice though – he's too busy stuffing the book into his messenger bag.

There's an awkward moment when I stand in front of him and sort of wave, as if *that's* how you greet someone. He goes in for a hug and I thank God that at least one of us knows how to be normal. He smells so good: sort of fresh and zesty. He's definitely wearing aftershave. I do my best to ignore the little voice in my head that gleefully shouts, 'Aftershave = date!' I also do my best not to bury my face in his shoulder and stay there forever. Because that might scare him.

After the hug there's a little silence.

'So . . . the Natural History Museum . . . ?'

'Um, yes. As soon as I sent that text I realized you'd think I was a complete weirdo. I just . . . really like it here.' He looks like a bashful little boy.

'No, no, it's fine! I haven't been here for years.'

'Oh man, you're gonna love it! There's so much cool stuff here.' He winces and puts his hands on my shoulders. I think I might pass out. 'Alice, there's something I have to tell you.' Oh God. 'OK, here goes. I am a *massive* geek. I never quite got over my dinosaur obsession. I've seen *Jurassic Park* thirty-seven times. I have a lot, and I mean *a lot*, of dinosaur books at home.' He takes a deep breath and hangs his head. Then he looks up at me through his hair. 'So now you know my secret. I completely understand if you want to bail. I just thought you should know what you're getting into . . .' Getting into? What does *that* mean? Nothing. It means nothing. Calm down.

His eyes sparkle with mischief. 'So now that's out in the open, I reckon it's your turn . . . What's *your* dirty little secret?'

21

My stomach contracts and I think I might vomit all down Jack's T-shirt.

I manage to pull myself together, somehow. 'Where do you want me to start? How about the fact that I used to obsessively collect elephants – not real ones, obviously. Or the fact that my Dad and I play Scrabble at least three times a week. Or, here's a good one . . . I spend most Friday nights in the library.' What. Have. I. Done?!

'Wow. That is truly impressive geekery. You win. You are *definitely* a bigger geek than me. I bow down to you, Queen of Geekdom.' And he actually does a little bow.

I pout and frown at the same time, until I realize this might not be the most attractive look in the entire world.

Maybe the whole pouty/frowny look was too

convincing, because his smile slips. 'I'm sorry! I don't think . . . You're not . . .'

I laugh and grab his arm. 'It's OK, I've been called worse!' Mostly by your sister. 'Now come on, show me some dinosaurs.' He lets me drag him in the direction of the dinosaur gallery. His arm feels wiry and strong beneath my fingers.

So we trawl round the dinosaurs, and it's about a million times more fun than I would have thought. Jack really knows his stuff, and he's very cute when he gets all enthusiastic and stumbles over his words trying to get me interested too. It doesn't take much — before long I'm asking him questions (and genuinely wanting to know the answers).

A couple of times he stops himself mid-sentence. 'I'm not boring you, am I?' I laugh and tell him that I'm enjoying myself, and his smile makes me forget everything but this exact moment. Here. Now. Jack. Me. And a room full of dead lizards.

As we trawl round some of the other galleries I somehow manage to forget about the obvious non-dateness of the occasion. And even more surprisingly, I manage to forget about Tara for minutes at a time. But then Jack will say or do something that reminds me of her and it's like all the breath in my body whooshes out at once.

It's not that Jack *looks* like her or anything. But there's a definite family resemblance in some of his features. His eyes and hair are darker than hers, but his nose is the same and his lips are perfectly lip-shaped, just like hers. If I had any artistic ability whatsoever, that's how I would draw a mouth. I need to stop thinking about Jack's mouth now.

It's not the way he looks that makes me think of Tara though. It's the little things. Like the way he runs his hand through his hair. And the half-smirk on his face when he teases me. And the really intense look he has in his eyes when he thinks I'm not looking.

Three hours of museuming and my feet are killing me. Luckily, Jack seems to sense I've had enough and suggests we go and sit on the steps outside. Snogging Couple have snogged off somewhere else, thank God, but I can't help but smile when Jack sits in the exact same spot.

It's a lot colder now. We're the only ones sitting on the steps.

'Thank you, Alice.' The intense look is back and this time it's got me pinned down.

'For what?' I say softly.

'For helping me forget for a little while. I didn't think it was possible.' He exhales loudly and continues before I can say anything. 'I shouldn't forget though, should I? It's not right . . .' A tear springs from nowhere, surprising us both. He swipes it away. 'Sorry. Man, this is embarrassing.'

I put my hand on his shoulder. 'Don't apologize. There's nothing to be embarrassed about.'

Another tear, this one treated with the same disdain as the first. 'It's just . . . how can I be here with you, having an amazing time and laughing and stuff, when she's . . .' He stares at nothing in the distance.

Before I can think about what I'm doing, I grab his hand. 'Jack, listen to me. It's OK. You're allowed to have fun sometimes. It doesn't mean you miss her any less. And you're allowed to cry.'

'I don't want to cry any more. I've cried enough. She wouldn't want me moping around feeling sorry for myself. She'd want me to get on with my life.' He looks down at our hands and I wish I knew what he was thinking.

And then he looks right at me. His eyes are shining and melty brown and I would do anything to make the hurt in them go away. And suddenly I know what he's thinking after all. He's thinking about kissing me. He moves his head closer to mine, ever so slightly. You wouldn't even notice if you weren't looking for the signs. I tell myself I'm imagining things – Jack would never want to kiss me. Never ever in a million years. But somehow, I *know*. His lips are parted a little. I can almost . . .

I can't do this. I can't.

I squeeze his hand and then release it and jump to my feet. 'Um . . . we should go. Are you cold? I'm getting cold.' I rub my arms as if that proves something. Jack looks like a puppy. A puppy I've just kicked.

I grab his hands and pull him to his feet. He looks dazed and confused. He's not the only one. My head is spinning, but I can't think about it.

'So . . . where do you want to go now? London is our oyster!' I link arms with him, trying to show that I DO want to touch him.

He recovers quickly — I'm impressed (and relieved). 'The choice is yours! As long as it involves pizza. Lots of pizza.'

The rest of the day passes without incident. We gorge on pizza and we talk about nothing. Nothing important anyway. Jack's doing a really good job at pretending nothing happened earlier. Probably because nothing *did* happen.

After a while I start to wonder if I was imagining

things. Maybe he was just going to hug me, or flick a bug out of my hair or something. That would make a lot more sense.

But I know. Deep down, I *know* I was right. And it makes me feel nauseous and guilty and excited all at the same time.

I try my very best to listen to everything he says, but every so often I find my eyes straying down to look at his mouth. It really is perfect, even when there's a little bit of pizza sauce nestled in the corner.

We sit next to each other on the tube later. There's no one sitting opposite us, so I can look at our reflection in the window. I like the way the reflection looks. Something about it seems right and normal. I try to be subtle, but he catches me looking and waves at me and laughs. All I can do is wave back and laugh too.

There's a girl sitting a little way down the carriage from us. I think she's giving me evils, but it's hard to say for sure. Maybe her face is just made that way. Nope – *definite* evils. She probably fancies Jack and thinks I'm not good enough for him. Or maybe she just hates the fact that we're having fun and she's not. I feel sort of sorry for her. Until I remember my rather unfortunate situation: I'm starting to really, really like a boy I should really, really be staying away from. And even worse, I think he's starting to like me back.

We come out of the tube station and it's time to say our goodbyes. There's a silence between us as Jack scuffs his trainers on the pavement and I check the time on my phone. I want him to speak first and eventually he obliges.

'So . . . this has been fun.' He looks at me questioningly, as if he's not altogether sure.

'Yeah, it has. Thanks for the pizza. Are you sure I can't give you some money towards it?'

He rolls his eyes at me. 'Alice, how many times do I have to tell you? This was *my* treat . . .' He lowers his head then looks up with a cheeky smile. 'Besides, you can pay next time, can't you?'

'Next time?'

He shrugs, trying his best to be casual. Or maybe he just *is* being casual. It's hard to tell. 'I'd like there to be a next time. If *you'd* like there to be a next time, that is . . .'

Our eyes meet and we're really *looking* at each other. I feel a weird hotness spread through my body. I've never felt anything like it before.

And then I say the words I hope I won't regret. 'I'd like there to be a next time.'

Cass is going to kill me.

22

It is five days since I saw Jack. Most of my awake-time during those five days has been spent thinking about him. Most of my asleep-time has been spent dreaming about him. Ghost Tara has left me alone. It's a relief to be able to think my thoughts in peace for a change.

The Almost Kiss. I can't stop thinking about the Almost Kiss. What would it have been like, kissing him? I play it several different ways in my head, and each time is better than the last.

I should have done it. I might not get another chance. He was feeling sad and vulnerable and confused. He didn't really want to kiss me. Not really and truly. And even if he did want to kiss me, the way I reacted will have put him off for good. I might as well have slapped him in the face. But then again, he *did* say he wanted to see me again, didn't he?

My brain is battling itself. The things I *know* to be

true (e.g. no boy has ever shown the slightest bit of interest in me, he is super-hot so why would he like me?) versus the things I think/hope might be true (e.g. he *was* going to kiss me, he *does* seem to like me). My mind flits between the two extremes so fast it makes me dizzy.

I wish I could talk it through with someone. But the only someone I'd want to talk to is Cass, and that would definitely not be a good idea. She doesn't know I saw Jack on Saturday, and I intend to keep it that way. Besides, boy talk has never been a major feature of our friendship. Whenever I talk about a boy I like, her default reaction is to mock me mercilessly. And something tells me that if I was to talk about this particular boy, being mocked would be the least of my worries.

Cass is right though. Of course she's right. Spending time with Jack is the baddest of bad ideas. But not for the reasons she thinks. She's convinced I'll let something slip about Tara. The fact that she even thinks that's a possibility is insulting. The truth of that night is so tightly wrapped up inside me there's no way it could ever escape.

No. Spending time with Jack is a bad idea because every time I look at him, every time I think about him, I think about Tara.

I think about what we did to her.

I think about the well.

I think about the rocks.

Sometimes I manage to *not* think about her for a couple of minutes here and there. And those minutes are so precious. But they're fleeting. How can those minutes go faster than the Tara-minutes? Time should not be allowed to play tricks like that.

I'm pretty sure I'd be thinking about her all the time anyway, even if it wasn't for this thing with Jack (what even *is* this thing?). Cass tries to think about anything *but* Tara, and I wouldn't be surprised if she actually manages it too. Her brain is like a filing cabinet – everything neatly stored in categories. My brain is more like soup – everything all blended and mushed together.

Tonight is my worst nightmare. Well, it's what *used* to constitute my worst nightmare. Before. My nightmares are much bigger and badder now. But it's unpleasant nonetheless: parents' evening.

I used to quite look forward to parents' evening. Yes, I was (am) a big loser. Mum and Dad (and later, just Dad) would dress up in their semi-smart clothes and head off into the night. A couple of hours later

I'd pounce on them as soon as they came through the front door. They'd sit me down and I'd fire questions at them – essentially just fishing for compliments. None of my teachers ever said anything bad about me. Unless you count 'Alice could perhaps benefit from contributing more in class discussions'. Which I don't. Luckily Mum and Dad didn't either. Mum was a shy sort of person. She never talked for the sake of talking. Never felt the need to fill those awkward silences with meaningless chatter. Dad's a bit louder, but not much.

I felt sorry for Dad when he had to start going to my school things by himself. He never complained though. And he went to every event he was supposed to. He never missed one – even when he was mega-busy at work.

These days we're expected to go along with our parents. It's excruciating.

You might think it would be fine, sitting there while teachers say nice things about you. But it's not. It's painfully embarrassing. The stupid jokes the teachers make. Dad being on his best behaviour. Me trying to react appropriately when Mrs Cronin says things like, 'It's a complete *pleasure* to teach your daughter, Mr King. You must be *so* proud.' (Turns out my reaction is usually a grimace/wince followed by a semi-smile.)

Dad and I get the bus to school. Almost everyone else will drive. The bus is packed with weary commuters heading home from work, but we manage to get seats together on the top deck.

'Here we go again. Anything I should know before we head into the lions' den?' He smiles and elbows me gently in the side.

'Um . . .'

'Got into any fights recently? Graffitied the premises with profanities? Headbutted any teachers?'

'I'm saying nothing,' I smile slyly, 'but if Mrs Cronin has a broken nose and a black eye . . . try not to stare.'

'I'll do my best. She probably had it coming anyway.'

We both laugh and it feels nice.

Mrs Cronin doesn't have a broken nose and a black eye. Instead, she has baby-pink eyeshadow (which makes her look like she's got a weird eye infection) and an over-powdered face. The powder seems to collect in each and every one of her many wrinkles. She looks dusty.

Her praise is more effusive than ever. Her eyes go all misty as she says, 'Well, what can I say about my little star? She's doing *so* well this year, especially considering the *terrible* tragedy.' I somehow manage to refrain from rolling my eyes. Mrs Cronin has been in her element ever since it happened. Maybe it would be slightly unfair to say that she's been revelling in it – but I can't help thinking that's true. She keeps mentioning it in class. At first she tried to set aside ten minutes at the end of each lesson to talk about how we were feeling. This lasted all of a week before it became abundantly clear – even to her – that we'd rather talk about the Great Depression and the Holocaust and cheery stuff like that than talk about our feelings in front of everyone else. Cronin was gutted – you could just tell. Still, when the bell rings at the end of each lesson, she usually says something along the lines of, 'Remember, girls, I'm here if you want to talk. About *anything*.' Not bloody likely.

The rest of the evening goes S-L-O-W-L-Y. Nothing particularly interesting is said. Dad smiles a lot. I cringe a lot. And before I know it, it's time for our last appointment. The one I've been dreading. I'm not even sure why I've been dreading it; it's not like I think she *knows* or anything. But she was there. And that's enough.

Daley's the only teacher Dad hasn't met before. Most of the others have been knocking around for years. Relics of a bygone era. My school is like an elephant graveyard or something. They could use that on the big advert they've put up by the school gates: *Bransford Academy — where good teachers come to see out their days.*

When we arrive at her classroom Daley is sitting at her desk taking tiny sips from a plastic cup. Dad walks in ahead of me, all easy and confident. He stretches out his hand across the desk. 'Miss Daley? It's great to finally meet you.'

She half stands and reaches to take his hand. 'It's a pleasure to meet you, Mr King.' Her smile is huge and genuine.

We sit down opposite her, she says hello to me and I say hello back. She looks small and fragile, dwarfed by her huge desk.

'So how's Alice doing this term?' Dad sits back in his chair, legs loosely crossed. He's obviously expecting the same spiel he's had from all the others.

Daley looks down at her notes, shuffles them a bit, then meets Dad's gaze. 'I have to be honest with you, Mr King. I'm a little worried about Alice.' I stare at the whiteboard just over her head. Someone hasn't done a very good job of cleaning it. I can make out what looks like the word 'Chancer' but I'm guessing it's actually 'Chaucer'. That would make more sense.

'Worried? Why's that?' Dad uncrosses his legs and leans forward in his chair.

'I'm not sure she's coping so well, after . . .' Why can't she say it? Why can't anyone just *say* it?

'But her marks have been fine, haven't they?' Yes. They have. You tell her, Dad.

'Yes, her marks *have* been fine. The essay Alice handed in last week was well written and well argued and just . . . fine.'

Dad shrugs. 'So what's the problem then? Everything's fine.' WILL EVERYONE STOP SAYING FINE?! Please.

I finally risk a look at Daley. She looks like she wants to crawl into one of the desk drawers and hide. She sighs. 'Alice is one of the brightest students I've ever taught.' This statement is ridiculous for two reasons: 1) She's been a teacher for all of ten minutes. This makes me one of the ONLY students she's ever taught, and 2) I've always been OK at English. Never great. Never crap. I've never won any prizes or anything. Never had one of my essays chosen to enter those competitions they put people up for every now and then. She goes on, 'But she's not reaching her full potential. Not even close. She's been distracted since we got back, which is perfectly understandable. A lot of us have had trouble . . . adjusting.'

181

Dad's sitting so far forward in his chair I think he might topple over and whack his chin on the edge of Daley's desk. At least that would put a stop to this. 'Of course Alice has been distracted! What happened was . . . terrible. I don't know how she even manages to get out of bed in the morning.' He pauses to squeeze my knee and give me a sad smile. 'She copes with anything life throws at her.' Oh God. Please don't bring Mum into this.

'Yes, that may be so. But I've noticed she's not been concentrating in lessons.' What is this woman's problem?!

'Surely you can give her a bit of leeway, considering what she's been through?' Dad's pissed off. His voice has an edge to it. Maybe Daley won't notice, but to me it's as obvious as if he had a wailing siren attached to his head.

'Mr King, I don't want you to get the wrong idea. Alice isn't in any trouble or anything like that.' Now she leans forward in *her* chair. Their body language is exactly the same. Didn't I read something about that happening when people fancy each other? I think it's called 'mirroring'. Dear God, please don't let there be any mirroring happening in this room.

Daley turns to look at me. Finally. 'Alice, I want to help you. I'd like for us to meet after school, once a week perhaps. We can go through the week's work and any questions you might have. And we can talk. About anything you like.' She's all hopeful and expectant, like I'm supposed to jump at the idea or something. Not gonna happen.

'Um . . .' Every word in the English language seems to have momentarily fallen out of my head.

Daley and Dad both wait for me to say something coherent. They'll be waiting a long time. I have the right to remain silent, etc.

After an extraordinarily long pause – filled only by the ticking of the clock above the whiteboard – Dad finally pipes up, 'I think that sounds like a good idea.' No! Traitor!

Daley breaks into a grin. Her teeth are slightly too small for her mouth. 'I'm so pleased you think so!'

Dad smiles back. I would like them both to stop smiling now. It's making me nauseous. 'It'll be good for Alice to have someone to talk to. I think she's lucky to have a teacher like you – someone willing to go above and beyond.'

Daley blushes way too easily – just like me. 'Oh, it's no trouble. Really.' She glances down at her notes again and then back up at Dad. 'Alice is worth it.'

Dad nudges my arm and laughs. 'Y'hear that,

Alice? Because you're worth it!' The smile I give him in return is like weak tea versus his double-bloody-espresso, high-beam Smile of a Thousand Teeth.

'This *is* OK with you, isn't it, Alice?' asks Daley. Nice of her to bother.

I know when I'm beaten, but I'm not going to give them the satisfaction of thinking I'm actually *happy* with the idea. 'I suppose so.'

They take my agreement as a sign to ignore me completely and talk about anything *but* English, schoolwork, Bransford Academy and me. I can't believe they're making small talk. Dad never bothers with any of the other teachers. It's usually a matter of pride with him — how he can get a fifteen-minute appointment done and dusted in six minutes. But not this time. Now he's acting like he's got all the time in the world and he'd like to do nothing more than to spend it in this bloody classroom, talking to bird-lady.

I do my best not to listen. I try to tune it out the way I've been trying to tune out Ghost Tara recently. It doesn't work. They end up talking about cycling. Apparently it's a '*shared* interest'. FFS. Maybe I should stab myself in the eye with Daley's biro? Anything to make this stop.

I will not let myself think about what this might mean. They CANNOT be interested in each other.

It's impossible. He's, like, fifteen years older than her or something. No. He's just being friendly. That's all there is to it. He hasn't been interested in anyone since Mum died. He's perfectly happy on his own. He told me. It's his motto or something: 'Just me and you, kid – me and you against the world.' We like it that way. Of course, we liked it a whole lot better with Mum around.

An ugly screeching sound interrupts my thoughts – Dad's chair dragging across the floor. I stare at Daley and Dad as they say their goodbyes. It's all perfectly formal and fine. They shake hands again, and it's not like he keeps hold of her hand for too long or gazes into her eyes or anything like that. But Daley *does* smooth down her skirt and fidget a bit. It's like she doesn't know what to do now there's no more hand-shaking to be done.

'I'll see you tomorrow, Alice?' I can tell Daley's trying to catch my eye, but I don't want to look at her. I just nod vaguely and head for the door. I walk down the corridor as fast as I can without looking like one of those crazy power-walkers. Dad catches up just as I reach the front entrance. The doorway is clogged with overly glam mothers and tired, rumpled fathers (and a few overly glam fathers and tired, rumpled mothers). The girls trailing behind them are various shades of bored, disinterested and too-cool-for-school. I spot Rae and her parents. Her folks look normal. Not that I was expecting them to be all emo or anything. Rae's shoulders are hunched up and her arms are sort of wrapped round herself. She looks like she's trying to make herself as compact as possible so that no one will notice her. It seems to be working. *I* see her though. I always see her. I've become painfully aware of Cass and Polly and Rae whenever they're around. I can't stop myself from staring, wondering what they're thinking. How they're coping. How they manage to get through each day without breaking.

It's a relief when we finally get outside, and an even bigger relief when we pass through the school gates and escape from everyone milling around the car park.

Neither of us says a word until we're at the bus stop.

'So that was pretty rude.' Dad doesn't sound angry – not exactly.

I give him my best wide-eyed innocent shruggy sort of look.

Dad shakes his head. 'Don't give me that! You barely said two words to Miss Daley back there.'

'What was I supposed to say? You two seemed to be getting along just fine without *me* getting involved.'

'She's trying the help you, Al. The least you can do is *act* like you're grateful.'

'Grateful? For being kept behind after school like there's something wrong with me?'

'It's not like that, and you know it. She's taking an interest in you, and I for one am glad about that. It's more than the rest of that lot have ever done.'

'I don't need anyone to "take an interest" in me. I'm fine!' My voice betrays me and cracks in the middle of the word 'fine', breaking it into two syllables. Tears spring from nowhere and Dad immediately looks alarmed. He hates to see me cry. It's his kryptonite.

'Hey, hey, don't cry.' He gathers me up in his arms and I practically collapse into the hug. I have no idea why I'm so upset. I really hope no one from school drives by and spots us. Hopefully the tinted windows in their BMWs make it just as hard to see out as it is to see in.

The bus arrives but I can't stop my snivelling, so Dad lets it pull away without us on-board. Eventually he disentangles himself from the hug and says the one word that he *knows* will cheer me up. It works every time. 'Doughnuts?'

We catch the next bus and neither of us speaks on the journey. Dad has his arm around me, and that's enough. Just me and him. Against the world.

The doughnut shop is perfectly situated between the bus stop and our house. It's our favourite place. We sit in our usual booth and I have one glazed raspberry-jam doughnut and one maple-glazed. I can never quite finish the second doughnut, but Dad always manages to polish it off for me. Each bite of doughnut is like a little piece of heaven in my mouth. Each bite makes everything seem that bit better. Sugary goodness is my drug of choice.

We talk about nothing in particular and both of us manage to ignore the fact that I'm still all snotty and red-eyed from the random tears. It's only when the doughnuts are all gone and I'm starting to come down from my sugar high that he sips his coffee and looks at me out of the corner of his eye and says, 'I think you should tell me about Tara.'

23

I've been waiting for this. I knew it was coming. He's asked about it before – quite a few times, in fact – but never with *that* look. That Dad look that tells me that he can make everything OK, as long as I tell him the truth – Superdad will save the day. It used to be sort of true – he *could* solve my problems. But my problems were different back then. Smaller, simpler problems. *I haven't done my maths homework and it's due first thing in the morning . . . It's my turn to take Bruno for a walk, but I'm not feeling very well . . . Barbie's head's fallen off (well, actually I sort of somehow managed to pull it off) . . .* These were Dad-sized problems. Sort-of-but-not-really-murdering-one-of-your-classmates-and-throwing-her-down-a-well is most definitely *not* a Dad-sized problem.

I have an idea of what Dad's expecting to hear. So that's what I tell him. Tara's death stirring up memories about Mum. How I still miss Mum every day. How it doesn't get any easier, not really.

Most of what I say to him is true. But the lies I do have to tell come easily. Dad is silent for the most part, but he squeezes my hand once or twice and does a lot of nodding. I can tell all this talk about Mum hurts him. But I manage to convince myself that the truth would hurt him a whole lot worse. The truth would kill him. Maybe not literally, but something inside him would die. The part of him that thinks I'm his little angel. The part of him that thinks I'm his reason for soldiering on after Mum died. I will not let that happen.

I head straight to bed when we get home. I need to be by myself for a little while. Should have known she wouldn't let that happen.

She waits until I'm getting undressed. I'm in my bra and pants.

'Hmm . . . have you put on weight, Alice? Been comfort eating again? Maybe you should lay off the doughnuts. Especially if you want my little brother to be interested. I don't think he digs fat chicks.'

I grab my dressing gown and put it on as quickly as possible. Tie the cord around my waist as tight as it will go.

'Oh, come on, Alice, there's no need to be shy! I was only joking, for Christ's sake. The least you can do is laugh at my jokes.'

I can't do this. Not tonight. I climb into bed and pull the covers over my head.

'Talk to me. Please? I'm bored. Did you have fun this evening? Teachers falling over themselves to say nice things about you? And how was Daley? Has she got over it yet? Can't be good for your career, letting one of your students get a severe case of dead on your first school trip, can it?'

'Please stop this, Tara. I'm begging you.' I'm not even sure if I say this out loud, but she hears it anyway.

'Why?' Her voice is quiet. More thoughtful than usual. Or perhaps I'm reading too much into a single word.

'Because I don't know how much longer I can go on like this. I feel like I'm going mad.'

'Maybe you are.'

'Maybe I am.' I burrow deeper under the duvet and try not cry. The trying is a waste of time.

In English the next day Daley keeps glancing over and I do my best to ignore her. I concentrate on drawing hundreds and hundreds of tiny squares in the margin of my notebook. Towards the end of the lesson I realize that the nib of my biro has torn a hole in the page, ruining everything.

Daley keeps me behind after the lesson – again. As everyone else files out, Danni turns in my direction. Our eyes meet for maybe a second or two and then she's gone.

Daley's fussing around, putting papers back in her bag and pens in the desk drawer, waiting for the room to empty. I'll give her that. At least she's not broadcasting the fact that she's forcing me to have after-school lessons/counselling sessions for Special People. She wants to know what day is best for me. She can't do Thursdays apparently, as that's 'salsa night'. I try to picture her with a flower in her hair, wearing a stupid black dress and dancing with some Latin god. The picture evaporates in my head as soon as she says that she goes with Miss Schuman, my German teacher. I bet they end up having to dance with each other when there aren't enough blokes to go round.

I must have been smiling slightly, because Daley says something about me seeming a lot brighter today. I wipe the smile off my face immediately. I will not give her the satisfaction of thinking she's helping me somehow.

We settle on Tuesday afternoon. At least that way I've got almost a whole week before I have to face it.

On my way to history I see something that stops me in my tracks. There are flyers everywhere. And I mean *everywhere*. They're all different colours, but they all say the same thing:

The Tara Chambers Memorial Dance
Friday, 12 November
Special guest band: Blackdog Sundays
Please see Polly Sutcliffe for tickets – £5 each
All proceeds to the Tara Chambers Memorial Society

People are rushing past me, jostling me with their bags. I'm a rock in the middle of a raging torrent. I can't believe what I'm seeing. I can't even begin to understand what she's playing at. Blackdog Sundays is Jack's band. He's the guitarist (or the bass guitarist . . . something involving guitars anyway). He told me about them at the weekend – somewhat reluctantly. He didn't mention anything about this though.

I am going to kill Polly Sutcliffe. I mean, I knew the proceeds of the dance were going to her little society, but I didn't think they'd *rename* the thing –

it's been called the Bransford Bop for something like fifty years. I don't know what I'm angriest about: the dance itself or the fact that she's getting Jack's band to play. I feel hot and cold at the same time. My hands ball up into fists and I swear I'm about to punch something.

'Weird, isn't it?' Danni is standing behind me, a little bit too close.

'Um . . . what's weird?'

'*The Tara Chambers Memorial Dance?!* Have you ever heard of anything so ridiculous? If Tara was around to see this, she'd have a fucking fit. Here, hold this.' She shoves her bag into my arms and starts tearing down flyers. People are stopping to watch. They're staring at me like I'm an accomplice. She rids one whole wall of flyers before she turns to me. There are tears in her eyes.

'What on earth is going on here?!' It's Daley. Of course it would *have* to be Daley. And she's looking at me. God knows why, when Danni's the one standing there with bunches of scrunched-up paper in her hands.

'Um . . . nothing.' Very convincing.

'Alice, Danni, come with me.' Great. Just great. I wait for Danni to explain that I haven't done anything wrong. She doesn't. She just grabs her bag and follows

Daley down the hall, dropping the flyers as she goes. For the first time I notice Rae standing in a doorway, a purple folder clasped against her chest like a shield. Our eyes meet and she turns away. I should talk to her. I keep meaning to talk to her.

Daley leads us to her classroom and makes us sit down while she hops up onto her desk. She looks like a small child playing at being teacher.

'Now, does one of you want to tell me what that little scene was all about?'

I look at Danni as pointedly as possible. Tears are trickling down her face and she's not even trying to stop them. She says nothing.

'Danni, I realize you're upset, but that's no excuse for vandalizing school property!'

Vandalizing? That seems a little extreme, but I know when to keep my mouth shut.

'Danni? Talk to me, please.'

'That fucking dance,' she says quietly.

Daley doesn't even flinch at the swearing. 'What about the dance?'

'It's twisted! Tara's dead, for Christ's sake. We shouldn't be having a fucking party! Who does Polly Sutcliffe think she is anyway? She wasn't even friends with Tara.' I couldn't agree more.

Daley's sitting there nodding as if she agrees with

everything Danni says. But she's just biding her time, formulating her argument in her head.

'I can understand how you feel, Danni. But *you* have to understand that people grieve in different ways. And just because Polly wasn't necessarily friends with Tara, that doesn't mean she's not hurting too. I think Polly's doing a wonderful thing, dedicating so much of her time. I think Tara would appreciate that too, don't you?' Her eyes are big and wide and full of sympathy and I can tell she's so sure that she's saying exactly the right words.

Danni's expression is disdainful to say the least. The tears have dried up. 'No offence, miss, but you didn't really know Tara either.' I snort with laughter and try to mask it with a cough.

'Well, of course, you're right. But I——'

'Please can we go now? We're already late for history . . . Look, I promise I won't take down any more flyers. Polly can do whatever the hell she wants.'

Daley sighs. 'You can go. Just . . . remember, I'm here if you need to talk, OK?' I nod, half-heartedly. Danni does the same.

The hallway is deserted. Neither of us speaks, until the silence gets too awkward and Danni says, 'Listen, do you want to grab a coffee or something? I don't think I can face history right now.'

I look at her to see if she's joking. The idea that Danni Carrington would want to spend time with me out of choice is more than absurd. But she's not joking. And I have to say yes.

24

We leave school through the front gates, in full view of Mrs Cronin's classroom. Danni struts confidently, not even a little bit worried about being spotted. I sort of scurry, head down. I'm not used to skiving; Danni is clearly a pro.

She leads the way, and we end up in a tiny Portuguese cafe on some dodgy-looking side street. The waitress saunters over and Danni starts chatting to her IN PORTUGUESE. I don't know why I'm so shocked. Lots of people can speak foreign languages. I'm just surprised Danni's one of them. They babble away for a few minutes and I try my best to look perfectly at ease with the situation. Eventually the waitress heads back into the kitchen, laughing and shaking her head at something Danni said.

'I hope you don't mind, but I ordered for both of us. Tara used to love it here – the custard tarts are to die for.' Her smile falters, and it's obvious she's regretting her choice of words. I know exactly how she feels. I was the same after Mum. *OMG! It was so embarrassing – I almost died. Aw, man, I am SO dead.* My heart would squeeze itself up into a hard little lump every single time. *She's dead. Gone.*

I decide to help her out. 'A custard tart sounds perfect.'

Danni makes a visible effort to pull herself together. 'So . . . how annoying is Daley? As if anyone would ever talk to *her* about anything. Just how desperate would you have to be?!'

'She means well.' This is a stupid thing for me to say, because a) only old people talk like that, and b) why the hell am I defending Daley when she seems intent on making my life a misery?

'If you say so. I suppose you think the same about Polly Sutcliffe?'

'Not exactly.'

'You know the band she's booked to play the dance? The Blackdog Sundays? That's Jack's band.'

'I know.'

I fully expect her to ask *how* I know. But she doesn't. 'Do you think you'll go?'

'Dunno. Will you?' This is my number-one conversation strategy. Always throw a question back at the other person. Put the focus back on them. It works every time.

Danni sighs a huge sigh. 'Probably. It'll be *expected*. I can't not go, can I? I'm Tara's best friend.'

'I think people would understand if you didn't feel up to going . . .'

She stops suddenly and turns to face me. 'You have no idea what it's like. Having people watching you every minute of every day. I can't even smile any more in case people think I'm over it.'

I start to say something vaguely reassuring, but she cuts me off. 'No, I mean it. I have to be in Grieving Best Friend mode ALL the time. There's no escape from it, not even at home. My parents are driving me crazy. We never have conversations about anything *normal* any more — it's all "Do you want to talk about it?" and shit like that.'

'I know what it's like. My mum . . .' I don't need to say the actual words before she gets it.

'Ah. Yeah. Sorry.'

I shrug.

'It's hard, isn't it?'

I nod.

'It's like, I *do* want to talk about it — but not like they think. Not some therapy-style bollocks. It's just . . . the whole thing doesn't make any sense.'

'What doesn't make sense?'

'Tara going for that *early-morning swim* everyone keeps going on about.'

My breath catches in my throat and my stomach turns inside out. Luckily the waitress chooses this exact moment to bring our coffee and tarts. There's more Portuguese chatter, which gives me the chance to concentrate on the food instead of what Danni just said. My stomach rights itself and I take a bite. Perfectly flaky pastry. Smooth, creamy custard. Before I know what I'm doing, I've wolfed down the whole thing. And they haven't even finished talking. There are some crumbs left. Not for long though.

When the waitress leaves, Danni gives me a knowing look – a very Tara sort of look. 'Do you want another one?'

I shake my head and surreptitiously wipe a crumb from the corner of my mouth. Danni proceeds to sip her coffee and nibble her tart in a much more ladylike fashion.

'So, as I was saying. Tara would have never gone swimming. I told the police, but that Marshall idiot doesn't seem to want to listen.'

'Why wouldn't she have gone swimming? Tara loved swimming . . . didn't she?'

Danni snorts and chokes on her coffee a little

bit. 'You have GOT to be kidding? She bloody hated it.'

'But she was still on the swimming team.'

She looks at me as if my stupidity is beyond comprehension. 'So?! I'm on the debate team, but you don't see me arguing about euthanasia in the pub, do you? She'd have given up swimming years ago if it wasn't for her parents. They're *all* about the trophies.' Tara's parents have never struck me as particularly pushy, but I say nothing.

Danni looks around furtively, as if someone might be listening in. 'Can you keep a secret?' I nod, even though I'm pretty sure I could do without hearing whatever it is she's about to say. 'I think Duncan might have had something to do with it.'

If I had any coffee left I would probably be choking on it right now. 'What?!'

'Think about it. It makes total sense. You know something was going on with him and Tara?'

'I thought she was making that up.'

'She'd never lie to me about something like that.' I'm pretty sure she's wrong about that. 'So anyway, what if Duncan is some psycho rapist or something?' Like the psycho rapists we pretended to be that night? Christ.

'I don't think Duncan is a psycho rapist. He

seemed . . . nice.' Apart from the whole inappropriate-liaisons-with-schoolgirls thing.

'Yeah, he *seemed* nice, but maybe that's how he lures in his victims?' Danni's eyes fill up with tears.

I reach across the table and touch her arm. 'You don't really believe that, do you?'

The tears spill over and trickle down her cheeks. 'I don't know what to believe any more. I told the police my theory about Duncan, and they said they were "investigating all possible avenues", but then they were on the news saying she'd drowned, and I just . . . can't believe she's gone. How can she be gone?' And then she loses it completely, and I jump up from my seat and sit next to her and put my arms around her.

25

Danni was ridiculously grateful to me for 'being so nice and understanding and everything'. She hugged me again when we said goodbye. She even asked for my mobile number. And I asked for hers too, because that's what you're supposed to do. Anyone would have thought we were actual friends. It's too weird to think about — how death seems to rewrite all the rules. People who never talked to each other can suddenly cry together. People who used to be close can hardly bear to be in the same room. Or maybe that's just this particular death. It's hard to tell.

When I got home Ghost Tara started on about me stealing her best mate. But as soon as I told her she was a figment of my imagination, she disappeared. I'm getting good at this. Maybe I haven't lost my marbles after all. Or rather, maybe I *did* lose my marbles but I'm gradually finding them again, one by one. Of course, it's got nothing whatsoever to do with the fact that Jack called. He called! That is at least ten times better than texting.

It was the first time we'd talked on the phone and it wasn't even awkward. He asked me about my day, and what I'd been up to since we saw each other. I lay back on my bed and rambled on, and he seemed genuinely interested in the banalities of my life. He got the edited version, obviously. I subtly (OK, not really) asked him about Blackdog Sundays.

'We've booked another gig.'

'Cool. I'd love to come. Where are you playing?'

'Well, it's actually a bit of a weird one.' I fought the urge to shout, 'Then why are you doing it?!' down the phone.

'Weird? How?'

'Um . . . it's at your school. Polly Sutcliffe asked us to play at a dance . . . in memory of Tara.' There was a shaky sort of sigh, and I wondered if he was trying to fight back tears.

'Oh.'

'Yeah, I know. I could hardly say no though, could I? Well actually, I *tried* saying no, but Polly went on and on at me. And it is for charity, I suppose . . .'

'I think it's the right thing to do.' I thought this was what he wanted me to say.

'Really?' His voice was soft and hopeful.

'Yes, really.'

'Will you come to the dance? I mean, will you be there? Um . . . unless you'd like to come with me? Because that would be good too.'

'I'd love to go to the dance with you.' Which was not strictly true. I'd love to go almost anywhere with him. Except for the dance commemorating the life of his sister.

'Awesome! It's a date.' A date! A real one. Not a trip to some musty fusty dusty museum. 'But it's sort of a long way away though, isn't it? I'd like to see you before then. That is, if you'd like to see me too.'

'I'd like to see you too.' My cheeks flushed with heat. Thank God Jack couldn't see me. Anyone would think I'd never been asked out on a real proper date before. Um. Yeah.

But there's a catch: I'm going to his house. Tomorrow.

This should be interesting.

I don't know why I agreed to it. The thought of being in her house . . . It's almost more than I can deal with. But I'll be with Jack. And being with Jack is exactly where I want to be.

I get a text from Cass just as I'm thinking that she must never find out about me going round to Jack's. It's like she read my mind from ten miles away. We've barely spoken since I lied to her about going to see Nan and Grumps. It's not like I'm ignoring her or anything. We see each other at school and say hi, but that's about it. I just . . . have nothing to say to her. There's only one thing worth talking about any more, and I definitely don't want to talk about that. And she's hardly been bombarding me with texts and IMs, so maybe she feels the same way.

This is the real way a friendship ends. Not with some huge screaming row, but with a gradual withdrawal. You'd think it would be less painful this way. Of course, not many friendships have the added burden of a dead body to deal with.

The text message is a surprise: *Hey, think we need to talk. After school tomorrow? My house?* No 'x' at the end. Cass doesn't go in for that sort of thing.

It's much easier to lie in a text message than face to face: *Sorry, can't. Dad's cooking a special dinner. He's been planning it for ages. x.* I sometimes play the 'lonely Dad card' when I want to get out of something. I've just never had to use it with Cass before.

She doesn't text back, which is her way of telling me she's pissed off without actually starting an argument. It's a relief that she doesn't try to fix up a date for this 'talk' she has in mind. One less thing to worry about – for now.

I spend the next day feeling mildly nauseous and strangely jumpy. I manage to avoid Cass by having lunch in the library. Eating in the library is STRICTLY FORBIDDEN, but I've done worse things in my life. And it's not as if I spill my Diet Coke on the carpet. Well, maybe I do just a little bit. But I scuff the stain with my shoe until you can hardly see it.

I make it home in record time, grab a slice of two-day-old pizza from the fridge and find myself standing in front of my wardrobe wondering why all my clothes are so *boring*. I really wish I was better at shopping. It would help if I actually enjoyed it, but I get hot and tired and impatient because nothing ever fits the way I want it to.

After careful consideration of my options, I pull on some jeans because I can't think of anything else. For once I'm actually glad when Ghost Tara turns up. 'I reckon you should show a bit of cleavage. Boys like boobs. Fact.' Unfortunately my wardrobe isn't exactly heaving with revealing tops. Eventually I find this old grey jumper of Dad's. It has a deep V-neck, and I've never worn it without a T-shirt underneath. It looks good though. Sort of almost sexy in an understated way.

I go for a little bit more make-up than usual – nothing too full on. As I'm rummaging for one of Mum's old bracelets I do my best to ignore Tara's ring, but something makes me pick it up. A sudden flashback almost floors me. Tara's cold hand slipping through mine. The sound of rocks hitting fragile flesh. It still stuns me just how physical the pain is. My heart hurts and my insides feel like they're clambering over each other to escape from my body. Tears roll down my cheeks. I rush to the toilet, Tara's laughter echoing in my ears.

By the time I've redone my make-up and am feeling vaguely human again I'm already late. I fire off a quick text to Jack, scrawl a note to Dad (telling him I'm off to the library), scratch Bruno behind the ears and run out the front door. I hope my eyes have lost their redness by the time I get to Jack's. I'm so flustered and shaky and rushed that I almost manage to forget that it's Tara's house I'm going to. It's only when I turn the corner onto the street that the memories come flooding back and all of a sudden I'm drowning.

26

We were eight years old and Tara and her family had moved here in the middle of the school year. Miss Murray gave me the Very Important Job of showing Tara where to hang up her coat and where the toilets were. Miss Murray made Jamilla move desks so that Tara could sit next to me. I was secretly pleased that out of a class of twenty-two girls *I'd* been chosen.

Tara was super-shy and only made eye contact when she absolutely had to. Back then her hair was a nondescript light brown and she always wore it scraped back in a ponytail. It was usually wet from her morning swim. Everyone thought it was weird that Tara had to go swimming before school. I couldn't think of anything worse than crawling out of bed two hours early on a freezing cold morning in the middle of winter, but Tara didn't seem to mind.

Her mum picked her up every lunchtime so she

could have lunch at home. That made people think she was even weirder. I didn't though. I would have gone home too, if Mum and Dad hadn't both been at work.

It took a while to break through Tara's defences and actually become her friend. She was so serious all the time – her brow scrunched up in concentration whenever the teacher was talking. She chilled out eventually, giggling at my stupid jokes and passing notes under the table. Sometimes I'd notice Jamilla staring at us from across the classroom.

Tara had been to my house four times before I got invited back to hers. She got on really well with Mum and Dad. Tara was parent-friendly to the point of ridiculousness. I used to tease her about it: *How was your day at work, Mr King? . . . Oh, Mrs King, this pasta is delicious. It's even better than the pasta I had in Italy last year! . . . Mr and Mrs King, don't you prefer me to your not-so-perfect daughter? . . .* Needless to say, Mum and Dad lapped it all up.

When Mum dropped me off outside Tara's house for the first time, one look at the HUGE place she called home and I knew why she'd been so reluctant to invite me round. Our house was half the size of hers. There was a fancy black sports car in the driveway (a driveway!), parked next to a huge white

4x4. Mum's Ford Focus suddenly seemed a little bit rubbish.

Tara answered the door and introduced me to her parents. I remember thinking they were shinier than my parents somehow – like someone had polished them up with a cloth. Before I had a chance to practise my parent-impressing techniques Tara dragged me away, pausing only to roll her eyes disdainfully at her grubby-faced little brother. Jack had a gappy smile and very messy hair. Not much has changed on the hair front.

Tara's room was heavenly. The ceiling was painted to look like the sky on a summer's day. The furniture all matched perfectly – white and artfully distressed. I thought it looked French, but that assumption was based on nothing whatsoever. The mantelpiece was crammed with trophies. Medals, mostly gold, hung in a row. Someone had put little hooks all the way along the wood to hang them on. Tara said she wanted to keep all that stuff in a cupboard but her mum wouldn't let her. Apparently it was important for positive visualization or something.

We sat on Tara's bed and chatted for a bit. Then she got this funny shy look on her face. 'Do you want to see the most precious thing I own?'

'Not that HUGE trophy in the middle there? It's

almost bigger than me.' I giggled to show I was only teasing.

'Urgh, no. Not *that*.' She leaned over to her bedside drawer and pulled out a green velvet box. She opened the box ever so gently and held it out for me to see.

'My grandma gave me it just before she died. She said that whenever I wore it, she'd be watching over me . . . keeping me safe.'

'It's beautiful. Why aren't you wearing it now?'

'Mummy says I should only wear it on special occasions,' she muttered.

'I think you should wear it every single day and never take it off. That way your grandma can be looking after you all the time.'

She was hesitant. 'Do you . . . Do you really think so?'

'Definitely. Here . . .' I slipped the ring onto her index finger.

I never saw her without the ring after that day.

It kept her safe for a little under eight years.

27

There are no cars in the driveway today. The house looks the same though. Pristine.

Don't think about Tara. Think about Jack. Think about his smile.

I knock on the door and wait.

The door swings open and there he is. 'Alice! Hi!'

He wraps me up in a hug and I want to stay there forever. His hair smells so good. I wonder if he's been using Tara's shampoo. So much for not thinking about Tara.

'Come in. Don't worry – the parents are out, thank God. It's the first time I've had the house to myself since . . . in ages.' It's painfully obvious what he was going to say. When someone dies, everything neatly divides into two categories: since and before. Before is always better. 'Mum and Dad are starting to loosen the reins a little bit, thank God.'

A black cocker spaniel bounds up to me and Jack introduces me to Rufus. He's gorgeous.

We sit in the kitchen, on either side of the breakfast bar. Rufus settles down for a snooze at Jack's feet. The kitchen's changed since I was last here. It used to be all English country kitchenish, but now it's all white gloss and black granite. I preferred it before.

Jack pops some crumpets in the toaster and slathers them with butter when they're done. I could seriously fall for a boy who gives me crumpets.

We talk about the band. He's worried they won't be ready for the gig, and I do my best to reassure him. He talks about his parents. They've been arguing a lot recently, and even started going to counselling.

'What have they been arguing about?'

'Tara, mostly. Dad reckons it's all Mum's fault for being so pushy about swimming. She was on at Tara all the time about training. I guess Tara had kind of gone off the whole swimming thing recently, but Mum wouldn't let her quit. She wouldn't hear of it. Reckoned Tara was good enough to swim for England one day. I don't know . . . maybe that *is* why she went swimming that morning . . .'

I need to change the subject. Pronto. 'Can I see your room?'

Jack's eyes widen ever so slightly and I can't tell

if he thinks I'm rude for interrupting him or just incredibly forward. 'Um . . . yeah, sure.'

He chucks our plates in the sink and leads the way up the stairs. Tara's room is at the end of the hall. The door is closed. I try not to look at it. There used to be a sign saying 'KEEP OUT! This means YOU, Jack Chambers!!!' I wonder when the sign came down.

Jack opens a door on the left and makes a sweeping gesture with his hands. 'Welcome to my humble abode!' I'm relieved that he doesn't say something gross like *This is where the magic happens.*

The room is perfectly Jack. The walls are a warm grey colour. (Who knew grey could be warm?) There are three guitars hanging on the wall above his bed . . . his *double* bed. There's a huge bookcase stuffed with more books than I've ever seen in one place. Obviously the bookcase is not quite huge enough, because there are towering piles of paperbacks on either side of it. There's even a sofa – big and squishy and orange. Jack flops down on it while I wander over to the bookcase.

'So I'm guessing you like to read?' I trail my fingers along the spines of a row of books. I don't think I've heard of any of them. The whole bottom shelf is dedicated to dinosaur books.

'Yeah, I suppose I do. Mum's always on at me to

chuck out some of my books, but I can't bear to do it. It just seems wrong, you know? Someone slaved over writing that for months and months — maybe even years. And even if it's crap, they deserve some respect for making the effort, don't you think?'

'Mum was like that. She even hated breaking the spine of a book. And she went mental if I turned over the corners of the pages instead of using a bookmark.'

'Your mum sounds brilliant.' Jack's smile is a heartbreaking mixture of happy and sad.

'She was.' Something in me cracks open and tears leak out. Not now. Please not now. I turn to face the bookcase so Jack can't see. I can't avoid raising my hand to wipe away the tears though. A total giveaway.

There are hands on my shoulders. Warm, strong hands. 'Hey, Alice. It's OK . . . Don't cry.' His honey voice trickles into my ears.

We stay like that for a few moments before he gently turns me around. He's standing so very close. I look up at him, but he's all blurry. I try to blink away the next round of tears, but they spill over. Jack's hands cradle my face, his thumbs wiping away the tears. I think I've forgotten how to breathe.

'I . . .' I've forgotten how to form words too.

His mouth is achingly close to mine. I have to kiss

him. If I don't kiss him now I never will. If I don't kiss him now I will never, ever forgive myself.

My eyes meet his, just to check that we're thinking the same thing. I move closer. Little by little, closer and closer, until my lips are touching his. It's a tiny little butterfly of a kiss . . . more fragile than I could ever have imagined.

Jack pulls away to look at me. There's a question in his eyes. I answer it by kissing him again, harder this time. He's kissing back just as hard. And I find myself pressing into him, wanting to get closer and closer until I disappear into him. My hands curl round his neck, fingers tugging at his hair. His mouth fits perfectly on mine.

I lose myself completely. There's no one in the world apart from me and Jack. Nothing else matters. Not even . . . her. There. Ruined it. I cannot carry on kissing Jack while I'm thinking about his dead sister.

I pull away too quickly, breathing heavily. Jack's face is flushed and he's breathing hard too. Tara is not breathing at all.

Jack tries to pull me back towards him, his mouth reaching for mine. I want nothing more than to kiss him again and stay kissing him and stop thinking. But I can't.

'What's wrong?' There's hurt in his eyes and I hate that I'm the reason for it.

'Nothing.' I run my hands through my hair and turn away from him.

'Alice, talk to me. Please.' His hand is on my shoulder again, hesitant this time, as if he expects me to shrug it off.

I want to leave this place. I want to run home and curl up on the sofa next to Mum, where nothing is confusing and everything is good and right and pure. But Mum's gone too.

I turn to face Jack because there's nothing else for me to do. 'Sorry. I . . . I'm fine. Really.'

'You don't look fine. You look like you've seen a ghost! Am I . . . was it *that* bad?' He stares at the carpet as if there's something fascinating there.

I almost laugh. 'No! Don't be ridiculous! It was . . . exactly how I wanted it to be.'

He brightens at this. A sly little grin appears from nowhere. 'Really?'

My smile mirrors his. 'Yes, really.'

He moves towards me. 'Then why don't we do it some more?'

The way I see it, I have two options. I can concoct some lie about what's wrong and leave right now. Or I can kiss him again.

Kissing wins.

28

There was a lot more kissing. I thought it might get a bit boring after a while, but it definitely didn't. After a while we moved to the sofa, and that was good too. Except I started to worry about what would happen next. Turns out I needn't have worried — Jack was the one who put a stop to things.

In between kisses, he whispered, 'I . . . think we should . . . stop.'

'Why?' Except it didn't sound quite like 'why', because I spoke the word directly into Jack's mouth.

'Because if we carry on, I really, really won't want to stop. And I won't be held responsible for my actions . . .' He wiggled his eyebrows, which made me laugh. Then he kissed my neck and it felt so good that I knew he was right. We had to stop. But I didn't want to. Yes, I was scared about what might happen, but I was also curious as hell. Somehow I'd gone from barely having kissed a boy to (maybe sort of just a little bit) wanting to get naked with one in the space of a couple of hours.

We straightened out our clothes and headed downstairs. Suddenly everything seemed a bit strange and awkward.

'So . . . um . . . I guess I'll see you.' That was Jack. He was biting his lip, which made *me* think about biting his lip.

'Yeah . . .' That was me, sounding gormless.

'We should do something soon, maybe?'

'Yeah. We should.'

It was painful. You wouldn't have thought we'd had our tongues in each other's mouths a few minutes ago.

'Alice, I really like you.'

'I like you too.'

'So maybe this could be, y'know, sort of official.'

'What do you mean?' I was pulling the cuffs of my jumper down over my hands and twisting them around my thumbs.

'We could be . . .' He trailed off into an unconvincing cough. 'Maybe you could be my girlfriend? God, that sounds really crap, doesn't it?' A blush crept up from his neck. It was possibly the cutest thing I've ever seen.

Suddenly I didn't feel shy or awkward. I felt a burst of confidence like nothing I've ever felt before. I felt invincible. I grabbed him by the front of his shirt and pulled him to me. Not that he put up much of a fight. I kissed him. 'It doesn't sound crap at all. Not even one little bit.'

Jack's smile was pure magic.

She was waiting when I got back.

'It's disgusting. The thought of you and my little brother . . . urgh.' She shuddered, and it reminded me of her shivering that night. 'I don't know what you think you're playing at. It's never going to work. You know that, don't you? In here.' She poked my chest hard with one bloody, grubby finger. 'You'll never be happy, Alice. Never. You don't deserve it.'

That was all. She disappeared when my phone rang. Instead of answering, I pulled at the front of my jumper, checking carefully for the mark where Tara touched me.

There was nothing there, no matter how hard I looked.

So now I have a boyfriend. I. Have. A. Boyfriend. I've said it out loud a couple of times and it sounds ridiculous. How can it possibly be true? This is *me* we're talking about. Me. It's just plain weird. Girls like me are not supposed to have boyfriends like Jack. It's not how the world works.

I should be the happiest I've ever been. But I am not allowed to be happy. I am allowed to have small, Jack-filled pockets of happiness, but that's all. Then real life comes crashing back, and the enormity of what's happened sweeps away the happiness in an avalanche of shame and guilt. I'm left with sadness and anger and a kind of dread about the future. The dread sits in the middle of my chest, always.

There's a broken-record voice in my head too: *There is no way you'll get away with this. Someone will find out. Somehow.*

29

I look through the window of the classroom and Daley's sitting at her desk, staring out the window. My phone buzzes in my bag, so I nip back round the corner. It's a text from Jack. We've been texting approximately thirty times a day. Not that I've been counting. We hung out on Saturday, which somehow cemented everything that had gone before. It convinced me that I was not delusional: Jack DOES like me. God knows why, but let's not dwell on that.

It was a perfect day. Walking down by the Thames, hand in hand. One of hundreds of couples doing exactly the same thing. I felt something close to smug. There was a slight wobble when Jack told me about a song he'd written for Tara. He wanted to play it for me before the dance; he was worried it might be too cheesy. I said I'd like to hear it (and prayed that he'd forget all about it).

I didn't want to say goodbye to Jack at the tube station. But he had to go to band practice, and I had Dad's Extra Special Spaghetti Bolognese Night to attend. Dad's Extra Special Spaghetti Bolognese Night turned out to be not *that* special – hardly surprising since it happens almost every Saturday.

Jack's message is silly and vaguely mushy and makes me smile. Until I remember that I'm about to face some nightmarish Daley pseudo-counselling session. It'll be over in an hour though. You can put up with anything for an hour.

It doesn't start off too badly. We talk about the last essay I handed in. I got a 73, which is pretty damn good if you ask me. But Daley keeps on pointing out things I'd missed in the text. Metaphors and symbolism and stuff like that. It seems so obvious when she explains it all. Still, I can't help imagining some long-dead writer screaming from his grave, 'THERE'S NO BLOODY SYMBOLISM! IT'S JUST A STORY!'

The work chat takes up a good forty-five minutes and I'm pretty sure I'm in the clear. Daley shuffles the pages of my essay and hands them back to me. Then she clears her throat and takes a deep breath. Uh-oh. This calls for a diversion.

'Miss Daley, could you possibly explain that

last bit again? I'm not sure I quite got it . . .' I arrange my features into a vague approximation of confused/willing to learn.

'We can talk about that next week. Let's just have a little chat, shall we? We don't have much time left.' Fail.

'Um . . . OK.' I stare at the desk in front of me. Someone's used a permanent marker to scrawl something filthy about Gemma Jones.

'Is there anything you'd like to talk about?'

I pretend to ponder for a moment. 'Um . . . Not that I can think of.'

She sighs. 'It's been such a terrible time. How are you doing? Are you sleeping OK?'

That's a new one. 'Yes.'

'You look tired, Alice.' She reaches across the desk and puts her hand on my arm. It feels cold and a little clammy.

'*Thanks*, miss.'

Daley laughs a little. 'You know what I mean. You look like you've got the weight of the world on your shoulders.' You'd think an English teacher would be able to avoid a cliché like that.

'I'm OK, really.'

'Does it bring back memories about your mum?' The question slams into me so hard I have to grip

226

the sides of the desks to steady myself. What does she know about Mum? 'Your dad told me about her. About how hard it was on you.'

I gulp down the lump in my throat.

'When?'

She's confused. 'When what?'

'When did he tell you about that?'

'We . . . We talked on the phone the other day.' Daley at least has the good grace to look slightly sheepish.

'Did you call him or did he call you?' The words are pointed, sharp. I'm staring at her now, daring her to lie to me.

'I phoned him.'

'Why?'

She gets up from her chair and starts packing things into her bag. 'I . . . needed some advice about my bike. I need to get the gears fixed, and since your father's such a keen cyclist I thought he might be able to tell me the best bike shop in the area. He said that there's a really good one on Essex Road . . .' She's talking so fast my ears can't keep up. She looks up at the clock over the whiteboard. 'I think that's enough for today, don't you? Same time next week? I think this has been useful. Yes, very useful.'

'We've still got ten minutes.' I smile sweetly.

She looks at her watch — an utterly pointless gesture. 'Actually, I've got a meeting with Mrs Flanagan. I completely forgot — how silly of me! Right, Alice, I'll see you next week. Same time, same place. And of course I'll see you in class . . . Yes. Right. Bye.' Her spindly legs can't carry her out of the room fast enough.

Well, that was interesting.

And disconcerting.

My head is full of disgusting Daley/Dad thoughts as I leave the classroom. I don't see the ambush coming (which is kind of the point of an ambush, I suppose).

'Why are you avoiding me?' Cass. Shit.

'What are you on about?' I start walking, and Cass has no option but to walk with me.

'Um . . . let me see. You haven't been round to my house, you never reply to my texts and you're nowhere to be seen at break and lunch. What the hell is going on?' I was kidding myself if I thought I could avoid this conversation forever.

I look around to check we're alone. We are. No one in their right mind would still be roaming the corridors at this time. 'Look, in case you hadn't noticed, we did something pretty terrible, and maybe I'm finding it a little hard to deal with, OK?' I can hardly bear to look at Cass. I want to punch her and slap her and scream in her face, 'THIS IS ALL YOUR FAULT!'

Cass shakes her head in disbelief. 'And you think I couldn't care less, right? This isn't affecting me at all. Yeah, I'm totally fine, couldn't be happier . . . Thanks, Alice. Thanks *a lot* for being such a great friend.' Her voice wobbles slightly, but she holds it together.

I feel nothing. I say nothing.

'You blame me, don't you?' A small voice that doesn't sound like it belongs to her. Her eyes search mine for an answer.

This is the moment. One of those moments in your life where the words you say could change everything. Lie or tell the truth? Lie. Truth. Lie. Truth.

I say nothing. But it does the job.

She shakes her heads and walks away. And suddenly I feel bad. Suddenly I have to say something to make this right. She's my best friend.

'Cass, wait! Please?'

She's halfway down the corridor before she turns. 'Don't talk to me. Just . . . don't. Oh, and by the way, I know all about you and Jack. Polly told me.' What?! No. Not possible. There's no way. 'Yeah, that's right.

Clearly you're not so good at keeping secrets after all. Bodes well, doesn't it? I hope you know what you're doing. For all our sakes. Because if you don't . . .'

The unsaid words hang in the air long after she's gone.

30

Jack and I are lying on my bed. Dad's out on one of his epic bike rides and Bruno has been banished to the kitchen.

I'm trying my best to focus on Jack – the feel of his mouth on mine, his hand running up and down my spine, the promise of what could be about to happen. But I can't. I keep coming back to Cass and Polly.

'Jack . . . can I ask you something?' It's hard to talk in between kisses.

'Mmm?' His tongue delves into my mouth again. It's nearly enough to kick any other thoughts right out of my head.

Nearly. 'This is important!'

'So's this . . .' Tiny feathery kisses down my neck and I almost lose all power of thought and speech and everything.

Almost. I push his chest, none too gently either. 'Jack!'

He sits up, his face serious, his hair all over the place. His lips red and tempting. He rubs his chest. 'Ow.'

'Sorry.'

'I think my heart might be bruised. You should probably kiss it better.' He starts to pull up his T-shirt. I throw a pillow at his face.

'Did you tell Polly Sutcliffe about us?'

'Polly? Nope. Why?' He props himself up on his elbow, finally ready to listen.

'Are you sure you didn't say *something*?'

'Er . . . I've talked to the girl twice in my whole life – and that was only to sort out the gig.'

'That's weird, because she knows we're seeing each other.'

'And?' The so-what look on Jack's face could not be any clearer.

'*And* . . . I don't like people knowing my business.' I sound like the rubbishest gangster in the hood.

'You're not embarrassed to be seen with me, are you?' He's laughing and then suddenly he's not. 'You *are*, aren't you? It's the age thing, right? God, I knew this would happen.' He runs both hands through his hair and looks away.

Jack is precisely one month and four days younger than me, but he's not in the same year as me. He's right – some people *might* think it's weird, me going out with someone who's not even in sixth form. I couldn't give a toss. But I'd rather he thinks it's *that* than the truth – that I hadn't wanted Cass, Polly and Rae finding out about us. Still, I don't want to hurt Jack's feelings (or his manly pride).

'No, it's not that . . .' I say in a way that makes it clear that it *is* that.

'Look, if you don't want to go out with me, just say . . .' His pout is so cute I want to take a picture.

I dive on top of him and straddle his legs. His face is a mixture of surprised, pleased and still a tiny bit pouty. 'I don't care what anyone thinks, Jack. I really . . . really . . . really . . . like you.' The words are punctuated by kisses, and I can tell by Jack's response that it's working. His hands snake around my waist and pull my body closer to his.

Later we decide to go for a wander down by the canal. Dad's due back in an hour or so, and I don't think I'm quite ready for The Talk. A couple of years ago, he tried to talk to me about boys. I ran from the room with my hands covering my ears, shouting, 'La la la,

I'm not listening.' I think he got the message. But now that there's an actual real live boy on the scene, God only knows the heights of awkwardness Dad will be able to achieve. Best that I keep him in the dark about Jack for as long as possible. Hopefully for as long as this relationship lasts.

Jack and I sit on a bench watching the ducks dipping their heads in the water and waggling their bums in the air. I can't even begin to imagine what they're looking for. Hypodermic needles and broken shopping trolleys?

'I never had any idea that it was possible to miss someone this much,' Jack says quietly. I squeeze his hand and say nothing. 'It's overwhelming – the sadness. It's there *all the time*. You'd think it would get better after a while, but it's getting worse. Alice, how can it be getting worse?' His eyes are imploring.

'It *will* get better, I promise. But it probably won't be anytime soon. You'll still feel sad, but it'll be a different kind of sad. Less painful, not so sharp. I'm sorry. I wish I could take away some of the hurt, even for a little while.'

Jack smiles sadly. 'I wouldn't want you to. Being with you is the only time things feel normal. Better than normal even. I know we haven't been together

234

all that long, but I . . . I don't know how I'd cope without you.'

I hug him hard and I don't want to ever let go. Maybe some of his sadness can seep into me if I hold him for long enough. I can handle it. Just add it to the guilt and worry and scrunch it up into a little ball. Store it somewhere so that Jack and I can be happy for a little while.

We sit in silence as a couple of sweaty joggers pass by. I'm hyper-aware of everywhere my body touches Jack's. I'm hyper-aware of everything about him. The knees of his jeans are worn and faded. There's some faint writing on the back of his right hand. He wears all these bits and pieces round his wrists. Strips of leather and fabric. I've never really looked at them before, but now I try to imprint them on my brain. Suddenly it seems vital that I memorize everything about him, and I can't work out why until panic wells up in my gut.

I'm going to lose him. It's unavoidable.

I lean into him and rest my head on his shoulder. His unruly hair tickles my forehead, but I don't care. He leans his head towards mine, so now we're basically holding each other up.

'Why did you and Tara stop being friends?'

31

I was hoping it wouldn't come up. It's something I try not to think about. And definitely something I don't want to talk to Jack about. There is no way to describe what happened without me sounding like a horrible person.

The truth of the matter is that I realized I didn't want to be friends with her any more. My reason was simple: she was holding me back.

Tara was *so* quiet. A group of us would sit in the cafeteria at lunchtime and she would never say a word. If someone asked her a question, she'd mumble the shortest possible answer, hardly even looking up from her plate. Everyone stopped bothering after a while. I'd sit there watching her, willing her to say something, willing her to act normal.

It was fine when we were younger. I didn't mind that Tara didn't talk to anyone but me. In fact, I liked it a lot. But things were different at senior school. You had to fit in. Being weird was not an option — not if you wanted to survive.

The final straw was when I found out that Tara and I were the only girls in our class who weren't invited to Stephanie de Luca's birthday party. It wasn't just any old party either. Her dad (who was loaded, obviously) had rented one of those old red London buses to ferry everyone round for the day. And his whole restaurant (well, one of his *five* restaurants) was closed to paying customers for the evening and the chefs cooked all of Stephanie's favourite food. There were ice sculptures and an enormous chocolate fountain.

We heard all about it on Monday. Everyone went on and on about how it was *the best day EVER*. They didn't even care that Tara and I were within earshot. They didn't even *notice*.

At break, Tara and I meandered round the school playing field, exactly like we did every single break time.

'I can't *believe* we didn't get invited! Even Maddie Fletcher got invited . . . Maddie Fletcher! Can you believe it?' Now I was stomping rather than meandering.

Tara shrugged. 'I'm not that bothered.'

'What do you mean, you're not bothered? Everyone was invited except for us — EVERYONE!'

Tara bent down to pick a dandelion. 'So? Stephanie de Luca isn't a very nice person.' She twirled the dandelion between her fingers and I wanted to grab it and rip it to shreds.

'It doesn't matter whether she's a nice person or not. She's *popular*. As in "has more than one friend".'

'What's wrong with having one friend?' Tara was genuinely confused.

I would have pitied her if I wasn't so angry. 'God, Tara, don't you get it? We're the lowest of the low at this school.'

'Why does it matter so much to you?'

I sighed theatrically. 'Why *doesn't* it matter to you? You can be so weird sometimes. You know that, don't you?'

Tara shied away. 'Sorry.'

I rolled my eyes and sighed again. 'Come on, let's go back. We *have* to sit on Stephanie's table this lunchtime though, OK?'

Tara smiled a very sweet smile through her braces and put her arm through mine. 'OK. Did I tell you what Jack did the other day? It was *sooo* annoying . . .' And she was off on yet another irritating-little-brother anecdote. But I was only half listening; I was already plotting.

The first step was to separate myself from her in

everyone else's eyes. I needed to not sit next to her in every single lesson. Ideally I needed to not sit next to her in any lessons. I didn't want to hurt Tara's feelings though (yeah, I was all heart). So I stayed behind after school one day and told Mrs Hodgson that Tara was distracting me and I was finding it hard to concentrate, but I didn't know what to do about it because she was my best friend. Mrs Hodgson was brilliant. She arranged for us to sit apart in every single class. I'd really laid it on thick about wanting to study law at university. She didn't seem to think it was weird that a twelve-year-old was worried about getting into uni.

When the desk move happened, I pretended to be as confused and hurt as Tara was. It was easy. After that, it was a simple matter of a gradual phase-out over the next few months. A few unreturned phone calls. Making up excuses as to why I couldn't go round to her house after school. Trying to become Stephanie de Luca's shadow. It was pitiful. Tara got the hint eventually. She never confronted me – she wouldn't have dared. I felt guilty about the whole thing, but not quite guilty enough to change my mind.

Then one day it happened. Everything I'd ever wished for. Stephanie invited me to a sleepover at her house. I'd made it.

The day of the sleepover arrived and I was so

excited I quite literally could not sit still. Mum had been out all morning. Dad was in the garage working on his bike. I was busy packing my bag and worrying whether my pyjamas were too babyish. Mum called me downstairs. She looked different, but I wasn't sure how. She made me sit on the sofa, then sat down next to me, holding my hand. Bruno jumped up and tried to muscle his way onto my lap despite being at least three times too big. Mum pushed him off, none too gently. She said there was something she needed to talk to me about, something important, something serious, and there was no easy way to say it. Then she said the words. The worst words in the world.

'The cancer's back. It's bad.'

I didn't go to Stephanie's party.

I didn't infiltrate the in-crowd.

Mum died.

Tara transformed.

My mind has never been able to separate Mum's illness from my treatment of Tara. It's not like I thought the cancer came back because I'd been such a terrible person. OK, I *did* think that for a while. But near the end I knew it couldn't be true. When I saw her ravaged by pain, her face pinched and sallow, her skin paper-thin, I knew. No God would ever inflict such suffering on her to pay for my crime. No God would allow such a terrible thing to happen to our family. God did not exist. Obviously.

I stopped blaming myself for Mum's death; I didn't stop blaming myself for the way I'd treated Tara. But by the time I'd worked up the courage to apologize, she was at least three rungs above me on the social ladder. Slowly but surely she'd reinvented herself. She'd stopped coming to school with wet hair (which was now streaky and blonde). Her skirts were shorter. She'd started wearing make-up. I swear she made one tiny change every day, so that no one really noticed what was going on. *I* noticed though. The transformation in the way she looked was enough to get her in with the in-crowd, and the transformation in the way she acted was enough to cement her place. They never even realized that it would only be a couple of years before the girl they'd so graciously invited into their hallowed circle would *own* them.

The reinvention of Tara Chambers was so dramatic, so all-consuming, that it erased the memories of the girl who'd been my best friend. I'd tried talking to Cass about it once, but she claimed not to remember a time when Tara hadn't been the Tara she knew and hated.

Sometimes I feel like I *created* Tara the über-bitch. Then I tell myself not to be so egotistical. But there's no denying the fact that Tara was a good person, a nice person, until I abandoned her.

In some parallel universe Tara and I are still best friends and neither of us cares in the slightest that no one else seems to like us. We're both happy. And more importantly, we're both alive.

I tell Jack that Tara and I drifted apart after we stopped sitting together. We both agree that it was a shame, but *just one of those things*.

I don't feel bad for not telling him the truth. The truth would hurt him.

And it would hurt me.

32

It's Monday morning and Mrs Cronin is subdued. Normally her energy levels are inexplicably high after the weekend, but today she puts on a DVD about Stalin and sits quietly at the back of the classroom (sparing us the usual running commentary).

That new teacher whose name I can never remember knocks on the door and scans the darkened room before spotting Mrs Cronin. Everyone turns and watches their huddled conversation, because anything's got to be more interesting that whatever Stalin's up to on-screen. I tell myself I'm just being paranoid when I catch Cronin and Teacher X glancing my way, but then they do it again and I know I'm right to be worried.

They know. Oh my God, they *know*. They've found the body. This is it. I knew it would happen sooner or later, but this is definitely sooner than I thought.

Adrenaline shoots through my body and saliva floods my mouth. I fight the urge to bolt from the room, because what good would it do, really?

Mrs Cronin doesn't even bother to pause the DVD. 'Alice, please could you make your way to Miss Daley's classroom?' Daley's classroom seems an odd choice for the interrogation. I pack my books and pens away with shaking, clammy hands and try to ignore everyone staring at me. My ruler clatters to the floor, but I don't bother to pick it up. It's not like I'll be needing it.

Gemma stage-whispers to no one in particular, 'Uh-oh . . . someone's in TROUBLE.' A couple of girls giggle. Danni tells her to shut up. I catch Danni's eye and she actually looks sympathetic – the way a friend might look in this situation. She won't be looking at me that way when she finds out what happened. I doubt anyone will ever look at me that way again.

The empty corridor stretches out before me and I walk on legs that feel like they don't belong to me. I peer through the window of each classroom I pass. Rows and rows of normal girls, sitting at their normal desks, living their normal lives.

I turn a corner and someone's coming towards me. It's Cass. The tiny part of me that hoped this whole thing is unrelated to Tara is crushed.

Daley's classroom is exactly halfway down the corridor, so Cass and I meet in the middle. I wonder if I look as scared as she does. I expect so. We don't speak. There's nothing left to say.

I follow Cass through the open door and Daley's at the front of the room, pacing back and forth. The pacing stops as soon as she sees us. She beckons us forward but doesn't say anything. Her face is red and blotchy and her mascara's a mess.

Polly's leaning against a radiator on the far wall, twisting her hair round her fingers. She doesn't look scared; she looks like she's waiting for a bus. Rae's not here yet.

There is no one else in the room. Not quite what I'd expected. Maybe the police are going with a softly, softly approach, letting Daley explain the procedure before they swoop in with the handcuffs.

I drop my bag on the floor and slump into a chair in the second row. Cass takes a seat a couple of desks to my left.

Daley takes the deepest of deep breaths and lets it out somewhat shakily. She closes the door and Cass and I exchange confused looks. Why isn't she waiting for Rae? A horrible idea creeps into my brain: maybe Rae told the police. Maybe she's brokered some kind of deal to protect herself? We are well and truly fucked.

Daley wipes away a tear and takes yet another deep breath. 'Girls,' she pauses to look at each one of us in turn, 'I'm afraid I have some bad news.' Yes. We *know*.

'Rae Morgan . . . um . . . Rae passed away on Friday night.'

No.

Polly's eyes widen. She stops twisting her hair.

No.

Cass shakes her head ever so slightly.

No.

And then I say it out loud. 'No.'

Daley turns to me, pity oozing out of every pore. 'I'm sorry, Alice.'

Polly speaks up. Her voice is strangely calm. 'How did she die?'

Daley winces. She looks at the door as if the answer might come strolling in at any moment. 'I . . . You have to promise me that this will stay between us. The family doesn't want rumours flying around. I'm sure you understand.' She waits for nods from each of us before continuing, 'Rae took her own life.'

No. This cannot be true.

'How did she do it?'

I want to strangle Polly for being so crass, but I want to know too. I need to know.

'I really don't think that's important, Polly.'

'I think we deserve to know.'

Daley's eyes flick towards the door again. 'She overdosed.'

'So they don't know for sure that she meant to kill herself? She could have done it by mistake,' says Cass. There's so much hope wrapped up in her words.

'I'm afraid they *do* know – there was a note.'

I pray that Daley doesn't notice the look of pure panic that flashes between Cass and me.

'What did the note say?' Again, Polly is the only calm one in the room, asking the questions that we so desperately need answers to.

I don't breathe again until Daley answers. '"Sorry." It just said, "Sorry."' She shakes her head at the tragedy of it all.

I can't help but let a sigh of relief escape. Sorry. Sorry could mean anything. Sorry is vague, ambiguous. Sorry is whatever you want it to be.

'There's going to be a special assembly this afternoon. Everyone else will be told then. We just thought that you girls should know now. After what you went through together in Scotland, I thought . . . you might have become close to Rae. Now, can you tell me who else she was friends with? None of the teachers seems to know.'

The other two look at me. 'I . . . um . . . Rae didn't really have many friends. I mean, she probably had friends outside of school that we don't know about.'

Polly chips in, 'She kept herself to herself really.' This pisses me right off. It's the kind of thing you hear on the news when some old lady's being interviewed because her apparently normal neighbour has just massacred a bunch of people. But Rae *did* keep herself to herself. I genuinely thought she preferred listening to music to talking to people. Well, if I'm completely honest, I never really gave Rae much thought at all up until the Scotland trip. Or after, for that matter. I never even thought to check how she was doing. Maybe there's something I could have done. Maybe I'm kidding myself.

I think Daley is going to cry over the thought of Rae not having any friends, but she manages to get a grip. 'Right, I've got a meeting with Mrs Flanagan now. You girls can stay here as long as you like. All your teachers have been informed. If any of you wants to talk about anything, you know where I am.' She hovers for a second or two, and I'm sure she's going to hug each of us. Luckily she comes to her senses and settles for a watery smile mostly aimed in my direction.

I think Cass sums up the situation perfectly as soon as the door closes behind Daley. 'Shit.'

33

Polly moves from her radiator perch to sit behind Daley's desk. I let my head fall forward onto the desk in front of me. Cass swears under her breath.

'I can't believe she actually *did* it.' Polly sounds a bit in awe. Which is more than a little bit disturbing.

'What do you mean?' My voice is slightly muffled by the desk.

'I thought she was *joking*.'

I don't like what I'm hearing.

'You talked to her about this?' Cass sounds as incredulous as I feel.

There's no answer, so I can only assume that Polly shrugged or something. I really should get my head off the desk and see what's going on. But I don't want to look at these people. I'm afraid of what I'll see in their faces.

'Since when were you such good friends with Rae?' asks Cass.

'I'm not. I wasn't. We talked sometimes. About . . . you know.' Of course we know.

'And she said she was thinking about topping herself?' I wish Cass would choose her words more carefully.

There's a pause and I wonder if Polly is working out how much to reveal.

'She thought we should go to the police. I managed to talk her out of it, thank God.'

'And now she's dead.' I finally manage to look up to find Polly staring right at me.

'Yes, she's dead. Don't look at me like that, Alice. It's not my fault.'

I sigh. 'I didn't say it was your fault. I wish there was something we could have done, that's all. This whole situation is completely out of control. Maybe we *should* go to the police. Maybe Rae was right.' I can't believe I am talking about Rae in the past tense. How many more people am I going to have to talk about in the past tense?

'NO!' Cass's voice is unnecessarily loud and the word echoes around the room. 'We are *not* going to the police. Alice, you promised, remember? Rae's gone and there's nothing we can do about it. There's no point ruining *our* lives as well.'

'Cass is right.' It's like that night all over again.

Polly and Cass ganging up on me and Rae. Except there's no Rae.

'Two people are dead! And it's our fault. Doesn't that mean anything to you two?'

Cass says, 'It was an accident,' at exactly the same time as Polly says, 'It's not our fault.'

I shake my head and get up to leave. The room tilts slightly and I have to steady myself for a moment. 'You're wrong.'

Cass pushes her chair back so hard it topples over. She's in my face before I know what's happening. 'OK, fine. You go to the police. But make sure you explain everything to your boyfriend first. I'd like to be a fly on the wall for *that* conversation.'

I don't back down. Instead, I step forward so Cass and I are practically nose to nose. 'Don't you dare bring Jack into this. You don't know anything about him.'

'I know that he wouldn't want to go out with the girl who killed his sister.' There's a twisted smirk on Cass's face and a sing-song voice in my head saying, 'She's right, you know she's right!'

'I thought you said it was an accident.' I push past her and leave the room without looking back.

I need to be somewhere else.

Somewhere I can think.

The library is my safe place. I secrete myself in a dark corner, far away from the librarian.

Cass knows I won't go to the police.

I know I won't go to the police.

I hate Cass and Polly for being right about this.

I hate myself for being the worst kind of coward.

I hate Rae and Tara for being dead.

I stay at the library till closing time, switching off my phone after the first three missed calls from Dad.

He's really, really angry when I get home, and I'm too tired to argue with him. And I know he's only cross because he's been worried. I know how much *I* start to panic when I can't get hold of him – always sure something terrible has happened. The scenario in my head usually involves him losing control at the wheel and ending up in a lake, struggling and failing to open a window or a door as the car rapidly fills with icy water. Not that north London has a lot of lakes.

Daley called to tell him that I hadn't been seen in school since this morning. She told him about Rae. I hate the thought of Daley and Dad talking about me.

Dad's anger is extinguished by an accidental onslaught of tears from me. He wraps me up in one of his hugs and tells me everything's going to be OK. Then he makes me some cheese on toast and sits me down in front of the TV, but not before making it clear that if I want to talk about things, he's there to listen. Maybe I should tell him. Maybe he can sort everything out. He'll give me another hug and say, 'Oh, you daft thing. You've been worried about *that*. Let me see what I can do.' I *wish*.

Ghost Tara is not in the least bit upset about Rae. 'Maybe you should do the same thing,' is all she has to say for herself.

I hardly sleep. All I can think about is Rae and how desperate she must have felt. And I can't help wondering why *I* haven't thought about suicide. Was her guilt so much worse than mine? Does that make her the better person?

No matter how bad things get, I can't imagine choosing to die. I couldn't do it to Dad.

And I *want* to live. There are things I want to do. I want to learn to snowboard. I want to go to university. I want to be fluent in Spanish. I want to have a job I'm really, really good at. I want to live in a cottage in the countryside and maybe keep chickens. I want to fall in love.

I wonder what Rae wanted to do with her life? Maybe she wanted to be a doctor or a scientist. And maybe if she had been a doctor or a scientist, she'd have done something really important – like discover a cure for cancer. Rae could have been destined to change the world, to stop people like Mum from suffering. And now that won't happen. Because of us.

We killed two people in the woods that night.

34

As the dreaded Tara Chambers Memorial Dance looms, all anyone can talk about is Rae. Despite the family's wishes, everyone knows it was suicide. The rumours are vicious. *Rae was in a cult. Rae was pregnant (with twins) after having sex with Mr Miles while his wife watched. Rae was secretly a lesbian and had been in love with Tara and was so distraught about her death she couldn't go on living.* I have no evidence, but I suspect a good half of the rumours were started by Cass.

I'm so relieved I don't have to sit through another funeral – Rae's is family only. A sensible decision, I think. Otherwise everyone would just end up comparing it to Tara's, and there's no way Rae could beat that turnout.

Polly, in another display of truly terrible judgement, decides to change the name of the dance. *The Tara Chambers and Rae Morgan Memorial Dance* is quite a mouthful. Some people try to protest that Rae doesn't deserve equal billing, since killing yourself is not as worthy of pity as accidentally drowning. But Polly isn't having any of it. Apparently there was a committee meeting and the vote was unanimous. No one seems to have any idea who else is on the committee.

The flyers now bear the new, supposedly committee-sanctioned name of the dance — although I've heard some people whispering about the *Dead Girls Dance*. It just goes to show that while one dead classmate is a tragedy, two is fair game for all manner of sick jokes.

The psychologist is back, and the parents are summoned to yet another meeting. The worry now is copycat suicides. Dad came home with a leaflet entitled *Is your teen suicidal? Ten signs to look for*. I bin it and tell Dad he has nothing to worry about. He seems to believe me.

I have a couple of uneventful after-school sessions with Daley. She tries to get me to talk about my feelings; I refuse to talk about anything unrelated to the syllabus. It's probably a relief for her. She can still reassure herself that she's at least making an effort. Needless to say, neither of us mentions Dad.

I spend a lot of time with Jack over half-term.

He invites me to watch Blackdog Sundays rehearse. There are four of them in the band. Spike is the lead singer (his real name is George). Jenks is on bass. I don't think that's his real name either. The drummer is Dave. I'm pretty sure Dave *is* Dave's real name. I find Dave vaguely reassuring.

They all dress a bit like Jack (but not quite as well, in my humble opinion). They're perfectly friendly if a little monosyllabic – except for Spike, who keeps on saying my name like he's some super-smooth talk-show host.

I haven't exactly been looking forward to this moment, dreading having to lie to Jack. *Yeah, you're amazing. You could TOTALLY get a record deal.* But much to my surprise they're really, really good. And Jack is brilliant. He doesn't even have to concentrate – he keeps on looking over at me and smiling.

When they take a break I can't help myself. 'You're *amazing*. You could *totally* get a record deal.' Jack's modest and tells me I'm deluded, but you can tell he's pleased.

The last song they play is the one Jack wrote for Tara. He takes over lead vocals from Spike and the atmosphere in the room changes immediately. The laughing and joking and messing around are gone. Jack sings with his eyes closed, and every word is infused with sadness. Every note is haunting. Jack's voice cracks a little during the last verse and my heart cracks a little bit more.

We're supposed to be going to the cinema afterwards, but I can tell Jack's not in the mood. Instead, we go to a quiet cafe and Jack talks about Tara. The words come pouring out of him. He cries once or twice, and he's not in the least bit self-conscious about it. A lot of what he says is hard for me to listen to, but I make no effort to stop him or change the subject. It's obvious that this is exactly what Jack needs to be doing. The least I can do is listen.

The night of the dance arrives. A tiny part of me is excited – the shameful, girly part of me that's stupidly pleased with herself for going out with the lead guitarist in the band that's playing. The rest of me is filled with foreboding.

I should stay at home and watch TV with Dad. That would be the sensible thing to do. I'd hear all about it on Monday morning, but the horror would be diluted by hearing the details second hand. But Jack wants me there. And *everyone* is going. If I don't go, people might talk. And the last thing I need is people wondering why I'm shunning the Dead Girls

Dance. I have to do whatever it takes to avoid drawing attention to myself. Even Cass is going. I only know because Saira told me, since Cass and I still aren't talking. I try to picture us getting ready at her house, doing each other's hair, dancing around and singing into our hairbrushes or whatever girls are supposed to do. The image disintegrates before it has a chance to make me feel wistful.

When I come downstairs, Dad's lounging in front of the telly, his feet tucked under Bruno's furry bulk for warmth. I have to cough loudly to get his attention, but when he turns to look at me a huge grin spreads itself across his face. He actually says the words 'My little girl . . . all grown-up'. I roll my eyes and he laughs. 'What?! Isn't a father allowed to be proud of his daughter any more? What *is* the world coming to?'

'Dad!'

'OK, OK, I'm sorry. Embarrassing Dad will not say another word.' He pretends to zip his mouth shut. 'ExcepttosayyoulookreallyreallybeautifulandI'mvery proudofyou.' He claps his hands over his mouth as if the words escaped by accident.

His playfulness transforms into melancholy; I'd suspected it might. 'I wish your mother was—'

'Don't say it. Please don't say it.' I can't bear to

hear the words one more time. The words that mar pretty much every happy occasion. There are different variations, but the sentiment is always the same. I used to nod vaguely whenever he said them, even though they made me flinch. I will not allow him to say them tonight. *I wish your mother was here to see you. Your mother would have loved this. If only your mother were here . . .*

Dad looks hurt, which obviously makes me feel terrible. But he recovers quickly and grabs his camera from the cupboard behind the TV. 'You wouldn't deny an old man a picture, would ya?' For some reason he says this in a terrible Cockney accent and I have to laugh. He deserves to get a laugh at least.

I make him delete the first four photos. They are hideous, even though Dad says they're perfectly fine. The fifth picture is barely acceptable but it will have to do if we're not going to be late. Dad insists on driving me there (chauffeuring me, he calls it) and he bows when he opens the car door for me. 'Your carriage awaits, milady.' I'm too busy trying to stop my dress from digging into my armpits to roll my eyes this time. The dress is so bloody uncomfortable. It's too tight, too short, too . . . everything. I bought it in a moment of madness, thinking only of Jack. He'd better appreciate the effort because I won't be doing this again in a hurry.

The butterflies in my stomach turn into vampire bats as we pull up to the school. There's a pink limousine hogging the space right in front of the main entrance. It's not hard to guess whose rich-yet-strangely-lacking-in-taste father hired that for the evening. My suspicions are confirmed when Stephanie de Luca and her tacky friends spew out. Even the ghost that's rumoured to haunt the second-floor music room can probably hear her braying voice complaining when her Jimmy Choos sink into the soggy gravel. It's hard to believe I ever cared what she thought of me.

There are suited and booted Knox Academy boys milling around outside. Dad eyes them suspiciously before driving off. I don't want to go in by myself so I pretend to check my phone for messages. My phone buzzes in my hand and I get such a fright I almost drop it. It's a text: *You look sexy as hell*. A thrill rushes through me and I look up, scanning the crowd for Jack's mop of hair. Then, from nowhere, a pair of hands slinks round my waist and I squeal – much to my embarrassment. I whirl round and there he is.

35

He kisses me and I kiss him back, and I know that people are staring but I don't care. Jack's wearing his version of smart — grey jeans, a black shirt and an undone purple bowtie. The other guys in the band are milling around behind him. Their clothes make no concessions to the occasion — in fact, I reckon Spike's wearing the same T-shirt as the last time I saw him.

Jack grabs me by the hand and pulls me towards the door, but not before I see Cass standing a little way off, watching us. She shakes her head and turns away. Her dress is plain and fits badly.

Jack leads us to the desk at the entrance. Gemma and Sam are taking money and handing people wristbands in exchange. Jack's already got one — I didn't notice it among all his other wrist adornments. As we edge to the front of the queue I pull his wrist towards me to get a better look. The band is bright pink and clearly modelled on those anti-cancer/anti-bullying/anti-insert-bad-thing-of-your-choice-here ones. It says: 'Tara Chambers . . . . . always in our hearts'. The parents of whoever chose the wording should ask for their school fees back. Some people just don't know where to stop when it comes to dots in an ellipsis.

Sam doesn't even bother to hide the blatant up-and-down look she gives me when Jack and I reach the desk. One perfectly plucked eyebrow arches in obvious disdain. She looks from me to Jack and back again and her eyes widen. Gemma is oblivious, as always. Jack takes a crumpled fiver from his pocket and hands it to Sam. Gemma hands him a bracelet and he gestures for me to hold out my wrist. He slips the bracelet over my hand, and it seems a strangely intimate thing to do among all these people. I can feel myself blushing for no good reason. I start to offer to pay, but Jack silences me with a fake stern look.

'I can't wait to see you play later, Jack,' says Sam, her voice confident and purring.

Jack says a vague, 'Thanks,' and turns away. Sam's sultry smile slips off her face and onto the floor.

'OK, so I think you'd better brace yourself, Alice. It's pretty full on in here. I've had a while to get used to it – we got here early for the sound check. But when I first walked in . . .'

Shit. He's not kidding. The hall has been transformed. The colour scheme is black and pink – the same shocking pink as the bracelets. I suppose the black is there to retain some sense of mourning. There's really no excuse for the pink though. There are huge screens on either side of the stage. A picture of Tara flashes up on both screens simultaneously for a few seconds before fading into another picture. And another. And another. It's hypnotic. Jack's grip on my hand tightens and we stand in the doorway, transfixed.

No one else seems that bothered. They all head straight for the bar, where a couple of barmen are showing off to the crowd – chucking glasses over their shoulders and stuff like that. There's no alcohol being served, of course – strictly mocktails only.

I'm finding it difficult to think or speak or do anything. The photos of Tara overwhelm me. She looks so beautiful up there. It doesn't seem possible that she's gone. Surely she's going to skip onto the stage at any moment and take a bow to rapturous applause. 'Thank you! Thank you! Sorry about the whole pretending-to-be-dead thing, but it was the only way I could think of to make you have a massive party all about ME!' And then the adoring crowd will storm the stage and hug her and congratulate her on her terribly cunning plan.

'It's . . . wow.'

'Told you. I kind of like seeing her up there though. Tara would have loved it, don't you think?' Jack pulls his gaze away from his sister to look at me, but his eyes flicker back towards the screens every couple of seconds.

'Probably.' I see something out of the corner of my eye and drag Jack along to get a closer look.

It's an easel displaying a big sheet of black cardboard. Someone has written 'Rae Morgan R.I.P.' at the top in silver pen. The letters get smaller towards the right-hand side, as if the writer misjudged the amount of space. There are three pictures, overlapping each other at inappropriately jaunty angles. The picture in the middle is a school photo of Rae, from last year by the look of it. The other two were obviously taken years ago. In one of them she has the kind of tragic bowl-cut you always dread when you go to the hairdressers. In the other, she's perched on a shiny new mountain bike and sporting a neon-green baseball cap.

This is the best they could do? *Really?* It's like someone's done it on purpose – created the crappiest memorial they possibly could to make it clear that this is all about Tara. Rae is an afterthought. A support act who must not be allowed to distract from the headliner. If Tara would have loved the big screens bearing her image, then there's no question that Rae would have hated this. She wouldn't want her pictures or her name anywhere near this morbid carnival.

Jack reads my mind. 'Doesn't seem right, does it? You'd think they'd have made more of an effort.'

All I can do is nod.

We spend the first hour or so hanging out with the band in a reasonably quiet corner. Spike's hand brushes my bum a couple of times and I resist the urge to slap him. Maybe he just struggles with the concept of personal space.

A couple of Jack's mates from school sidle over and Jack introduces me as his girlfriend, which is pretty much the best thing I've heard anyone say – ever. While we're all chatting he keeps his hand on the small of my back. It keeps us connected, even when we're talking to different people. I like it.

I try my best to forget about where we are and why we're here. It's not that easy when I can practically feel Cass's glare on the back of my head. I *know* she's watching — I caught her when I nipped to the loo. She's sitting on the edge of a group of girls I don't know all that well.

Every time I turn around I see Polly chatting to someone else. A couple of times I notice her eyes glistening with unshed tears.

Polly is almost unrecognizable as the girl who got on that bus to Scotland.

While the rest of us have become *less*, somehow she's managed to become more. Has this version of Polly been biding her time all these years, watching, waiting? Like those cicadas that emerge from under the ground after seventeen years or something. I can't help wondering where the old Polly is. Whether she's gone for good. I hope not — this new version makes me uneasy.

The boys are caught up in some kind of drinking game, which strikes me as slightly pointless until I realize that Spike has smuggled in a bottle of vodka. There's nothing 'mock' about what they're knocking back. I hope Jack doesn't get too drunk before their set. I almost say something, until I remember that I'm not his mother, so telling him not to drink would be decidedly not OK.

'What a fucking circus.' The voice is slightly slurred. I turn to see Danni practically collapse onto the seat behind me. Her hair is a state and her make-up is smudgy. She smells like she's been showering in alcohol. Clearly Jack's mates aren't the only ones who've smuggled in some booze to liven up the party.

'How are you doing?'

She shakes her head and says nothing.

'This must be hard for you.'

'Nice of you to notice. No one else gives a flying fuck. Funny how I seem to have been relegated from the position of Tara's best friend. How come Polly Sutcliffe is the centre of the universe all of a sudden? Tara would be laughing her arse off. Everyone seems to have conveniently forgotten that she DESPISED that girl. How can they have forgotten? How is that even possible?'

But I know all too well how quickly people forget. Social boundaries are fluid – not set in stone like people think they are. People can rise up the popularity scale faster than you would believe. No one knew that better than Tara. The irony does not escape me.

I'm about to say something vague and reassuring to Danni when a hush descends on the hall. The lights are dimmed and a spotlight flashes onto a lone microphone in the middle of the stage. Polly emerges from the darkness.

'Oh, you have GOT to be kidding me,' Danni says way too loudly. People turn and stare, before returning their attention to the stage.

Polly clears her throat and wipes a non-existent tear from her eye. 'Thank you all for coming tonight. I know it would have meant a lot to Tara. And to Rae. I don't think there's a person in this room whose life has not been profoundly changed by these tragedies.' She stops and looks around for a moment or two. I can hear sniffling coming from the direction of Stephanie de Luca's table. Jack's face is inscrutable. Danni's face is murderous. 'Let's have a moment of silence to honour our lost friends.'

Polly bows her head and everyone else does the same. I go for a kind of halfway option, bowing my head a little bit so I can still see what's going on. Some of the girls are holding hands. Some of the boys are fidgeting and looking awkward. Someone sneezes. The pictures of Tara are still flashing up on the screen. You'd think someone might have paused them or something.

Just as I'm beginning to think that this is the longest minute of my life, Danni jumps to her feet. She stumbles against the table so hard that a glass falls off and smashes on the floor. A vivid red stain creeps across the white tablecloth. Every single bowed head snaps up and all eyes are on Danni. I can hardly bear to look.

'You people . . .' She shakes her head in disgust. 'This is a complete joke.' She points at Polly and the look on her face is pure venom. 'YOU are a complete joke.' Polly's expression is a careful blend of sadness and pity, but it looks like a mask that could crack any minute.

Daley rushes over and grabs Danni's arm, gently but firmly manoeuvring her out of the room. Danni does nothing to resist.

The room is filled with whispers and awkward laughter. Everyone loves a bit of drama.

Jack's hand is on my arm. 'Do you think you should go and see if she's OK?' It shames me that he suggested it before it even crossed my mind. As I leave the hall I hear Polly start to sing some terrible ballad, unaccompanied. Good grief.

36

Danni was fine. Well, not fine exactly: drunk and emotional and sweary. But sort of OK. Daley was grateful to palm her off onto me while she went and called a taxi to take Danni home.

'I probably shouldn't have done that, should I?'

I shrugged. 'I don't think anyone would blame you.'

She smiled weakly. 'You're OK, you know.'

'Um. Thanks. I think.'

'I don't know why Tara hated you so much.' She clapped both hands over her mouth and laughed. 'Oops. I mean, that's no secret, is it? You knew that already?'

I nodded.

'Thanks for listening to me ramble on. I know I'm a teeny bit pissed, but I won't forget this. You're being more of a friend to me than my so-called *best* friends. Well, the ones I have left anyway.'

271

I walked her out to the taxi when it arrived. She hugged me and there was nothing for me to do but hug her back. 'Nice one getting it on with Jack, by the way – he is FIT . . . but I'll kill you if you tell anyone I said so.'

Daley cornered me on the way back in, enquiring about Danni's mental state. I told her Danni would be fine. She didn't look like she believed me. Probably worried that Danni would go home and slit her wrists. I left her looking fretful in the foyer.

Everyone seems to have forgotten about the disturbance by the time I get back to the table. Spike asks me about my 'crazy friend', comments on her 'awesome rack' and says he 'SO would'. Jack rolls his eyes and gives my hand a reassuring squeeze.

I'm left alone when the band heads off to get ready for their set. It's nice to be on my own for a while. I watch the images of Tara and work out there are thirty-one photos in all. My favourite is the one where she's looking over her shoulder at the camera. Her hair is windswept and glossy. The picture looks completely spontaneous – like the photographer called her name and just snapped away. Knowing Tara, she probably planned it that way.

Every time a new photo comes up, I think *I'm sorry*. Over and over again. It turns into a weird sort of game with myself, where I have to think the words at the exact moment when one photo fades into the next.

And then a new photo comes up. This one stays on the screens. This one breaks my heart into a million tiny pieces.

Jack and Tara. Their arms slung loosely around each other's shoulders, laughing. They look like twins.

The band come onstage to cheers and applause. Jack's eyes seek out mine. He waves at me and I wave back. It takes him a few seconds to notice the screens, but when he does he stops in his tracks. I want to go to him, hold him, touch him, tell him everything will be OK. Tell him I'm sorry.

His hands are shaking as he plugs in his guitar and fiddles about with some pedals at his feet. It looks like he's muttering to himself, trying to pull himself together.

Dave's drums kick in and people surge towards the stage. I can't take my eyes off Jack. He's on autopilot for the first couple of songs. He barely looks up from his guitar and I know it's not because he needs to concentrate.

It was Jack's idea to start with a couple of cover versions. Clearly a stroke of genius – loads of people are dancing like crazy. There are still a few people (me included) standing or sitting around the edges of the dance floor. Cass is leaning against the wall by the door, still watching. It's getting creepy.

A few songs in and Jack's loosening up, starting to enjoy himself. He looks so bloody good up there. He's sweating and his hair is sticking to his forehead. The muscles on his forearms are taut. His fingers move up and down the frets almost faster than I can see. I want to eat him up. Or tear his clothes off.

We make eye contact and there's something different there. Something powerful and raw. I'm surprised no one else can feel it.

The end of the set comes round too quickly and there's no avoiding what's next. Jack steps up to the microphone and I brace myself for a big, emotional speech.

'This one's for my sister.' That's all he says. It's enough though. The mood in the room shifts. People are suddenly still.

The song is even more haunting than the first time I heard it. Jack's eyes are closed and his voice is surprisingly rich and strong – different from before. I look around to see that everyone's eyes are on Jack. Even Cass has stopped staring at me for a little while.

Gemma and Sam are right at the front, their elbows resting on the stage. Gemma could probably reach out and touch Jack if she wanted to. She'd better not. The teachers are all grouped at the back of the room. Mr Miles has his hand on Daley's shoulder. She's crying in great big heaving sobs.

Daley's the only one crying at first, but somehow the tears infect the room, and by the time Jack gets to the really quiet bit at the end of the song I'd guess that a good half of the girls in the room are crying. As far as I can see, none of the boys have succumbed. A few of them are awkwardly patting the shoulders of the girls they're with. Probably working out if this heightened emotional state increases (or decreases) their chances of getting some action tonight.

Jack sings the last line and this time his voice doesn't crack and I'm glad for him. He bows his head for a second or two and I wonder if he's praying. It takes a few seconds for the crowd to shake off their stupor and begin to clap. The applause is quiet and respectful at first, but it soon builds and builds and some cheers and whistles are added into the mix. It goes on and on. Jack's embarrassed. He keeps ducking his head and acknowledging the reaction with a half-raised hand. Spike isn't so modest: he bows theatrically again and again. Jenks and

Dave are loving it too. They've obviously never had a reception like this before. The biggest gig they've played before now was some crappy under-eighteens night at a club in Camden. Apparently it did *not* go well.

The band disappear offstage and emerge ten minutes later. Spike is acting like some kind of minor celebrity. He even manages to work in a few high-fives on his way through the crowd.

Jack looks exhausted and I wrap my arms around him. 'You were amazing,' I whisper into his ear.

'Really?' he whispers back.

'Yes, really . . . and you looked ridiculously good up there.'

He squeezes me a little tighter. 'Oh yeah? You like the whole Rock God thing then?'

I kiss his neck, surprising myself. Public displays of affection seem to be my new thing. 'I like it a lot.'

We kiss properly and Spike asks if I'm willing to congratulate all the band members in the same way. We ignore him and kiss some more.

Jack pulls away too soon. 'Um . . . maybe we should stop?' he murmurs. He doesn't sound sure, so I choose to ignore him.

'Alice . . . people are staring.' Who cares? But a quick look over his shoulder confirms he's right. And one person in particular is watching us closely. That does it for me.

'Right, come with me.' I pull Jack by his hand and he almost loses his balance. We head out into the foyer, passing my would-be stalker on the way. 'Jack, could you wait here for a second? I'll be right back.' I give him a quick kiss and leave him looking puzzled.

I stomp back into the room and stop in front of Cass.

'What is your problem?'

She smiles sweetly and tilts her head 'Problem? I don't have a problem. What makes you think I have a problem?'

'Stop staring at me. I mean it, Cass.'

'Oh, you *mean* it. That *must* be serious.'

'Just . . . stop it.' I'm so angry I can't think of anything else to say.

'Ah, but it's so hard to resist watching love's young dream. You two really are perfect for each other . . . What could *possibly* go wrong?'

'Nothing's going to go wrong.'

She's glittering with malice now. 'Hmm . . . you don't sound so sure about that, do you? Aw, don't look at me like that. I'm sure you two will be fine. I mean, it's not like you've got some big, dark secret that would ruin everything, is it? Oh wait – you *do*. I *know* you, Alice. The guilt will eat away at you, more and more each day until you can't take it any more. Until you tell him.'

'For God's sake! When are you going to start listening to me? I'm not going to tell Jack anything!'

'Tell me what?'

37

It's like something off a terrible daytime soap. I didn't think things like this actually happened in real life. Turns out I was wrong.

Jack's face is relaxed and open. Cass looks almost as freaked out as I feel.

'I . . .' That's the best I can do. And here I was, thinking I was a good liar.

'Tell you that she's crazy about you,' says Cass. 'I said she should tell you how she feels, but she wanted to wait. Our Alice has always been shy when it comes to boys.' She laughs and pats me on the cheek. She knows how much I hate that, but I'm so grateful for her quick thinking that I could forgive her anything right now.

I shrug and hopefully look just the right level of bashful.

'Oh, right. Er . . . cool.' The poor boy doesn't

know where to look. 'I'm Jack, by the way. I don't think we've met?'

Cass sticks out her hand. 'It's nice to finally meet you, Jack. I'm Cass.'

They both look at me as if it's my turn to speak. My heart still feels like it's trying to burst out of my chest like some kind of alien.

I need to extract Jack from this situation as quickly and painlessly as possible. 'Jack, do you want to come with me? There's something I want to show you.' Makes me sound like a paedophile . . . *Do you want to come and see some puppies?*

'Consider me intrigued . . . OK, let's go.'

Jack and Cass say their goodbyes and I lead Jack away. I turn back to Cass as I steer Jack through the door. I mouth the words 'thank you' and she nods.

Jack and I walk through the deserted hallways. It's dark and eerie, and I might be scared if I was on my own. But Jack's hand in mine is all it takes for me to feel safe.

'So what is it you wanted to show me? I bet it's your locker, plastered with poems about me.' Since when did he get so cocky? Oh yeah, probably since being told I'm *crazy* about him.

I refuse to rise to the bait. 'You'll see soon

enough,' I say, aiming for sexy and mysterious. The truth is, there is nothing worth showing him in this place, unless you count Ernie the skeleton in the biology lab. He's pretty special.

I stop when we're far enough away from the main hall so we can't hear the music any more. I peek in the window of a classroom I've never been in before.

'In here. Follow me.'

'Your wish is my command.' He can be such a perfect geek sometimes.

Pale moonlight glances off the teacher's desk. Jack moves to turn on the lights, but I stop him. I hop up onto the desk and swing my legs back and forth. Jack wanders round the room, eventually stopping in front of me.

'Ah, so *this* is what you wanted to show me . . .' He gestures to the whiteboard. 'I can see why. I've always wanted to know more about the shanty towns of São Paulo. How did you know?!' He laughs.

'Shut up and kiss me.'

He's surprised at my forwardness, but he doesn't mind. He is a boy after all. 'Whatever you say.'

I kiss him hard. My tongue seeking out his with a new kind of desperation. My fingers run through his hair. His hands are on my waist, but I want them everywhere.

I pull him even closer to me so that he's standing between my legs. My dress rides up my thighs and I don't care.

After a few minutes he pulls away. 'What if someone comes?' The choice of words makes me giggle.

'Who cares?' I slip my hands up under his shirt and my fingers roam up his spine. 'I just want you to kiss me and not ever stop.' My mouth finds his and I feel out of control with lust.

My fingers find his belt buckle and get to work. I'm struggling with the zipper when Jack grabs hold of my hands. 'What are you doing?'

I laugh. 'What do you *think* I'm doing?' My breathing is ragged. 'I want you, Jack.'

'You mean you want to . . . ? *Here?*' It's funny how these things are so hard to talk about.

'Yes, I want to. Don't you?'

Jack sighs and winces. He leans towards me so our foreheads are touching. 'Of course I want to. I've wanted this for longer than you can imagine. But not like this. Not here.'

'Why not?' I think I'm going to cry.

'It doesn't feel right, you know? And anyway, I don't have any . . . um . . . condoms.'

I kiss him, biting his lip a little. 'I don't care.'

And that's when I know I've lost my mind. What a monumentally stupid thing to say.

'Alice! You don't mean that.'

Of course I don't. I'm not stupid — just horny. And embarrassed. My vision blurs with tears and I turn away, hoping Jack won't see.

'Hey, don't cry . . . Come on, it's OK.' He puts his hands on my shoulders and tries to get me to look him in the eye.

'I'm fine. Really. Let's go back to the party.' I hop down from the desk, straighten my dress and take a deep breath.

'Are you . . . ? Are we OK? I don't want you getting the wrong idea. I want this to happen, but I want it to be right.' Isn't it supposed to be the girl who says things like that? *I want my first time to be perfect.* He must think I'm a right slag. I can't work out whether it's better if he thinks I'm a slag or a virgin. Tough call.

'We're fine. I don't know what I was thinking. This is really embarrassing.'

Jack puts his arms around me and kisses me on the forehead. 'Don't be embarrassed. I'm flattered. Oh God, that sounds really arrogant, doesn't it? That's not what I mean. What I'm trying to say is, I feel very lucky that you want to be with me.'

This makes me feel a bit better. 'Sorry for throwing myself at you.' I smile to make sure he knows everything's fine.

He smiles back. 'Next time I'll be ready. I can promise you that.'

38

The rest of the night went quickly, thank God. I couldn't quite manage to shake off the shame, but at least I managed to hide it from Jack. We danced and laughed and talked. I kept an eye out for Cass, but she must have left early. No such luck with Polly. She seemed to be everywhere I looked – to such an extent that I started to wonder if she was doing it on purpose. But that seemed like a weird thing to do, even for her.

When Jack and I said goodbye, he said one word: 'Soon.' And suddenly I felt terrified and not at all ready. This is all very confusing.

Dad picked me up and we stopped for doughnuts on the way home. I gave him a (very) edited version of the night's events and he asked lots of questions without ever crossing the line into nosiness.

Of course Ghost Tara had a thing or two to say. She was disgusted at how prominent Polly had been in the proceedings. She was worried about Danni. And she called me a 'right little minx' for 'trying to get in Jack's pants'.

As I tried to sleep, all I could hear was Tara whispering in my ear. At least I think it was Tara. Sometimes I swear the voice is inside my head. And sometimes I swear the voice is mine.

You don't deserve Jack.

You don't deserve to sleep.

You don't deserve to live.

I've been dreading Monday the whole weekend: the inevitable, interminable talk about the dance. I swear most people enjoy that bit more than the event itself. It's all about who was wearing what, who was getting off with who and who was sick in the toilets.

The last thing I want to hear is any gossip about me and Jack. Not that I think I'm particularly gossip-worthy, but I saw the way a lot of girls were eyeing him up onstage. Some of them will definitely have something to say – probably along the lines of *he could do SO much better.*

I swear more people are paying attention to me than normal as I trudge through the corridors. And I know for sure it's not all in my head when Stephanie de Luca says, 'Hi,' as I approach my locker. I say a quizzical 'hi' back and turn to concentrate on finding my books. Daley wants us to hand in our copies of Chaucer today. Mine must be lurking underneath the miscellaneous detritus at the bottom of my locker.

Much to my surprise, Stephanie leans against the lockers. There's such an air of nonchalance about her that you'd think she stopped by for a chat every day.

'Did you have a good time on Friday?'

'Um, yeah. It was OK, thanks.' I get down on my knees and start piling up books beside Stephanie's feet. She's wearing sparkly ballet pumps, for Christ's sake.

'So . . . you and Jack Chambers? What's the deal there?'

Oh God, here it comes. 'What do you mean?' I'm glad I don't have to look at her, but I don't exactly feel comfortable scrabbling around at her feet. I find a Spanish textbook I thought I'd lost.

'You're together, right?' I find a grubby pair of gym socks.

'Yes.' That's all she's getting from me.

'Since when?' There's something wedged down the back of the locker, partially hidden by my mammoth German dictionary. I pull it out. It's a plain white envelope, slightly creased and grubby. My name is written on it in fat black capital letters. I wonder how long that's been there.

Stephanie fake-coughs. 'Alice? Helloooo?'

I stand too fast and have to ride out the wave of dizziness. Stephanie's lucky it's the locker door I grab hold of rather than her. 'Sorry, I was miles away. We've been together a while. Why?' I turn the envelope over and over in my hands.

She shrugs. 'Just curious. He's cute. Soooo . . . I don't suppose you know the rest of the band, do you? Cos that lead singer was smokin'.'

'Yeah, that's Spike.' I wedge my thumb under the flap of the envelope and start to tear it open.

'Spike? Sounds *dangerous*.' And you sound pathetic. The envelope contains a single piece of white paper, folded once in the middle.

'Maybe you could introduce us sometime? Oh, BTW, I'm having a party on Saturday if you're interested?' This catches my attention. Firstly, I can't believe she actually said 'BTW' out loud. And secondly, I can't believe she's inviting me to a party. I've only been waiting four years. Also, I can't believe she's not even bothering to hide the fact that she's only talking to me to get to Spike. How could I have ever wanted to be this girl's friend?

I unfold the letter slowly, just to leave Stephanie hanging.

At first I don't understand what I'm seeing. The words don't make any sense, even though they're written in the same thick letters as my name on the envelope.

I glance up at Stephanie, worried that she might be looking at the note. I needn't have bothered though – she's busy examining her nails. I need her to leave – now. But there's a planet-sized lump in my throat. Somehow I manage to force out some croaky words. 'I'm busy on Saturday.'

This was clearly not the answer she was expecting. 'Um . . . OK. Well, let me know if you change your mind. Facebook me, yeah?'

I nod vaguely, and Stephanie walks away looking puzzled.

A quick, furtive glance around at the now empty corridor before I risk looking at the letter again, hoping it will say something different.

It doesn't.

You have to do the right thing.
Tell someone. Please.

The note is signed: 'R'.

A bizarre thought flits in and out of my head: the letter R is only worth one point in Scrabble.

39

My hands were shaking as I folded the note and put it back in the envelope. I put the envelope in my bag, shoved everything else back into my locker and slammed the door. I went straight to the school nurse and told her I'd just thrown up. She told me I did look a bit peaky and let me lie down in the sick room. When she popped her head round the door an hour later I asked her to call my dad.

On the way home, Dad kept on asking if I was OK. I said that talking made my head hurt.

I went straight up to my room, closed the curtains and got into bed still wearing my school clothes. Bruno jumped up next to me and rested his head on my legs. I couldn't stop shivering.

I read the note again. One question steamrollered over all the others in my head: how long had it been there?

I tried to convince myself that Rae had put it there just before she killed herself. I really, really wanted this to be the case, because the alternative was too horrible to think about. But I forced myself to think about it anyway. What if Rae put it there weeks and weeks ago, waiting to see what I would do? And when I did nothing, she . . .

I didn't sleep for four nights. I mean, I'm sure I slept a little, but it definitely didn't feel like it. I felt groggy and confused and sick with anxiety. Dad tried to get me to go to the doctor, but I refused. I told him I was on my period and he left it alone.

Rae's letter was all I could think about.

I felt terrible. A whole new level of terrible I never knew existed. The kind of terrible that makes you want to lock your bedroom door and stay in there forever. That makes you scared to look anyone in the eye in case they see what kind of person you really are.

I stayed home from school for the rest of the week – which stretched Dad's belief in my 'women's troubles' as he called them. Jack wanted to come and visit me, but I put him off. I was scared to see him. The only other person to get in touch was Danni, who messaged me on Facebook: *Just wanted to check you're still alive. Hope you haven't topped yourself. Sorry for being a dick the other night.* I didn't reply.

Ghost Tara taunted me, repeating the words of Rae's note in a crazy sing-song voice that never went away. Even when I was downstairs with Dad and Bruno, I could still hear it. On Thursday morning Dad caught me banging my head against the kitchen table in a vain bid to silence the madness. I somehow managed to convince him I was annoyed with myself for pouring orange juice on my cereal instead of milk. He didn't seem to notice I was eating toast at the time.

By Sunday afternoon I realize there's no way I can avoid going to school tomorrow. If I stay cooped up in this room I may well end up in a mental ward. Or worse. I put Rae's note in the drawer next to Tara's ring. It seems like the right place for it.

There's a knock at the door and I slam the drawer shut, throw myself onto the bed and close my eyes. I'm sure Dad must be able to hear my thumping heart from the other side of the door.

'Alice? Can I come in?' It's not Dad. The voice is so out of context in these surroundings – in *my* surroundings – that it takes a moment or two for me to place it.

'Yeah, come in.' I manoeuvre myself into a sitting position as the door opens.

Danni closes the door behind her and tiptoes into the room like she's creeping through a graveyard in the dead of night. 'Sorry. Were you asleep?' Before I have the chance to answer she looks around and her eyes widen. 'Wow.'

'I know, I know, I've heard it all before. My room looks like an eight-year-old's . . . blah blah blah.'

Danni shrugs and strokes the zebra-print curtains. 'I was just going to say how much I like zebra print.' I'm pretty sure she's lying, but I appreciate the effort. She pulls the curtains open and the light hurts my eyes. 'Can I open the window? It smells a bit . . . stale in here.'

'Charming! Yeah, go for it. Um . . . how did you know where I live?' I try my best to sound nonchalant, as if I'm used to random people popping over all the time.

'I asked around.' Danni throws herself down on the beanbag in the corner. 'I wanted to see how you were. Did you get my message?'

I shake my head. 'Danni, why are you here?'

Her eyes narrow. 'I wanted to talk to you about something. And I was worried about you . . . but mainly I wanted to talk to you. You're the only one who gets it.' Somehow I have become Danni Carrington's confidante.

I draw my knees up and tuck them under my chin. My body language could not be any more defensive if I'd adopted the brace position they show you on aeroplanes. 'What do you want to talk about?'

Danni leans forward and I can hear the polystyrene balls inside the beanbag rearrange themselves. 'I think Tara was murdered.'

My stomach twists itself into a complicated knot and I hope against hope that my facial expression has stayed neutral. 'Is this the Duncan thing again?' Please God, let it be the Duncan thing again. Or any crazy story that Danni has concocted, as long as it's nowhere near the truth.

'No. I mean, yes. Sort of.'

'Danni, we've been through this before.' My sigh comes out more shakily than I would have liked.

'I know, I know. But I can't stop thinking about it. Sometimes I feel like the whole world is going crazy and I'm the only one thinking about this logically. And then sometimes I think *I* must be the crazy one because no one else is even considering other explanations. They've got their neat little story and there's no need to look any further. But it makes no sense. One, Tara would never have gone swimming.

She was looking forward to a week away from all that . . . she said as much. But even if she did go swimming – which she didn't – there's no way she'd have had an asthma attack. Swimming never brought on her asthma before, and anyway, she'd have had her inhaler with her. Definitely.' Danni's words tumble out fast, as if she's worried I'm going to stop her or contradict her at any moment.

'You can't *know* that, Danni. Not for sure.'

'I can. I do! Tara never went *anywhere* without her inhaler. She was pretty chilled about most things, but not about that. She had a scare about a year ago when we were doing cross-country. It was bad.'

'What happened?'

'She was in the lead by miles, but she started to have trouble breathing. Of course, being Tara, she decided to power on through it – she couldn't bear the thought of losing.' That sounds about right. 'She collapsed near the finish line. I was way back so I didn't see what happened. Apparently it was really scary. Thank God Polly was there.'

The room shrinks and the walls start to pulsate in time with my heartbeat. Somehow I manage to spit out a single, ugly word. 'Polly?'

'Yeah, she pretty much saved Tara's life. Knew exactly what to do. You know her asthma's really bad? Way worse than Tara's.' I shake my head. Why would I know this? 'Yeah, she's like, obsessive about it. Carries at least two inhalers wherever she goes. That's why she always gets out of doing sports at school. Tara probably could have too, but she likes . . . *liked* pushing herself as far as she could go . . . Anyway, Polly was at the finish line, being the official timer or whatever. Tara was lucky.'

'Polly saved Tara's life?' There's a scrabbling sound in my ears. I think it's my brain trying to make a break for it. It can't compute what Danni is telling me.

'Yeah. Mad, isn't it?'

'How come I never heard anything about this?' Everyone knows about everything at our school. There's nowhere on earth that gossip spreads as fast as at a girls' school.

'It's not exactly something you'd want getting around, is it? Polly Sutcliffe coming to your rescue? Tara made sure no one said anything.'

It makes sense now – Tara letting Polly follow her around like a lapdog. Polly would have been so grateful to be hanging on to the edge of the in-crowd that she wouldn't even care that they still despised her.

'She always had this thing about never wanting to look weak. She always had to be the strong one. You know, I never once saw her cry?'

That was my fault. Tara was like that because of me.

'I . . . Danni, I'm not feeling too well. Would you mind . . . ?'

She nods. 'I'll head off. But do you think I should go to the police? I mean, I know I don't have any evidence or anything, but they might listen to me. Don't you think?'

I can't think. Not while Danni's looking at me as if I have all the answers. 'Let me think about it. Don't do anything rash. We can talk about it next week.' I sound strangely calm and in control.

'OK.' She struggles up from the beanbag. 'Thanks for this, Alice. I feel a little less crazy now – sometimes it's just good to get stuff out, you know?'

I nod.

'See you at school.'

'Yeah.'

I'm left alone with too many thoughts clashing against each other in my head.

What the fuck am I going to do?

40

This is what I know to be true. Polly has asthma. She carries inhalers with her wherever she goes. She knows what to do when someone's having an attack. Polly *knew* Tara had asthma. She saved Tara's life once. She did not do it twice.

The place my thoughts are leading me towards is so disturbing that I can't look at it head-on. I have to squint at it out of the corner of my eye. Danni must be wrong. It's as simple as that.

I text Cass and ask her to meet at the coffee shop we used to go to before our lives were over. Cass likes it because it's got a pinball machine; I've never understood the appeal of pinball.

She texts back — she'll be there at five. That gives me half an hour to shower and make myself fit for public viewing. I haven't left the house for six days. I haven't washed my hair for three. I am officially disgusting.

Dad's shocked to see me in actual clothes. He makes a half-hearted effort at persuading me to stay home (*You can't go out with wet hair . . . can you? Doesn't that mean you'll catch a cold . . . or something?*), but I think he's just pleased to see me vertical again. Bruno looks up hopefully from his favourite lounging spot in front of the fire, but puts his head back on his paws when he clocks that I'm not brandishing a lead.

Cass is there when I arrive – playing pinball, of course. She looks up when I call her name, and the little ball drops down through the hole at the bottom of the machine. I know enough about pinball to know that this is undesirable.

'Sorry. Didn't mean to ruin your game.'

'Don't worry about it. I wouldn't have got anywhere near my highest score anyway – haven't been practising enough recently,' she says pointedly. The point being: we haven't been here for ages and it's all your fault.

Cass has already got a drink – a can of Coke (not diet) is on the table next to the pinball machine. *Our* table. At least it used to be. I grab a can of Diet Coke from the fridge and pay at the counter. For the first time my hands are as clammy as those of the boy at the till. Cass and I always tried to get our change from him without actual physical contact. It was a challenge – one that Cass excelled at. I failed pretty much every time, and today's no exception.

Cass looks at me warily as we sit down opposite each other. She fiddles with the ring pull on her can until it breaks off. 'So . . . ?'

It's weird seeing her here; I wish I'd chosen somewhere else. It doesn't seem right to stomp all over those memories. 'I need to talk to you about something.'

She makes a big show of looking at her watch – a huge diver's watch that dwarfs her tiny wrist. 'I haven't got all day, you know.'

'Sorry. Yes.' The cafe is empty apart from the boy behind the counter. He's busy watching the football on a tiny TV in the corner. The volume must be turned up as far as it will go. Which suits me just fine. 'It's about Tara.'

Cass winces and looks around before leaning across the table towards me. 'There's nothing to talk about. I think you've made your feelings quite clear, don't you?'

'Cass, listen to me. I need to know what happened.'

'What do you mean?'

'That night. In the woods.'

She scrunches up her face and shakes her head. 'You *know* what happened,' she says in a fierce whisper.

'No. I *don't*. When Rae and I went back to the cabin . . .'

Cass holds onto the edges of the table with both hands as if to steady herself. 'No.'

'What do you mean, *no*?' This isn't exactly what I was expecting.

'I mean, "I don't want to talk about it." It's pretty simple really.' There's real hatred in her eyes and it makes me so sad I could cry.

'This is important, Cass. *Please*.' I put everything I've got into that *please*.

The only sound is the roar of the crowd on the TV. Someone must have scored. Clammy boy is clutching his head in his hands, so I'm guessing it wasn't Arsenal.

'You never asked. Not once.' Cass isn't looking at me. She's not looking at anything. 'I kept on waiting for you to ask. I mean, why wouldn't you? Surely you'd want to know what happened? Surely you'd know how awful it must have been? Surely my *best* friend would want to know if I was OK, having been through something like that?' She's firing the words at me like machine-gun bullets. Each one hits me smack-bang in the heart.

I'm stunned. Cass is right. I never even thought about it – not once. I didn't think about how terrible it is to watch someone die. Ironic, really.

'I . . .'

'You were too busy blaming me, right?' She leans forward again, eyes blazing. 'Well, you know what, Alice? You could never, *ever* blame me more than I blame myself! So if that's what this little reunion is all about, you can save it.' She pushes her chair back and it hits the wall behind her. The boy looks up from the TV. 'What are you looking at?' Cass shouts at him, and he returns his gaze to the screen pronto.

This isn't going to plan. One last try. I look up at her, my eyes pleading. 'Did you *try* to save her? Did Polly try to save her?'

She stands over me for a second, making up her mind. Then she shakes her head and slumps back down in her seat. 'It was the scariest thing I've ever seen. I didn't know what to do. I mean, I don't know first aid or anything, and you know how squeamish I am.' She's not kidding. Cass can't bear being in the same room as an ill person. She never goes to the doctor, even when she's really unwell – she can't bear breathing the same air as 'those diseased freaks' in the waiting room.

'So what *did* you do?'

'I was going to try giving her mouth-to-mouth or something. I mean, I didn't know what I was doing, but I've seen it on TV enough times.'

'What happened?' I say.

'Polly stopped me. She said it was too dangerous. She was the one who knew first aid, so I had to listen, didn't I?'

'She said it was too *dangerous*?'

Cass nods vigorously. 'But Tara needed air, right? She needed to *breathe*. It was like watching a fish out of water. The panic in her eyes . . . I think she knew she was dying. Can you imagine what that feels like?'

I ignore the question. 'What did Polly do?'

Cass shrugs. 'She just . . . watched. I think she must have been in shock or something. There was nothing else we could have done, right?'

I find myself shaking my head slowly, as if agreeing will make this nightmare go away.

'Alice, are you OK? You look . . . I dunno . . .'

'I'm fine.' I reach across the table and take her hand. She looks taken aback but she doesn't snatch her hand away. 'Cass, I need you to understand something. You did everything you could. You were out of your depth — we all were. You can't blame yourself.' I don't know why I don't tell her. It's not like I make a conscious decision *not* to tell her. Not really.

'But it was my idea. The stupid joke.' There are tears in her eyes. She tries to blink them away.

I squeeze her hand. 'Yes, but you had no idea what would happen. None of us did.'

Cass shakes her head. 'I took it too far though. Putting the pillowcase over her head . . . pretending to be that guy. Polly said it was too much, but I didn't listen.'

'When? When did Polly say that?'

The tears are flowing freely now. She doesn't bother to wipe them away. 'When we were orienteering – remember when we were supposed to be lost? I wanted to talk it through with Polly before telling you. I just wanted to scare Tara, you know? *Really* scare her. She deserved it.' I can't argue with that. She deserved a scare. She did not deserve to die. 'At first I was just going to jump out at her wearing that stupid balaclava. But then I had a better idea – to drag her out of bed in the middle of the night and lock her out of the cabin. Then Polly said she'd seen this film once where they staged a kidnapping – made it look really real and everything. Said they tied this guy to a tree and pretended to be a gang of psychopaths . . . I jumped on the idea – thought it was genius. Way better than my plan. Polly said it was too cruel, but I wouldn't let it go . . . Why the fuck didn't I just let it go?' She's sobbing now, out of control.

I feel sick.

Why can't she see that Polly played her from the start? Planted the idea in Cass's head, then pretended to be horrified by it.

Why can't I tell her?

'Cass, you made a mistake. We all did. We're all to blame.'

She looks up, her face a blotchy, tear-stained mess. 'You don't really believe that, do you? What about Rae?'

'We all had a choice – Rae included. You can't blame yourself for what she did. You just . . . can't. Look, I've got to go. Dad wants me back by six. Are you going to be all right getting home?'

She nods. 'I think I'll stay here for a bit. Get my head together – play some pinball . . . Alice, is it going to be OK?' She whispers the question.

I don't know whether she's talking about our friendship. Or something bigger. Whatever she means, I know there's only one answer. And I know it with a cold, sharp certainty.

No. It is not going to be OK.

'Yes. It's going to be OK, I promise.'

41

Three in the morning and still no sign of sleep. I don't know if I'll ever sleep again.

Ghost Tara and I have been talking, and I'm actually glad of the company. Maybe this is how madness works. At first you're worried you're going crazy, but in the end you don't even care. You embrace it; it's the only thing you've got left. The only thing you can trust when the rest of the world has gone to shit.

'She fucking killed me, didn't she?' Tara's pacing the room. Her legs are pale and goosebumpy. I shiver.

I lean over to scratch Bruno behind his ears. His tongue lolls out of his mouth.

'Polly Sutcliffe killed *me*? Christ, that's embarrassing.'

If this girl wasn't a figment of my imagination I would throw something at her head.

'Is that all you can say? It's *embarrassing*? It's . . . fucking fucked up is what it is.'

'Well, yeah. *Obviously*. Who'd have thought Polly would turn out to be a bona fide psychopath . . . or is it sociopath? What's the difference between those two anyway? I've never been quite sure . . .'

'Tara, will you please shut up for a minute? I'm trying to think.'

She throws herself down on the bed with such gusto that Bruno should have been catapulted off, or at least woken up. He wasn't and he hasn't. 'What are you thinking about? Maybe I can help. Tell me tell me tell me.'

I close my eyes and press my fingers into my eye sockets. It hurts, but the pain feels good and right. It grounds me – anchors me to what is real. My hands are real. My eyes are real. I wonder if my eyeballs would pop right into my brain if I pushed hard enough. I wonder if anyone's ever committed suicide that way.

I'm trying to form coherent, ordered thoughts, but it's like trying to knit with candyfloss. 'She didn't kill you. Not really. It was an accident.' My voice rises up at the end of the sentence. It's an almost-question mark. I open my eyes and blink away the red spots in my vision.

'Yeah, course it was. I *accidentally* got dragged

out of bed and tied up in the middle of the night. A pillowcase *accidentally* fell over my head and Cass *accidentally* pretended to be some sleazy fucker who wanted to rape me.' She counts off each 'accidentally' on her muddy, blood-encrusted fingers.

'We didn't know you had asthma!'

'*She* knew. She knew and she didn't say anything, and she stopped Cass from trying to save me. Open your eyes, Alice.' My eyes are open, but that's not what she means. 'This isn't going to go away. You can't escape this. Rae couldn't escape, and she didn't even know the truth. Or maybe she did.'

Maybe she did, maybe she didn't. We'll never know. That's part of the joy of the whole 'being dead' thing. The unanswered questions, the secrets, everything you never said. A laugh escapes from my mouth and I have no idea what's so funny. But I can't stop. The laughter is manic and high-pitched. It doesn't sound like a noise I would ever make. It doesn't sound like a noise a normal, sane person would ever make. And then before I know it I'm crying so hard I have to stuff my fist in my mouth to keep from screaming.

'Alice, will you please shut the fuck up? You sound like some kind of rabid animal. Seriously, you're making my ears bleed.' I look up and she's right. Blood is trickling over her ear lobes and tracing a precarious path down her neck.

Everything goes blurry and fuzzy. Then dark.

I wake up with a wet ear. My first thought: blood. My ears are bleeding. I'm dying.

My second thought: Bruno. He's now slobbering all over my mouth. Gross. But it's a relief. It's normal. I get a saliva wake-up call at least twice a week.

Dad's banging on my bedroom door and banging on about me being late. This is also normal. I lie in bed and breathe. Breathing means I'm alive. And being alive is a good thing.

Isn't it?

I need to think about this. But I really, really don't want to think about this. It's too big to fit inside my head. It's too big and serious and not the kind of thing a sixteen-year-old girl should have to deal with. This sixteen-year-old girl cannot deal with it.

I have to do something. Ghost Tara is right. This isn't going to go away, no matter how much I want it to. But I need more time.

I get the bus to school. I go to lessons. At

lunchtime I throw my sandwiches in the bin. I talk to Danni. I tell her not to go to the police – not yet. For some reason, she listens to me. For some reason, she seems to respect me. God knows why. I see Cass. We talk. But not about *it*. We talk about the latest episode of that crappy MTV show she loves so much. We talk about the new biology teacher who started last week. Cass says his teeth are so white they must glow in the dark. We talk about her brothers. Jeremy lost a tooth and there was five pounds under his pillow when he woke up the next morning. 'Five quid?! FIVE QUID?! Can you believe it? I got a pound if I was lucky. It just backs up my argument that Mum loves the boys more than she loves me.' We laugh, or rather we both make a sort of laughing sound. Then we both stop because it doesn't sound right.

So I get through Monday, somehow. Tuesday is a repeat of Monday, with the added bonus of a session with Miss Daley after school. I say as little as possible. She doesn't seem to mind. She seems as distracted as I am. Her hair looks nice though. It's shinier than normal and I think she's changed the parting. Jack calls me in the evening. His voice soothes me. His laugh smooths the edges of my fragmented mind. He asks me to go over to his house on Saturday night. Something in his tone suggests that he wants Saturday to be *the* night. I don't know what to do about that. I say yes, because that's what he wants to hear.

Wednesday is the day I start to lose it. Wednesday is the day I spend two hours in the toilets in the art block. I choose the end stall, put down the toilet lid and sit there with my knees drawn up to my chin. If anyone looks under the door they won't be able to see any feet. They'll assume the lock is jammed. They'll leave.

I cry. As quietly as possible.

42

I don't see her until Thursday. Not that I've been purposefully trying to avoid her. Well, maybe just a little bit.

She's alone. Standing in front of the vending machine. I stop dead, not sure what to do. I watch. She's just standing there and staring. At first, I think she's having trouble choosing what to buy, but then she flicks her hair and turns her head to the side – still staring at the glass.

I take a step forward and then a step back. What should I do? *Fucking talk to her.* Tara's voice in my head makes my decision for me. I'd feel a whole lot better about this if I'd planned what I was going to say. Stupid.

'Polly, hi! How's it going?' My voice is loud and bright and as fake as it's ever been.

She takes a second or two to fiddle with her hair

before turning towards me. 'Hi, long time no see. I heard you were ill. Nothing serious, I hope?' Her smile seems genuine enough.

'No, nothing serious. So . . .' I run out of words. My idiotic, frazzled, sleep-deprived brain has finally ceased to function.

Polly reaches into her bag (Mulberry) and pulls out her phone. 'So, I'd better be going. Got to meet Stephanie for lunch.' There is no good reason for her to tell me this. She takes a couple of steps away and the Tara-voice in my head is screaming at me to say something – ANYTHING!

'Polly, wait. Um . . . could I talk to you about something?'

She turns and smiles uncertainly. 'Of course. What do you want to talk about?'

'I'd like to get involved with the memorial . . . thing.'

'Really? I thought you found it *distasteful* in some way.' There's suspicion there, but that's only to be expected.

'I was wrong. I'm sorry. I'd like to help – really.'

'Hmm. Well, I'm sure we can find *something* for you to do. There's the yearbook thing to sort out for starters. It's got to be sorted ASAP. Originally it was only going to be two pages, but I managed to get Mrs

Flanagan to agree to an eight-page spread, right in the middle. Isn't that great?'

'An eight-page spread of what, exactly?'

'Photos of Tara, maybe some quotes from her friends, things like that.' She snaps her fingers and points at me. 'I've got it! I know *exactly* what you can do. Why don't we get the lyrics of Jack's song? The one he played at the dance? We could get him to write them out and then we can scan them. Oh, it'll be perfect, don't you think?'

'Perfect,' I say. Not tacky, tawdry, sick.

'You'll be able to get him to agree, no problem. I'm sure you can think of some way to persuade him if he's not too keen . . .' Polly laughs and I somehow manage to smile back at her.

'Actually, I'm seeing Jack after school. Why don't I get him to write out the song and then I can meet you later?' Oh God, what am I doing?

Polly looks at the ceiling, her lips pursed. I wonder if she'll be able to fit me into her newly jam-packed social life. 'Yes, that could work. I think I'm free tonight.'

'Why don't I come round to your house around eight?'

I'm ridiculously relieved when she shakes her head. 'No, not there. It's . . . too far for you to come. Tell you what, why don't we meet here? Mrs Flanagan's given me special permission to use the media lab after hours. I've got a key and everything. The security guard will let you in if you tell him you're with me.' The word 'smug' doesn't go far enough to describe the look on Polly's face.

'Great. Um . . . perfect. I'll see you there at eight.'

Polly's phone suddenly blasts out a tinny rendition of a song I can't quite place. 'Oops, that's Stephanie. I'm so late! Must dash!'

And she's gone. And I am freaking out. What have I done?

It's not till later that I realize that Polly's ringtone was 'Don't Stop Me Now'. The song from Tara's memorial service.

Dad and I have an early dinner.

I manage to somehow give the impression of eating without actually ingesting much of anything. Normally Dad would be on my case, persuading me to have a second helping. He never did that before Mum died. Now he says things like, 'There's nothing of you,' and, 'You'll disappear down the plughole if you're not careful.' But not today. He's quietly eating his noodles and reading the recipe on the bottle of soy sauce. Five minutes later and he's still holding the bottle. I think it's safe to assume he's somewhat distracted.

'Dad? Earth to Dad?' I wave my hand in front of his face and he blinks and puts the bottle down.

'Sorry, Al, I was miles away.'

'Really? I'd never have guessed.'

'Enough of that sarcasm, young lady.' Dad can't stand sarcasm. He gets really cross about it sometimes; I'm pretty sure he just doesn't get it. I must have got all my sarcasm genes from Mum.

I look at Dad, and for the first time in weeks I really *see* him. I haven't been paying him much attention recently. I've been so completely wrapped up in myself that we haven't talked in ages – not properly anyway. Unless you count exchanges like, *Will you take Bruno for a walk? Aw, Dad, can you do it? I'll do it tomorrow – I promise.* Dad's looking kind of old. A few grey hairs are sprouting at his temples. I wonder when they appeared? Maybe they've always been there and I just haven't noticed. And is it my imagination or does his face look sort of grey? Fear body-slams me and suddenly I'm sure he's ill. Cancer. I bet it's cancer.

'You OK, Dad?'

'Mmm.' He shovels a huge forkful of noodles into his mouth.

'Is that "Mmm, yes" or "Mmm, no"?'

'It's "Mmm, I'm in the middle of eating, but yes, I'm OK, thanks".'

'So you're feeling OK? Promise?'

He gives me that sympathetic expression I've come to know so well. This is not the first time we've had this conversation. Dad got used to my paranoia a long time ago. 'Yes, I promise. I'm fine. Tip-top, tickety-boo, fine and dandy.' Exactly the same words he always uses.

'And you'd tell me if you weren't, wouldn't you?'

'You know I would,' he says as he reaches out and gives my shoulder a squeeze. 'I'm fine, kiddo. Strong as an ox, healthy as a . . . dolphin . . .'

'Dolphins get trapped in tuna nets all the time, you know.' I give him a sly look.

'OK . . . how about healthy as a highland cow?'

'That works for me.' I quickly stack Dad's empty plate on top of my full one, just in case he decides to go all Food Nazi on me after all.

'Leave that, Al. I'll stack the dishwasher in a minute. There's something I want to talk to you about.' Dad coughs and twists his paper napkin in his hands.

'Can it wait? I'm in a bit of a hurry. Got to head back into school later to help with the yearbook.'

He doesn't comment on the fact that I've never so much as mentioned the yearbook before, which adds to the evidence of him being massively distracted. 'This won't take long. It's . . . um . . . a bit of a sensitive subject, really. I need to ask your opinion on something. And I want you to know now that I'll listen to what you have to say, so don't you worry about that . . .'

'Dad, what are you on about?'

Dad winces, takes a deep breath and speaks really, really fast. 'I was wondering how you'd feel about me going on a date. With a woman.'

Not what I was expecting. At all. Weirdly, the idea doesn't horrify me as much as I would have thought. I've been dreading this day for years, and now it's here I feel kind of OK about it. It doesn't seem that big a deal.

'I think you should go for it, Dad.' And the look on his face is one of such relief that I can't help but pat myself on the back for my generosity. 'Are you thinking of trying Internet dating? I've heard that's a good way for old people to meet each other.' He doesn't admonish me for calling him old, and that's when a tiny needle of worry pierces my brain.

'I've . . . er . . . already met someone.' The needle

gets a little bit bigger. 'It's your . . . It's Miss Daley. Daisy.' He says the word 'Daisy' like it's something nice to savour – a toffee bonbon, perhaps.

The needle morphs into a whacking great sword. All I can think to say is, 'Daisy Daley is a ridiculous name for a person to have.'

'Alice! Don't be so rude! So . . . what do you think?'

'No.' The word pops out of my mouth before I know it. The wounded look on Dad's face is horrible to see, but I won't take it back. I can't.

'What do you mean?'

'No, I'm not OK with it. Isn't there some kind of law against going out with your kid's teacher? I'm sure there is.' I sound like the snottiest little brat imaginable. But how can I tell Dad that I was OK with the *idea* of some mythical future woman, but the thought of a real, live, present-day one that I actually *know* makes me want to cry.

'Don't be daft! There's no law against it. But . . . it's OK. I just wanted to see how you felt. I'm not going to do anything you're not one hundred per cent happy with. It's fine. It was a silly idea, really. I'm happy as I am. *We're* happy, aren't we? Us against the world, remember?' His voice is extra-bright, like the fluorescent lighting in the hospital.

'Yeah, us against the world,' I say. Now I'm the one doling out a reassuring shoulder squeeze.

Dad gets up and starts busying himself around the kitchen. He puts the radio on loud. I sit at the table and try not to choke on guilt. The fact that he didn't fight me on this, that he didn't even try to change my mind, makes me feel terrible. At least if we'd had a blazing row I could have mustered up some righteous indignation. I think he was *expecting* me to say no. Which makes me feel even worse. I have lived down to his low expectations of me.

I can't stand the thought of him and Daley together. It's so many different kinds of wrong I can't even begin to count them. Daley is not good enough for Dad. I mean, she's fine when she's just being a teacher and staying out of my business. She's kind and clever and sort of pretty if you think pretty = dainty and weak-looking. But Daley's like a wishy-washy yellow carnation from the garage. Mum was a prize rose – deep, gorgeous red.

The clock on the oven reads 7.06. I've got to get ready. 'Thanks, Dad.'

He turns and flips a dishcloth onto his shoulder. 'What are you thanking me for? You're the one who cooked.'

'I know.' I shrug, not sure what to say. I can't bring

myself to say the words he so obviously wants to hear, so what's the point of saying anything at all?

Dad purses his lips and nods. 'It's OK. Really. Now, you go and write some scandalous article to put in that yearbook. "The dark truth behind the friendly facade of Bransford Academy." I can see the headlines now!' He laughs easily and loudly and he's trying so hard to be a good father that I can hardly bear it.

The dark truth behind the friendly facade of Bransford Academy is darker than he could ever imagine.

43

I don't really have much getting ready to do so I lie on my bed and try not to hyperventilate.

I'm scared. Polly Sutcliffe scares me. How can I be scared of Polly Sutcliffe?

What the hell am I going to say to her when I show up without Jack's song lyrics? And *why* exactly am I doing this again? I'm hit with a sudden desire to stay home and forget all about it. Erase the knowledge from my brain. Go on living my life and avoiding what's ugly and real and impossible.

But I have to go. I need to hear what she has to say for herself. I need to convince her to do the right thing. Rae was right. We *have* to go to the police.

I lean over and reach into the drawer beside my bed. The ring feels warm to the touch, but maybe I'm running a fever or something. I look at it closely. It looks like an ordinary ring – nothing special about it whatsoever. But to me it has a sort of power. I slip it into the back pocket of my jeans. Perhaps Tara's grandmother will keep watch over me. Somehow I doubt it.

A scenario plays out in my head. I enter the media lab. It's dark. There's a huge leather chair at the other end of the room, facing a big console with lights and screens and stuff. I approach with extreme caution. The chair turns around to reveal Polly sitting there in a sharp black suit. Her hair is scraped back from her face and she's wearing red lipstick. She strokes a fluffy white cat on her lap and arches an eyebrow, 'Ah, Alice, I've been expecting you.' And I know I'm in deep shit.

The reality is slightly different. My footsteps sound ultra-loud, echoing around the deserted corridors. This would make the perfect start to a horror film. Suddenly I feel icy fingertips dancing down my spine and I'm sure that someone's watching me. When I look over my shoulder the corridor is empty. But someone could be watching from one of the darkened classrooms and I'd never know. Being at school is creepy enough in the daytime; at night it's just plain terrifying.

I've only been in the media lab once – when Mum, Dad and I came to visit the school before I enrolled. I remember being very impressed with all the flat-screen Macs that made our crappy old PC look like a remnant from the Dark Ages.

I glance through the little window in the door and see that the room *is* mostly dark. But Polly's not exactly looking like some budget Bond villain. She's leaning over a plan chest, with one of those desk lamps that look like an alien arching over her head. Her hair hangs in front of her face like a curtain.

I take a deep, unsteady breath and open the door.

'Alice, hi! Come and look at this – tell me what you think.' She waves me over and moves aside so I can see the yearbook pages in all their glory. There are pictures of Tara everywhere. All the photos from the dance, as well as some I've never seen before. One of her in her swimsuit holding an enormous trophy. I don't think she'd thank Polly for choosing that one. Her legs look mottled, exactly like the night she died. The other girls in the swimming team stand behind Tara, grinning and clapping. I look for Cass but she's not in the picture – maybe she was the photographer.

There's a photo of Tara, Danni, Gemma and Sam. Tara and Danni are in the middle, with the other two acting as bookends. Tara looks knowing and powerful somehow – like she's been given the key to the universe. She looks like a born winner, ready for whatever life can throw at her.

'So what do you think? Not bad, is it?' Polly's standing way too close, so when she turns her face to look at me I have to take a step back.

'I think it's a lot of pictures of Tara.'

'It took so long to sort through them all. Her parents have hundreds of photo albums of her. Well, maybe not hundreds, but *a lot*. There were three albums of her at various swimming competitions, if you can believe it.'

Tara's dad used to take his camera with him everywhere. I found it kind of creepy, and Tara hated it – back then anyway.

'Polly, why are you doing this?'

She shakes her head and frowns. 'Doing what?'

'*This*. The yearbook, the dance, the society. All of it.'

Polly shrugs and meanders round to the other side of the plan chest, her fingers trailing around the edge. 'Because I think it's the right thing to do.'

'Bullshit!' It's like an elastic band has snapped inside me. I wasn't expecting this to happen. I was planning on being calm and reasonable and other sensible things like that. 'You can't possibly think that! Can't you see how twisted this is?'

Polly blinks so slowly that I can see the unevenness of her eye shadow. It's much darker on the left than on the right. 'It's nothing of the sort. It's . . . I think of it as penance.'

'For killing her, you mean?' There. It's been said. The words are out there.

There's a sudden stillness in the room and it scares me. 'Have you got the song lyrics from Jack?'

Now I'm the one shaking my head. 'What?'

'The song lyrics you were bringing me. That *is* why you're here, isn't it?' Her voice is sugar-sweet and coated with a thick layer of insincerity.

'I'm here to talk about Tara.'

Polly leans her elbows on the plan chest, hands cupping her face. The light from the alien lamp makes her look ghoulish. 'OK. Let's talk.'

'What happened that night?'

She laughs as if I've said something hilarious. 'I think we both know what happened, Alice.' She clocks that I'm not smiling and carries on. 'It was an accident. A terrible accident.'

'An *accident*.' This whole confronting-the-villain thing always looks a lot easier on TV.

'Don't be so suspicious, Alice. All I'm trying to do is make things right.'

'And how exactly are you going to achieve that? Tara's dead, in case you hadn't noticed. And so is Rae. There's no possible way to make things right, and you know it.'

'Well, no. I'm not talking about bringing them back from the dead or anything.' The sound of her girly giggle makes me want to throttle her.

'This isn't a joke. Look, I *know*.'

'Know what?' she asks, but from the look on her face I think she might have an idea.

I speak quickly and quietly, wanting to get this over with as soon as possible – like ripping off a plaster. 'You gave Cass the idea of how to get back at Tara, and you knew Tara had asthma, and you have your inhaler with you all the time but you didn't give it to her. You stopped Cass giving her mouth-to-mouth – I thought you were supposed to know first aid.'

'Wow. That's . . . interesting.' Her head is down and I can't see her eyes – they're hollow black sockets. The effect is monstrous. She rearranges the yearbook pages between us so that they line up with the edge of the plan chest.

'Polly, I know you didn't mean for this to happen.' I don't know anything of the sort, but I have to hope it's the truth. If it's not, then I'm alone in the dark with a complete psychopath. 'You made some mistakes; we all did. But we have to tell someone. We have to go to the police.'

Polly finally looks up at me and her expression is hard to read. 'OK, now you've told me what you *supposedly* know, how about I tell you what *I* know? No one would believe that I came up with a plan like that – not in a million years. And traumatic circumstances can make you forget your own *name*, so it's hardly strange that I'd forget about my inhaler, or forget that Tara had asthma, or even forget my first-aid training. If I told Cass not to do mouth-to-mouth, it was only because I was scared out of my mind.' There's no smugness in her voice or on her face – there's nothing there at all.

I open my mouth to speak and then promptly close it again. She's right. I mean, she's not right. But that's how it would look to an outsider. That's how it would look to the police.

'We're not going to go to the police, because if we do, Cass is the one who'll get the blame. *She's* the one who organized it all. *She's* the one who's always hated Tara. I was Tara's friend, remember?'

'Lapdog, more like,' I mutter.

'What did you say?'

'You weren't Tara's friend. Tara despised you, and you know it. She humiliated you.'

Polly shrugs. 'It doesn't matter how she felt about me. All that matters is that I liked *her*. I looked up to her. That's what people think, and that's what really counts here. Why else would I be doing all this?' She gestures at the pages in front of her.

'How can you be so calculating?'

'I'm not calculating – just pragmatic.'

I walk away from the pool of light around the plan chest and slump in a chair in the darkness. My head is in my hands and I'm trying to keep it from exploding. This cannot be happening. This CANNOT be happening. My new mantra.

I hear footsteps and I think – hope – she's leaving. But the footsteps get closer and closer until they stop right by me. I hear chair legs scraping against the floor as she sits down next to me.

'You have to understand that not everything in the world is black and white. Things are hardly ever that simple.' She sighs. 'I didn't plan for Tara to die. I just wanted to humiliate her the way she humiliated me. She deserved it. I didn't think she'd *die* though. And I can't tell you why I didn't help her. I . . . I don't know. But I'm not going to lie to you, Alice; I'm glad she's dead. She was a horrible person and you know it. So many people are better off without her.'

'What about her parents? Jack? Danni? Are they better off?' My voice is dull, lifeless – defeated.

'Maybe not. But it's done now. And no one's going to benefit from knowing the truth.' She sounds so reasonable I can almost believe she's right.

'What about Rae? Did she deserve to die too?'

'That was . . . unfortunate. But for all we know she would have ended up killing herself over something else. All that depressing music, those weird goth clothes. Suicide is practically a religion for those people.'

I finally look up at her. 'How can you say that?'

'Sorry. That was crass of me. All I'm trying to say is, what's done is done. It doesn't matter who meant what or who did what. We're in this situation and we just have to make the best of it. It will be OK, Alice, I promise you.' She puts her hand on my knee and I stare at it. Her fingers are long and elegant, her nails are perfectly manicured. Her nails used to be bitten down to the quick, if I remember correctly.

'Is that why you're doing all this memorial stuff? Making the best of it?'

'I saw an opportunity and I went for it. I thought

it was about time people around here started showing me some respect. In case you hadn't noticed, I was *nothing* at this school. I was less than nothing. And now I'm not. Don't look at me like that. I'm not the only one making the best of this situation, am I?'

'What are you talking about?' I'm suddenly dog-tired. This conversation has ground me down to a fine powder. The tiniest puff of wind would blow me away.

'You mean to tell me you actually believe you'd be going out with Jack if Tara was still alive?' She snorts. 'Two words: as if.'

'He . . . I . . .'

'You know I'm right. Even if by some miracle he would have asked you out, Tara would never have allowed it to happen. She was not a good person, Alice. You have to remember that.' Polly's voice is gentle now. She thinks she's almost snared me with her words. She might be right.

'She used to be a good person – the best.'

Polly snorts. 'I find that very hard to believe.' She doesn't know, of course. She didn't know me or Tara back then. And even if she had done, she'd probably have conveniently forgotten – just like the rest of them.

'She didn't deserve to die. No one deserves that.' My eyes fill with tears and I tilt my head back as if that will pour them back to wherever they came from.

Polly says nothing.

44

She's right. Going to the police won't do any good. Tara and Rae are gone. We have to get on with our lives.

I'm still not sure whether Polly meant for all this to happen. There's something not quite right about her, definitely. But I can't believe she's a *murderer*. More like an opportunist or something. It's like she said – there's no black and white. Everything is murky grey, blurred at the edges. The distinction between murderer and opportunist seems an important one, but I could well be kidding myself.

I can't help thinking that maybe Polly's the way she is because of how everyone's treated her. Who can blame her for wanting to be popular? That's what most people want, isn't it?

She's right about Jack too, much as I don't want her to be. The thought of me going out with him if

Tara was still around is almost laughable. I may not be as bad as Polly – using Tara's death as a springboard into the higher echelons of the social scene – but I'm not far off.

Ghost Tara isn't talking to me. When she's around she sits on the floor in the corner, glaring at me. She was hoping I'd have a huge confrontation with Polly, ending with me frog-marching her down to the local police station. I've let her down. I try not to look at her; it hurts too much.

I can't help thinking about Tara's body at the bottom of that well. I can't help thinking about what she must look like now. There are bound to be bugs and worms and all kinds of awful creepy-crawlies down there. I wonder if the reality is worse that the horror-movie image in my head.

She shouldn't be down there. I bet it gets very cold at night. And what happens when it rains?

She must be lonely. No one ever comes to visit.

The next day at school I throw myself into getting back to normal. I eat lunch in the cafeteria. I talk to Cass. I even talk to some other people. But I do my best to avoid Danni; I don't know what to say to her. I pass Polly in the corridor between lessons and she gives me a look. It seems a very pointed look, but I'm not entirely sure what it's supposed to mean.

Jack's loitering at the school gates at home time, looking rumpled and knackered and good enough to eat. I embarrass myself by running into his arms.

'What are you doing here?! And how did you manage to get here on time? You lot finish at the same time as we do, don't you?'

Jack holds up his hands like he's shielding himself from my barrage of questions. 'Whoa! The answers to your questions are, in the order you asked: I wanted to see you; I nipped out early from my study period; and yes, we do finish at the same time as you.'

'It's good to see you. I've . . . missed you.' I bury my head in his shoulder and try to force down the lump that's mysteriously appeared in my throat.

'I've missed you too. I didn't want to have to wait till Saturday to see you.' He wraps his arms tightly around me and I lean into him. He smells of good, clean boy sweat mixed with Lynx deodorant.

We stand there for a minute or two. I didn't know just how much I needed to see him – needed to hold him – until now.

'Wait, don't you have band practice today?'

He pulls away and looks at his watch. 'Yes, in approximately twenty-three minutes.'

'And how exactly are you planning to get to Camden in approximately twenty-three minutes?'

'Ah, you're forgetting about my trusty steed.' He gestures over his shoulder at the battered old BMX leaning against the railing. 'She'll get me there on time, no probs. Never let me down yet.'

'You came all this way just to see me for a couple of minutes?'

Jack nods and looks bashful. 'Yeah, I suppose I did.' He is so close to perfect I don't know how I can stand it.

'Well you'd better hurry up and kiss me then, hadn't you?'

'Yeah, I suppose I should.'

And he does. And it's easy to fall into the moment and forget about everything – forget about Tara and Rae and Polly and Cass. I'd almost be able to forget where we are, if it wasn't for one or two people shouting, 'Get a room!' as they walk past.

Not for the first time I thank God that Jack has chosen to be with me. It's miraculous. Too good to be true. And it's *not* true, is it? This relationship is a house of cards resting on a fault line. But it's the only good thing in my life right now, and I won't let anything ruin it.

When Jack pedals away I feel like my heart is

trying to push its way out of my chest, like it wants to go with him – it needs to be where he is or else it will forget how to function. I had no idea it was possible to feel this way about another person. It terrifies me.

By Saturday, my head is seriously messed up from lack of sleep. My vision keeps on going wonky – like I'm seeing everything from underwater – and I can't concentrate on anything for more than a minute at a time. I waste the morning attempting to write a rough draft of an essay for Daley. I'm not helped by Ghost Tara repeating herself in my head: *You have to tell him today. You have to tell him today. You have to.* When I look down at the page I realize I've started to write Tara's words instead of my essay. I throw the pen across the room and scrunch up the sheet of paper into a tiny little ball. Then I head to the bathroom to splash my face with icy water. I don't like what I see in the mirror. I don't look normal. I don't look *right*. Why can't anyone else see that?

My hair looks OK and my skin is clearer than it's ever been – if a little pale. So I think it's my eyes. I think there's something not quite right with my eyes. They stare back at me lifelessly. Dull grey and brimful of secrets. There's a greenish tinge in a certain light, but it's muddy and mossy and about as far away from emerald as you can get. Mum was either colour-blind or lying.

Dad doesn't talk much at lunch. He sits at the table with the newspaper propped up in front of him and a frown on his face. He hasn't really had much to say since our little chat about Daley. I feel guilty every time I look at him. He must think I'm the worst daughter in the world, and he doesn't even know the half of it.

He's going out to watch the football with his mates, then he's off out to dinner with a 'business associate'. He won't be back until ten at the earliest, so I don't have to bother making up some lie about where I'm going. I don't even have to tell him I'm going out at all. Lying by omission is much less guilt-inducing.

I take a long bath after lunch and take extra care removing every last bit of unwanted hair from my body. That's when it hits me properly. This is the day. By tonight I will be an ex-virgin. Everything will have changed. I should probably be more excited, but all I feel is a squirmy sort of fear in my gut.

I never would have thought it would happen like this – planned and premeditated. I'd have thought it would just happen in a lovely, spontaneous sort of way. One thing would lead to another and then before I had a chance to start stressing it would all be over. And I would be happy and relaxed and probably more than a little smug.

I know it's going to be nothing like I've always imagined. I'm fully prepared for awkwardness, embarrassment and pain. But at least it will be with Jack, and there's no one I'd rather be awkward and embarrassed with. I could do without the pain bit though.

Choosing the right clothes is tricky. I can't help thinking the dress I wore to the dance would have been the most appropriate pre-virginity-losing outfit. At least that was easy access. I wish we'd just got it over and done with there and then. It's not *that* big a deal, is it? People do it all the time.

I try on a couple of skirts, but they don't look right. Too try-hard. I need to look like me. It has to be jeans – easy access or not. My favourite ones are still languishing on the beanbag where I chucked them the other night. I can't remember the last time they were washed, but they smell OK. A plain black top is the best I can come up with after a lengthy search.

Ghost Tara reappears when I'm spritzing on some

perfume. She's sitting in the corner again, looking small and vulnerable. I turn away and concentrate on applying some waterproof mascara.

'Don't do this.' Her voice is different, more serious.

'Why not? Because I'm not good enough for your little brother?'

'You're not, but that's beside the point. I don't want you to hurt him.'

'Me hurt *him*? From what I've heard, that's not the way it works.'

Tara sighs at my lame joke. 'That's not what I meant and you know it. He's falling in love with you.'

I say nothing.

'He's falling in love with you and you are going to stomp all over his heart. How do you think he's going to feel when you tell him the truth? You think he's going to give you a hug and say, "Don't you worry about my dead sister — I'm over it."? You honestly think he will ever be able to forgive you for what you did? God, Alice, I always knew you were stupid, but this really takes some beating.'

'I—'

'Don't say it. You *are* going to tell him. Today.' Suddenly she's standing behind me. Hallucinations can move faster than you can blink.

Before I can think of anything to say, she's gone again, leaving me feeling dizzy.

Once last look in the mirror before I head off confirms that I look adequate if a little bit queasy.

There is no way in hell I'm telling Jack anything.

45

The journey to Jack's house takes longer than expected. The bus gets diverted due to a burst water main on the high street. My stomach feels like it's made from lead. I can't seem to shake this jittery pre-exam feeling. I'd really like to know how a normal girl would be feeling right now. Surely there should be delicious anticipation mixed in there somewhere. What I'm feeling seems way too close to dread.

Looking out the window helps to calm my nerves, even though I have no clue where the bus is going or whether it's going to end up where I need to be. People are milling around outside pubs even though it's freezing cold. I suddenly worry that the diversion will take me past the pub Dad's at with his mates, and he'll happen to be outside, and he'll happen to look up at exactly the wrong moment, and I'll be so busted. Then again, that might not be so bad after all.

He'd drag me home and he'd cancel dinner with his 'business associate' and we'd order a Thai takeaway and watch a DVD together.

No. I *want* to see Jack. I *want* to do this.

If I can just get through the next few hours without thinking about Tara, everything will be fine.

Jack opens the door so quickly I haven't even finished knocking. My fist is raised as the door swings inward and I nearly lose my balance. Smooth.

He looks great. That smile is enough to make my doubts and fears slink away to the back of my brain. He's wearing a white T-shirt, jeans and odd socks. He catches me checking out the socks.

'What?! It's been scientifically proven that people who wear odd socks are forty-eight per cent luckier than people who don't.'

'So you're hoping to get lucky tonight, huh?'

'That's not what I . . . well, I kind of am, actually,' he says sheepishly.

'Yeah, we'll see about that.' I flounce past him, dropping my jacket on the back of the sofa. Then I turn and smile, and he smiles back, and everything is right with the world.

Jack orders a Thai takeaway, which makes me

wonder if he can read my mind. He apologizes for not cooking something himself – he reckons he's a terrible cook. Tara used to tell him he'd never get a girlfriend if he didn't know how to cook. Tara was wrong.

We sit on the living-room floor eating the food straight out of the boxes. There's a single silver-framed picture of Tara on the mantelpiece. It's very hard to ignore, but I try my best.

The pristine cream carpet is so thick it's probably comfier than most people's beds and I'm so paranoid about making a mess that I force myself to eat extra-slowly. And I only eat about half the amount I would normally eat. It's partly down to nerves, and partly that I don't want Jack to think I'm a greedy cow. And I'm more than a little bit worried about garlic breath.

Jack's super-talkative and super-attentive – he keeps asking if I need a top-up, or whether I think he should put the central heating on. It makes me feel more at ease, knowing he's just as nervous as I am. We haven't talked about it, but I'm pretty sure he's a virgin too. I can't know for sure without asking, and I would never ever do that. I wonder if I'll be able to tell when we're doing it.

He brings out some mint-choc-chip ice cream that he bought for pudding. 'Now I may not be able to cook, but I can create the most perfect scoops of ice cream you will ever see. It's a gift.'

'You are truly blessed.'

'Ouch! Your cynicism *hurts*. I feel actual, real pain. Right here.' He taps his chest and adopts a facial expression that would put Bambi to shame.

I have to admit, the ice cream is perfectly scooped. I pretend to inspect it carefully from every angle. 'Not bad, not bad. But I've seen better.'

'Oh, you are in so much trouble. You should never, ever disrespect a man's scooping abilities.' He scoots closer to me and before I know what he's doing he's stuck a finger in his ice cream and smeared it on my nose. It tickles.

I raise an eyebrow, seriously unimpressed. 'I seem to have ice cream on my nose. I suggest you do something to rectify this situation as soon as is humanly possible.'

'Or what?' he says, a cheeky, challenging grin working its way across his face.

'Or a world of pain is coming your way in the next five seconds . . . four . . . three . . . two . . . one.' At the exact moment the word 'one' passes my lips, Jack tilts his head towards mine and licks my nose.

He leans back and looks at me through narrowed

eyes. 'Nope, think I missed a bit.' He goes in for another lick. 'There, that does it. Good as new.'

'That was . . . gross.'

'Did you know that nose-licking is the greatest sign of respect in . . . um . . . Azerbaijan?'

I lean in close and he does the same. I pause when his lips are tantalizingly close to mine. 'You . . . are . . . full of it.' His laugh is stifled by my mouth on his.

The ice cream has melted into ice-cream soup by the time we get round to eating it.

We sit in silence for a little while. I know what's coming, but I'm not going to be the one to say something.

'Do you . . . I mean, should we . . . go upstairs? Only if you want to, of course. We can always watch a DVD or something if you'd rather . . .'

46

We head for the stairs, exchanging a couple of nervous glances. I make a quick diversion to the bathroom while Jack waits in his room.

I squeeze some toothpaste onto my finger and give my teeth a quick onceover. I check my hair in the mirror – it's looking only slightly dishevelled. Right. This is it. No turning back now. Unless I jump out the window. I doubt I'd fit though. Jack would break down the door to find my legs dangling over the sink and my arse well and truly jammed in the window frame. Something tells me that wouldn't be a good look.

Jack's sitting on the edge of the bed looking slightly anxious when I enter the room. There are no candles, no rose petals. The curtains are drawn and there *is* some mood lighting – if you count the desk lamp, which has been angled to shine its light on a poster of some obscure French film.

I stand in front of him and when he looks up I know this is going to be OK. I just need to muster up some fake confidence from somewhere.

'I think I'd like to kiss you now.' And I *do* sound confident. Not even a hint of wobbliness in my voice.

He nods. 'I think I would definitely be OK with that.'

I lean down and put my lips on his, gently at first. Then harder. I push his chest so he lies back on the bed and then I'm mostly lying on top of him, except our feet are still on the floor.

Jack stops kissing me for a second and says, 'Toothpaste? No fair.'

I kiss his neck. Tiny little kisses.

'Seriously. Now I want to brush *my* teeth. I don't want you thinking my breath stinks while you're all minty fresh.'

I laugh into his neck. 'I don't care, Jack. And you're not going anywhere.' I clamber over him so I'm properly on the bed. Then I pat the space next to me and give him what I'm hoping resembles a come-hither glance. Jack shrugs and flings himself onto the bed beside me.

We kiss for a long time and I start to worry about the time. I have to be back at the house before Dad, and I've no idea what time it is now. If something's going to happen, it had better happen soon. One of us has to make the first move and it looks like it's going to have to be me.

I reach down and pull at the bottom of Jack's T-shirt. Our lips have to part while I pull the fabric up over his head, but it only takes a second. His skin is hot to the touch. I like the way it feels beneath my fingers.

Jack tugs at my top and I help him out by yanking it over my head. And then we're skin to skin, with only my bra in the way. The kissing gets faster, hungrier. My heart is galloping as I start working on his belt buckle.

Jack moans into my mouth. My fingers are unzipping his flies when he pulls away from me, breathing heavily. 'Can we . . . stop for a second?' He zips up and sits up.

Shit. He's changed his mind.

I lie back on the bed and steel myself for the badness that's coming, but Jack reaches for my hands and hauls me into a sitting position.

My jeans are digging into my sides and I can't bear to look down to see how that looks. And I can't bear to look at Jack, so I concentrate on the door. My escape route.

Jack keeps hold of my hands. His breathing is

slowly getting back to normal, as is mine. 'Alice, why are you staring at the door?'

So now I have to look at him. At his messed-up hair, his flushed face, his chocolate-brown eyes. He's biting his lip.

Jack squeezes my hands in his. 'There's something I want to say. Before we do this.' I'm slightly reassured by the 'before' there. If he still wants to have sex with me, how bad can it be?

I wait.

'OK, here goes. I think I sort of . . . maybe . . . love you a little bit.'

Something ignites inside my heart.

'Shit, I messed that up. Let me try again. I love you, Alice King.'

Fireworks explode inside my heart. I feel like I've been waiting my whole life for him to say these words. I feel like I was born to hear him say these words.

I close my eyes to fend off a wave of dizziness that threatens to overwhelm me.

'Alice, are you all right? You look kind of weird. I'm sorry, I didn't mean to freak you out. It's OK if you . . . um . . . don't feel the same . . . yet. I just wanted to say it. I didn't want you to think I was taking advantage of you, or that I sleep with girls all the time or anything. I mean, I haven't slept with *any* girls, *ever*. You know that, right? This is special to me. *You're* special to me. I've never felt this way before. You're the best thing that's ever happened to me.'

'Tara didn't drown.'

47

'What? Yes, she . . . *What?*' Jack's eyebrows knit together in confusion.

Why? Why did I say that? *Because it's the right thing to do.* Tara's voice is back inside my head. I look towards the door again. If I leave now, we can pretend this never happened. I'll call him later and make up some excuse for being such a weirdo. *No, you won't.*

'Alice, talk to me. What do you mean?'

This is it. I am hanging from a cliff by my fingernails. I can try to scrabble back up to safety. Or I can let go and fall.

I let go. 'There's something I need to tell you. It's serious.'

Jack goes very still. His hands are still holding mine, but his grip has loosened. It won't take much to break the bond. 'About my sister?'

I nod. 'Maybe we should get dressed first?'

'Tell me now. Please?' He squeezes my hands a little too hard. My knuckles crunch together.

'I wanted to tell you. I really did. But I was so scared, and I know how bad it sounds. But you have to understand that it wasn't like that. It all went wrong.' Twin tears start trickling down my face.

'Alice, you're scaring me. Please tell me what you're talking about.' He lets go of my hands, as I knew he would. I know we will never hold hands again.

My jaw's so tight it feels like my teeth might crush each other and crumble in my mouth. *Tell him. Everything.*

I tell him all of it. Everything I missed out when I told him about the holiday. Duncan. Polly's humiliation in the cave and in the dining hall. The plan to get revenge on Tara. What went wrong. I tell him about Rae's note in my locker. My conversation with Polly in the media lab.

I stare at my hands the whole time. I can't look at him. He doesn't interrupt me once. I wish he would interrupt so that I can stop talking. There's just one thing I leave out. One thing I can't bear to tell him. It shouldn't be any more horrifying than what I've already said. But somehow it is.

The silence in the room stretches away into

infinity. I risk a glance at Jack, hoping he's not looking at me. He is. His face is hard, unforgiving. He looks like a man. I look away fast. 'Where is she?' Ice-cold words.

'Jack, I—'

'Where is she?' I want to touch him. Some gesture – anything – that will remind him of what we have. What we had.

'You have to understand . . . we were scared out of our minds. We didn't know what else to do.' I'm babbling and stuttering.

'Tell me. Now.' I flinch.

'There . . . there was an abandoned well.' If my voice was any quieter it would be inaudible.

Jack's jaw flexes a couple of times. His hands are bunched into fists. 'A *well* . . . ?' he croaks.

So now I've told him all there is to know. I don't feel relieved. I don't feel like a huge weight has been lifted from my shoulders. I feel like I would do anything to take back what I've said – to turn back the clock and tell Jack that I love him too. Because that's the truth.

Jack gets up from the bed and stalks to the other side of the room. He leans his head into the wall and hits it with his fist – hard. His shoulder blades stick out sharply. It's as if a pair of wings is lurking under his skin, ready to sprout. It's hard to believe that I was running my fingers up and down his spine only minutes ago.

I grab my top and pull it over my head.

After a couple of minutes and seven more punches to the wall, I have to say something before the silence suffocates me. 'Jack . . . say something, please?'

'Don't talk to me. I can't listen to you right now.' His words are clipped, harsh.

'Do you want me to . . . ? Should I go?'

'You're not going anywhere. Just . . . stop talking.' His head is still against the wall. If anyone walked in they might think he was counting to a hundred for a game of hide-and-seek.

I look at my watch. 9.03.

Eventually Jack turns away from the wall and lets himself slide down so he's sitting on the floor. His legs are pulled up against his bare chest. Tears stream down his cheeks and he swipes at them angrily.

I can't stay quiet. 'Jack, I'm so sorry. You have to believe me.'

He barks an ugly laugh. '*Believe* you? You honestly think I can believe anything that comes out of your mouth?'

'I'm telling the truth. Jack! Please . . . I love you.'

'Don't. You killed my sister. You left her to rot in

a fucking well.' His face crumples. 'My *sister*. What is the *matter* with you?'

'It was an accident.' Pointless words.

'If you say that one more time I swear I'll . . .' Then he lets go and starts sobbing. His shoulders shake and the sound is the second-worst thing I've ever heard.

I can't help myself. I get up off the bed and go to him. I sit down on the floor in front of him. Tentatively I put my hand on his knee. He flinches a little but doesn't say anything.

The sobbing subsides after a little while. 'Why didn't you tell someone?' he asks. His voice is thick with tears.

'I wanted to. But we were scared. We didn't know what would happen to us.'

'You should have told someone.'

'I know.'

'And Polly could have helped her.' It's hard to tell if this is a question or not – his words are so flat.

'Yes.'

'She hated having asthma, you know? She started having breathing problems a couple of years ago, but she didn't tell Mum for ages – not till she had a really bad attack. And when she finally got an inhaler, she hardly ever used it. Not at first. She said that only losers had asthma. Ridiculous, really.'

I feel something in the back pocket of my jeans, digging into me. The ring. It's been there for two days; I forgot all about it. It's almost as though it's waited for this exact moment to make its presence known.

I lean forward so I can get it out of my pocket.

My hand trembles as I hold it out for Jack to see.

48

Jack plucks the ring from my palm and closes his fist around it. 'Where did you get it?'

'It slipped off her finger.' There is no need for him to know the exact circumstances.

'You've had it all this time? Why didn't you tell me, Alice? Why did you let me fall in love with you? You should have stayed away.'

'I know. I wanted to, but I liked you so much. I just wanted you not to feel sad any more.'

He shakes his head. 'All this time . . . you lied to me all this time. This whole relationship was based on nothing.'

'That's not true. I've never felt this way about anyone either. I love you, Jack. That's why I had to tell you.'

'You don't know anything about love. You're a stupid, scared little girl.' He sighs. 'I suppose I'm meant to be grateful that you've finally told me? That you finally had the guts to give the ring back? Well, thanks a lot for killing my sister.' His normally open features are closed and narrow and hooded. He wants to hurt me. And I can't blame him. I don't look away. I *deserve* to see this.

Jack rubs his arms and I notice that he's shivering. I scoot over and grab his T-shirt from the bed. He takes it without a word and pulls it back over his head, inside-out.

'You're right. There's no excuse for what I've done. It doesn't matter that it was an accident. We should have gone to the police. *I* should have gone to the police. Or I should have told you sooner. I should never have let anything happen between you and me. I can say sorry a million times and it will never be enough. But you have to know that my feelings for you were – *are* – real. If there was anything I could do to make this better, I would.'

'So would I.' Some of the hatred on his face melts away, unless I'm just imagining the slight softening to his features. He rolls the ring between his fingers.

'Are you going to tell your parents?'

Jack shakes his head slowly.

'Are you going to tell the police?'

Another shake of the head.

'But . . . I don't get it. Why not?'

'Because you are.'

Oh. 'Jack, I can't. Please don't make me do this.'

His eyes burn a hole into my brain. 'You can. And you will. It's the right thing to do. And even after all this, I think . . . I *know* you'll do the right thing.'

That kills me. I'd rather he blackmailed me or threatened me or called the police right this second.

'I have to go. I'm sorry. Dad doesn't know I'm out.'

Jack nods and slowly gets to his feet. He holds out his hand to pull me up. I hesitate before taking it.

We trudge downstairs. The house is too quiet, too dark. The ticking of the grandfather clock in the hallway is the only sound. Jack opens the front door and steps aside to let me pass.

I turn to face him. His T-shirt is Day-Glo bright in the darkness, his face shadowy. 'I'm sorry this happened. I'm sorry I did this to you.'

'I know.' For a split second I think he's going to hug me. But he doesn't. Of course he doesn't.

The driveway gravel crunches under my feet. I turn around and he's still standing in the doorway. I can't tell if he's watching me. All I can make out is the bright white inside-out T-shirt.

The bus is busy and loud. People are talking to each other, or talking on their phones, or listening to music. How can their lives be so normal when mine is falling apart? Why does no one look at me? Can't they sense something's wrong with me?

I felt the same way after Mum died. I hated being around strangers who didn't know what had happened. I thought that everyone should know and everyone should behave differently. No one should be allowed to laugh and joke. It didn't seem right.

I shouldn't have told Jack. Polly was right. Jack isn't any better off for knowing the truth. He'll never be able to stop picturing what happened. And he'll never be able to shake the image of his sister lying broken at the bottom of a well.

Dad finds me sitting on the sofa in the dark, a blanket over my shoulders because I can't seem to stop shaking. He flicks on the main light and stumbles back into the door. 'Jesus, Al, you scared me half to death! I thought you were a ghost or something – the Lady of the Green Blanket!'

He's drunk. Not completely wasted, but far from sober. He kicks off his shoes and slumps down next to me, reeking of cigarettes and beer. 'So what are you doing sitting here in the dark? Meditating? Where's Bruno?'

I haven't seen Bruno. I have never once come into this house without Bruno bounding to greet me. Maybe he knows to stay away from me now. Maybe he knows I'm toxic.

Dad takes a second to look at me properly. Mum would have looked at me like that straightaway. Mothers know instinctively when something is wrong with their daughters. Fathers, it would seem, do not. Especially when they've been drinking. 'Hey, kiddo, what's up?'

Every molecule of me is screaming *NOTHING! I'M FINE*. That's all I have to say and Dad will turn on the TV to watch *Match of the Day*. It's very simple. Three little words. Say them, go to bed. Speak to Jack in the morning. Beg him. Do whatever it takes to make him keep this a secret. Forget this ever happened. Get on with your life. Tara and Rae are dead. Get over it.

'I have to tell you something. It's bad.'

'OK, shoot.' He glances towards the clock on the mantelpiece and I can tell he's itching to switch on the TV. He doesn't believe that what I'm going to say is truly *bad*. He thinks it's going to be I-got-a-D-in-an-exam bad, or I-broke-your-favourite-mug bad. He has no idea. I am going to break him.

49

He listens quietly for the most part. He tries to interrupt a couple of times but I beg him to let me finish. I watch his transformation from relaxed and tipsy to worried and tense. By the time I've finished, he's sitting on the edge of the sofa with his head in his hands.

'Dad? Say something, please?' I sound like a scared, stupid little girl. Just like Jack said.

'Let me . . . I'm thinking.'

'Dad? It's going to be OK, isn't it?' I start to cry. I really didn't want to cry, but I suppose it was inevitable.

He says nothing for a moment or two, then jumps up from the sofa and starts to pace. He always says his brain works better when it's on the move. I count thirteen trips from one end of the room to the other before he speaks. 'OK, Alice, I don't want you to worry about this any more. You made a mistake – you all made a terrible mistake. But that's what it was – a *mistake*. You didn't mean any harm.' Apart from Polly. I didn't tell him what I know about Polly. I'm not sure why.

My tears have settled into the occasional sniffle. 'I'm going to call the police. DI Marshall said we should contact him if we had any information.'

Dad's head snaps towards me. 'No!'

'I have to, Dad. You know I do.'

He kneels on the floor in front of me, grasping my hands in his. His hands are sweaty. 'No, Alice, you don't. I don't know much about this sort of thing, but I don't think it'll just be a slap on the wrist for something this serious. It's *manslaughter*, Al. Someone is *dead*. Two people, if you count Rae. You're sixteen years old – you'd go to prison. And I am *not* going to let that happen.' His face is fierce, but the fierceness isn't aimed at me.

'But think about her family – never knowing the truth. It's not fair.'

'I don't care about her family! I care about you. You're all I've got, Alice.' He starts to cry and I can't watch. When Mum died he was careful not to cry around me. I'd often come into a room and find him sitting there, red-eyed. He would cough and mutter something about contact lenses, and I'd say nothing. It was better that way for both of us.

'Please don't cry. I have to do this. What if it was me? What if I was the one who died? You'd do anything to make sure I had a proper burial, wouldn't you? A proper resting place where you could visit and bring flowers. Like we do for Mum.'

He sobs, but I can tell he's trying to pull himself together. Trying to be the strong one like he's always been. 'If it was you, I wouldn't want to know that you'd been lying at the bottom of a well all that time. It would kill me to know that.'

He's right. But so am I. 'Mum would agree with me.' It's a low blow, but it's all I've got.

Dad shakes his head fervently. 'You're wrong. Your mother would do anything to protect you, just like I would. I promised her I wouldn't let anything bad happen to you.'

'That's not a promise you could ever have kept. You've done everything right, but you could never have stopped this from happening. You do understand that, don't you?'

He hangs his head and I know that he blames himself for this. That somehow I wouldn't be in this predicament if only he'd been a better father. Or that this wouldn't have happened if Mum was still alive.

Nothing I can say will make him think any different. His shoulders are slumped. 'I can't lose you, Alice.'

'You won't lose me. Whatever happens. I'm still your daughter and I still love you.'

He won't look at me. 'Please hear me out. No one has to know about this. It's just you, Cass and this Polly girl, isn't it? And from what you've told me, they don't want this getting out either. There are four of us, Alice. Four people can keep a secret. The police investigation is closed. No one has to know.'

'That makes you an accessory.' I don't know why I'm even bothering. He's never going to agree to this. I should just tell him about Jack. That will stop him in his tracks.

'I don't bloody care what it makes me! I'm your father, Alice. Some day you'll have children and you'll understand what it is to be a parent. That's if you're not banged up in some women's prison!' he shouts.

I've heard enough. I get up from the sofa and head for the stairs.

'Alice King, you get back here right now. I haven't finished talking to you yet!' If I close my eyes it could almost be six or seven years ago. I can almost imagine he's cross with me because I've refused to eat all the carrots on my plate.

'Let's talk about this in the morning. We're both exhausted.'

He gets up and rubs his face with his hands. 'You're right. Come and give your old Dad a hug, will you?'

There was a time when I thought that Dad's hugs had magical properties. They always made me feel better when I was scared or worried. They even made me feel a little bit better when I was ill.

There's something final about this particular hug. I wonder if Dad feels it too, because he whispers, 'I'll always love you, Alice. Never, ever forget that.'

'OK, Dad.'

'Promise me?'

'I promise.'

The last thing he says to me before I leave the room is, 'You're a good girl.'

I don't know who he's trying to convince.

50

Bruno is lying on Dad's bed, illuminated by a shaft of light from the hall. 'Here, boy! Come here!' I whistle, but the sound doesn't come out right. He raises his head and looks at me. He puts his head back on his paws and closes his eyes.

My bedroom is cold.

I turn on my laptop and search through my desk drawers while it's booting up. There's a photo I need to find. It used to have pride of place on my bedside table. Until I put it away because I couldn't bear to look at it.

I find it wedged in the back of the bottom drawer. It's slightly torn in the corner. I should have taken better care of it.

Grumps took the photo on my eighth birthday. There's a cake on a table in the background. A cake with eight candles. I'm wearing a blue and green

stripy dress and standing in front of Mum and Dad.
I'm cowering and laughing because Mum has just
started tickling me. No one's looking at the camera:
Dad's looking at Mum and Mum's looking at me and
I've got my eyes squeezed shut from laughing so hard.
It's a bit of a rubbish photo really. The composition's
all wrong, and we're ever so slightly out of focus. But
it's the only one I have.

There are loads of photos of me and Mum, or me
and Dad, or Mum and Dad. But this is the only one I
have with all three of us. I don't know why that is. I'm
sure there must be others, maybe on Dad's computer.
I wish I'd thought to look for them before.

I carefully fold the photo and put it in the back
pocket of my jeans.

My ancient laptop has booted up at last. I sit on
the floor with it balanced on my thighs. It takes me a
while to find what I'm looking for. I don't know how
long I sit there staring at the screen.

There's a missed call from Cass on my phone.
She's left a message, but I don't listen to it. I send a
text: 'I'm sorry.'

The background on my phone is a picture of me
and Jack. I took it myself, angling the phone over our
heads. It's a nice picture. I delete it.

Ghost Tara appears next to me. Close enough to

touch, if she wasn't a figment of my imagination. Her hands are no longer muddy and bloody. And she's not sixteen any more. She's Tara Chambers, my best friend. Wet hair scraped back into a ponytail after swimming. School uniform a little too big for her. Braces on her teeth.

She doesn't say anything.

I enter a number into the phone.

My finger hovers over the call button.

I look at ten-year-old Tara and she nods. There's a hint of a smile there too.

I press the button and close my eyes.

'Hello? I'd like to speak to Detective Inspector Marshall. I have information about the disappearance of Tara Chambers.'

I open my eyes and Tara is gone.

I don't think she'll be back.

the end

Acknowledgements

Much of this book was written under difficult circumstances, so these thanks are especially heartfelt. I couldn't have completed *Torn* without the help, support and total awesomeness of:

Lara Williamson, Nova Ren Suma, Liz de Jager, Kaz Mahoney, Courtney Summers, Sarah Stewart, Irene Hodgson, Michael Bedo, Non Parish, Emily de la Mare, Liz Scott, Sam Meredith and Jessica Pitcairn.

Big thanks to the utterly marvellous Victoria Birkett, the legendary Nancy Miles, and Caroline Hill-Trevor — a rights-selling superhero if ever there was one.

Thank you to Roisin Heycock, Niamh Mulvey, Talya Baker and all at Quercus.

Thanks to my Sisters: Keris Stainton, Luisa Plaja, Kay Woodward, Tamsyn Murray, Keren David, Sophia Bennett, Susie Day, Fiona Dunbar and Gillian Philip.

Thanks to the brilliant bloggers of t'interweb for being incredibly supportive, especially: Lauren, Sya, Carly, Iffath, Becky, Caroline, Jo, Sophie, Andrew, Jenny, Sarah, Sammee and Ryan.

A special thanks to Rae at St Augustine's RC High School, Edinburgh, for letting me steal her name.

Music-wise, I'd like to tip my hat to My Chemical Romance, Imogen Heap and Owl City.

And finally, an extra-special big fat thank you to my family for being brilliant.